PURFIT

S.M. SAVOY

Published by
Ace Lyon Books
December 2025

Published by
Ace Lyon Books
Acelyonbooks.com
First Edition
Cover Design by S. M. Savoy
Purfit/S.M. Savoy
ISBN: 978-1-947122-61-1

CONTENTS

CONTENTS... 7

1 1

2 16

3 41

4 56

5 79

6 92

7 97

8 105

9 111

10 124

11 140

12 150

13 157

14 166

15 179

16 195

17 211

18 219

19 237

20 250

21 262

22 265

23 278

24 288

25 306

26 317

27 328

28 341
EPILOGUE...353
    THE END 356

1

"Will this take much longer?" I asked.

"Just a few more minutes," the doctor scrapping my head said absently. "Remain still, please."

She finished taking her swabs, which hadn't hurt at all since she'd numbed the skin, and she placed the bloody culture with the rest of them.

A nurse took the tray and hurried from the room.

"All done. You can dress," the doctor said briskly as she stripped off her gloves. She threw the gloves into a bin marked *Hazardous Hifis Material Burn Only* and began to wash at the sink. "I need to repeat the scan in an hour, but it appears that nothing was done to you."

I rolled my eyes, but my shirt was covering my face and I knew she couldn't see me. They'd given me a set of clean fatigues when they'd taken my clothing away. It felt odd to be wearing the two pieces instead of a one-piece BDU. The clothes were too big for me but better than wearing a hospital gown.

She said, "You won't be able to contact your ship in here, but as soon as you can, ask it to scan you too. We'll be sending you there directly on your release, but don't enter the hanger until the scan is complete. We can't take a chance that you harbor some sort of biological weapon intended for Zeus."

"How likely is that?"

"Very unlikely. We understand quite a bit about how Hifis works now and any deadly agent would kill you instantly or you could shift to heal it, but there's always a chance that the Geromi have other types of viruses available that wouldn't kill you but would decommission that ship."

"A virus can kill me?"

"Anything that can kill a human can kill you unless you reset. The onset of disease would happen slower for you. Your immune system is a measure of order stronger than a human. I couldn't say how much stronger without testing as it varies, but in general wounds will clot much faster and your stamina would be greater. If you begin to feel ill or more hungry or tired than your activity can account for, come back at once."

She strode to the door and wrote on the chart beside it.

An orderly entered and began neatening the room.

She said, "We probably shouldn't let you return to general population."

I said, "Whatever you say, doc."

She gestured dismissively. "I'll be back for further tests in an hour. Don't shift. We want the wounds to discharge into the bandaging."

She left and the orderly made a face at her retreating back and said, "Come with me, please."

I followed him to an elevator at the end of the hall where he used a retinal scanner, thumb print scanner, and then punched in a twelve-digit password to open the door.

A man spoke from the intercom in the ceiling as we descended.

"What do you have, Jack?"

"A subject of Doctor Kendall." Jack turned to me and said, "What's your designation?"

"My name? Recruit Mia Sutton, serial number—"

Jack interrupted by slashing his hand in the air. "Never mind. She must be new. They're still catching them all the damned time."

I said, "You have Hifis infected people here?"

He ignored me, and my feet began to tingle.

The elevator doors opened, and the tingles surged to the crown of my head. The man waiting at the doors wore black armor and carried a nightstick, but it was his disgusted smirk that made me back away from him.

Jack said, "She's a cooperative one and the doc wants her back upstairs in an hour."

"Where the hell am I supposed to put her? Every damned cage is full."

"You aren't caging me," I said. "I'll wait in my exam room."

Neither man even glanced at me.

Jack said, "Put her in with thirty-two. She's restrained and docile enough with the other animals."

"Take me back upstairs right now!"

"They shouldn't let them run around without restraints," the new man said. His lip lifted in a sneer as he gestured me forward with the stick. "Don't make this harder on yourself than it needs to be."

I hesitated. This was likely some sort of stupid test by the doctors but neither man wore a uniform. I didn't have to obey their orders. But if this *was* a test, I didn't want to fail it.

I hesitantly stepped forward. The hall was wide with doors on both side. The doors on the left side of the hall were metal with high-tech looking locks and small barred openings that closed with metal panels, and the ones on the right were simple bars or normal looking doors. The place was obviously undergoing upgrading.

I stopped when I reached the first barred door. Three naked men sat on the floor in a room no bigger than a supply closet. They were all shackled by one hand to the wall.

"No fucking way," I said and turned back to the elevator. It had a call button that I could use. I was sure the doctor hadn't meant for me to be sent down here with criminals. "I'm not a criminal."

"You're a filthy fucking animal."

I was too shocked to speak for a moment and in that moment he touched my hand with the stick he carried.

Fire licked along my nerves and my body convulsed so hard that I thought my bones might have broken. I bit my tongue hard enough that blood trickled down my chin and choked on blood and shattered remnants of teeth. The pain was excruciating but quickly became numb. I couldn't force my limbs to obey me.

"Easy, Nimons. You'll kill it. It hasn't acclimated yet."

"Just get it into the damned cage. They're going to kill us all letting these animals down here unchained."

"Doc doesn't want it to shift. They're testing something on its head."

As they were speaking, the two men picked me up by my hands and feet and carried me down the hall.

They dropped me by another grill door that locked with a key that Nimons took from his pocket. Jack dragged me inside and let me drop again. The girl already in the tiny cell was huddled against the far wall with her knees to her chest and her arms around them. She looked familiar but it might have been her shaved head. I was getting my wind back but remained motionless, deciding on my course of action.

I could shift, but I wasn't sure if I could do it fast enough to reach the door before it closed, and even if I could get into the hall, I'd be trapped down here. My only hope was the boys.

A sick feeling filled my gut. Bradly would have them somewhere just as secure as this. I was sure of it. They might even be down here already.

"Adan! Luke!"

"They always yell for their fucking pack mates first," Nimons said disgustedly with more than a hint of superior condescension as he nudged me hard with his boot.

The girl in the corner ducked her head, turning as far away as the collar on her neck allowed and huddling lower, trying to use the dirty hospital gown she wore to cover more of herself.

He slapped me hard, saying smugly, "Shut up. Keep quiet and do what you're told or you'll wish you had.

You might not feel much pain but there are other ways to make you cooperate."

Jack said, "I told you, she's a cooperative one. Leave her alone." He squatted beside me and tilted my chin. "I think you broke her teeth. Get her a towel or something." He wiped his hands when he stood, frowning at me as he said, "And don't try shifting. The doctor said not to. I'm sure it's uncomfortable but if you won't cooperate with the doctors, we'll need to shackle you."

Nimons reached forward with the nightstick, and I scrambled away. He laughed and tapped my leg. A soft tingle made me jerk and cry out.

"Lowest setting," he said smugly.

Jack grabbed his shoulder and pulled him from the room.

"Let her clean up a bit or we're going to catch hell."

The door clanked shut behind them, and I sank to the floor, shaking.

"How'd they catch you?" the girl asked.

"Because I'm a fucking idiot and turned myself in!"

She winced, lifting a hand to the collar.

I said, "Let me see if I can get it off you."

"Don't come near me!"

Her voice was high and frightened and her expression angry.

I held up my hand, scooting away from her. My tongue was still bleeding. I removed my shirt to wipe my face, leaving me in the too big t-shirt.

Nimons and Jack returned, and Jack handed me a damp cloth. I took it and cleaned myself as best I could.

"See, she's cooperative. I'll be back to bring you upstairs in an hour."

Jack left, and Nimons crouched in front of me.

"You're going to be a good little monkey, right?"

I said, "I'm a private in Afar and you're a thug in guard's clothing. You touch me again and you're going to be sorry."

He tapped me with the stick as I knew he would, and I laughed. "Is that all you got?"

"Don't," the girl said breathlessly, and Nimons tapped me again, turning to her while I was catching my breath. I wanted him to hit me with it. I needed to acclimate to it if I was going to fight effectively when they brought me wherever they were bringing me for their tests.

I figured they'd remove my coms next. I was betting whatever it was that they'd done to my head was meant to fool Whiroon somehow, which meant my DNA. Whiroon would scan for me in another thirty minutes and when it couldn't reach me, it would call my crew.

It would insist on seeing me, so they must think they could fool it. While I was imagining how they might be able to do that, Nimons was stroking the girl's hair. His expression was lecherous—mocking. I knew he meant to infer that I was next.

I was debating which form I should take or if taking one was the goal. They knew I had a rat form and rats were weak creatures, soft and easily frightened. My cat was strong, but they knew I had that too and a cat couldn't open doors. I could be my squirrel. It had hand-like paws and could hold things and fight, but it was a small soft creature too. But I had another form, one I'd never taken. Grots had hand-like paws too and they were fast with razor sharp teeth and they weren't small although they were dumb like an animal. I probably wouldn't lose much intellect though. It was the biggest of my forms.

He stood and tapped his leg with the stick, pursing his lips at me. "I like my rides a little livelier than this." He touched me with the stick again and while I shivered from the electricity coursing through me, he said, "Having friends here can make this easy. I'm a good friend to have. You're never getting out of here, but you can be sent to nicer quarters, and I can help make that happen. If you cooperate, and I mean fully cooperate"—he emphasized the word fully, adjusting his pants in an unmistakable way—"I'll take care of you."

I said, "I'm not going to cooperate in my own rape or in anything at all. And I doubt you have permission to treat us like this or any pull. We'll see what Kendall says."

"She'll say you're the lying animal you are, and when you're returned to me, I'll cut the lying tongue from your head and make your friend here eat it—You can count on that! And she's going to confirm your lies, or you'll be dining on her toes and any other part I cut off."

By the way the girl shook I knew he'd meant what he'd said.

Jack said, "Is there a problem in here?"

"No problem." Nimons grinned at me, tapped me again, turning to the grill where he waved Jack away.

"Just getting acquainted, filling her in on how we do things down here."

"Threatening to rape me and cut me up," I added in the same tone he'd used when I'd caught my breath.

Nimons adjusted a setting on the stick and reached, not to me, but to the girl.

She shrieked and shifted into a pitbull and began to choke on the collar that had tightened and retracted into the wall.

"She'll fucking rip you to shreds," Nimons said happily as I ran to help her.

She thrashed and snapped. Her paw cut a gash above my eye, but she wasn't snapping at me but Nimons.

Jack said, "Nimons...."

His tone was worried and angry, but I didn't have time to see if he meant to help her. She was suffocating, and I couldn't get the collar off of her.

Nimons put his hand on my neck and whispered, "Are you ready to be friends?"

I was suddenly my grot form. I slashed at him, catching him and myself by surprise. My pants tangled around my feet making me awkward. *Not fucking ideal* I thought angrily as my skin hummed and jumped as if it couldn't settle on the form. It didn't hurt but was deeply disturbing as if I might fall to pieces any second. Whiroon had warned that making a Hifis form from Hifis wasn't a good idea, so I knew it could be done but I was worried now it would dust me, but it was too late. I was stuck in this form for six minutes.

"Code Red!" Jack bellowed.

"It's a fucking alien!" Nimons screamed, trying to swing the stick at me. "Don't fucking toast them with me in here!"

I bit his arm, clamping down as hard as I could while reaching for his face with my paw. Blood sprayed and he shrieked as I ripped deep furrows across his face. I yanked the stick from his grasp and let him retreat while I grabbed the girl and used my teeth to rip the collar from her neck. My shirt dangled around my neck caught my front paw, making me awkward. It took me a second to rip loose.

She lunged forward and Nimons shrieked again as she bit into his leg. I ran for the door, ignoring them and the dangling shirt. Jack let Nimons fall to slam the door closed and ran down the hall. I whirled.

The girl continued to savage him, caught up in blood lust, ignoring me as I grabbed the keys from his pocket.

Making my arm small enough to fit through the grill made the disconcerting feeling of falling apart worse. Flecks drifted from me. I hoped it was my imagination and blood and not me turning to dust in slow motion, but it felt as if I was turning to dust. It was hard to make my paws work, but I continued and had the door unlocked within moments.

I ran down the hall. The movement firmed my body, making the shivery sensation fade. Jack had exited the corridor. I threw myself against the door, grasping the handle as sirens and lights flickered to life.

"You fucking idiot!" someone yelled angrily. "They'll fucking incinerate us!"

"It's a fucking alien. You think it cares? We didn't do anything! It isn't us!"

The men and women around me continued to yell. I turned and ran the other way. I might be able to force the elevator doors, and if I could force those doors that red intercom button might be our salvation. There was a chance Whiroon was monitoring it. I hadn't told the ship not to scan for me only to give me radio silence and I again cursed my stupidity for doing so.

I'd given them the time they'd needed. I bet Jacobs was in Bradly's office right now laughing over how he'd manipulated me so easily.

I snarled then howled, unable to control my reaction to the thoughts of my pack mates in their clutches. Clutches that I'd sent them into by sending them to look at the fucking nonexistent corpse.

My anger gave me strength. I forced my claws into the elevator door, whining at the pain of my claw tips tearing loose and the pressure of the doors squeezing my paws, but I continued to force them into the widening crack.

The pain faded leaving my paws numb and hard to manipulate like a tooth with Novocain. I howled more from fear than pain as my bones cracked but I managed to get the door open.

Shifting to my human form was a terrifying moment of nothingness. I was aware but not able to see hear or move, trapped in a black void unable to even scream.

Light, sound and motion returned simultaneously, and I fell hard.

Somewhere behind me a man was yelling for backup, and a siren was deafeningly loud above me.

I stabbed the red button and shouted, "Whiroon, run away! Execute plan release! Whiroon, run away! Execute plan release! Whiroon, run away! Execute plan release!"

"Mia!" Carr said sounding shocked and worried.

I spun, thrusting my arms through the dangling t-shirt. It barely provided modesty, but I'd done it to avoid tripping on it or leaving it to choke me.

"Get this elevator moving right fucking now or I'll tell it to execute last resort!"

"It can't hear you. Jesus, what the hell are you doing down here?" He spread his hands in a calming motion, saying, "Why is she down here?" to Jack and the two men with him.

All three men carried assault rifles and incendiary grenades.

Jack said, "Don't get too close. She isn't human. She's one of them."

The dog ran from the cell and leaped onto the closest man, clamping down hard on his armored arm. Gunshots knocked her loose, slamming her into the wall. I stabbed the red button and yelled! "Whiroon, fire on my location! I need a way out!"

14

I ran forward but halted when two of them shot into the floor at my feet.

I yelled, "Get the fuck away from her! She isn't a threat now!"

They might have killed me right then, but Carr jumped in front of them, spreading his arms and screaming for them to cease firing.

Angry tears streamed down my face. I knew Whiroon couldn't hear me and there was nothing I could do to stop them from killing her. There wasn't anything I could do to save myself. I was as trapped as she was.

2

Carr said, "Get back. Turn off the sirens and get me a secure line!" He knelt beside the dog, removing his belt to tie off the severed end of her hind leg.

"Get me ten cc's of adrenaline, stat!"

Jack ran back down the hall. One of the men had turned away and was speaking on the radio; the other kept his gunsights firmly on me.

"I'll fucking kill you all!" I clamped my lips together.

Threatening them was stupid. *Never let them know you're going to attack.* My father's advice rang through my head and I was furious with myself for not following it. He'd known that to reveal myself was a losing move— and I'd done it anyway.

Carr said, "Mia, let us help her."

"Get away from her!"

To my surprise, he did.

I ran forward, slipping in the blood and catching myself hard on my hands and knees.

Her pulse was thready but the blood was already slowing. I wasn't sure if it was slowing because she was dying or because her wounds were clotting. I knew they wouldn't heal until she shifted, and I needed her to wake but didn't trust that he'd actually give her the adrenaline.

Jack had no incentive to keep her alive and every reason to kill her.

I said, "Let me take her outside."

"She's dangerous, Mia."

"Let me go outside."

"I will after we talk."

I clamped my lips hard. I had no way to force him. I nodded as if I believed him as I examined the closest cells.

I'd dropped the key to my door. It lay in the hallway mere feet away. I couldn't grab it though with the gun aimed at me. That gun could cut me in half before I got two feet. I'd have tried it if I wore a vest but I only wore the damned t-shirt.

I said, "You can tell him to stand down or at least send him to the end of the hall."

Carr glanced at the dog then the soldier, licking his lips. "I think it's better if he stays here for the moment." He walked forward slowly to crouch three feet from me.

The soldier said, "Careful sir, that's a grot, and it can reach you from there."

I said, "Throw me my pants or her clothes to bind her wounds."

Carr said, "Do it."

The soldier hesitated. I was putting pressure on the bigger wound in her chest. The blood had stopped pumping and I couldn't feel her pulse anymore, but I didn't think she was dead. Her body still felt warm.

The soldier said, "I'm sorry sir, but my orders are to protect the staff here, and it would be a mistake to leave you alone with it."

Carr stood and ran for the open door of my cell.

I gathered my feet beneath me, trying to pretend my movements were to help the dog.

The people in the nearest cells were quiet but all of them stood in their doorways watching. A man on the left had his face pressed hard against the opening in his metal door.

He said pleadingly, "Get her water, Adam's, please! I'm begging you!" His gaze flicked to me and he said, "Is she alive? Molly, can you hear me? You need to shift back. Please, Molly!"

18

He began to cry, trying to push his hand through the bars. I gathered Molly into my arms. I knew where I'd seen her before now, she'd been on Gamma Team. I'd seen them together.

"Carr," the soldier said nervously as I advanced.

He backed away, letting me bring the dog to the crying man.

"Molly, please..." he begged frantically as Carr exited my cell.

His face was grim and his hands bloody. He threw my pants to me. I ripped them up to bind Molly's wounds.

Jack returned carrying a black bag followed by four more soldiers.

I said, "You better pray that whatever Kendall did to me worked because Whiroon will be looking for me soon."

Jack handed Carr a phone and I waited for him to accept it and dial before yelling. "Whiroon, run away, execute plan rescue!"

Carr punched buttons and then pressed the phone to his chest. I laughed.

"Think it heard me?"

Distantly a siren began to wail, and I laughed again.

"Guess so," I said triumphantly.

Carr looked scared, and the men confused.

"Who's in charge now?" I asked as I stood. I pointed at Jack and jerked my thumb at Molly. "Open his cage."

"He's dangerous."

Muffled explosions in the distance made everyone still for a moment.

"I'm fucking dangerous! Do it! Carr! Give me the phone or I'll let it execute my plan."

Carr hesitated and then handed me the phone.

He said, "I was calling the general. This is all a misunderstanding."

"Oh, I understand perfectly! Let him the fuck out!"

Carr said, "Let him out."

Jack said, "We can't. Even if we wanted to, we can't."

"Help her. Please, for the love god help her!" the man said.

I backed away from her, saying, "Help her. Don't let her die, Carr. I'm not in a forgiving mood."

I had his phone but no idea who to call. I had no allies at all, except Whiroon, and I hadn't thought to give it a phone number. Even if I could get my ship on the phone, I had no idea what to order it to do other than what I'd already ordered.

Carr took the black bag and knelt beside Molly. He injected her in the chest, and she moaned while the man in the cell cried and begged her to shift.

Her form shimmered and reformed to her human shape. Her long blond hair trailed through the blood on the floor. She tried and failed to stand, getting herself all bloody in the process. She'd lost the dirty gown in the fight. Her hair barely provided any modesty from the gawking men, which was infuriating.

I wiped my sweating face with my bloody hand. "Give her your shirt or something." I glanced at the man who was still trying to reach her through the bars where she was huddled, crying hard.

I said, "How do the doors open?"

The man in the cell said, "He'll have a key."

I ran for the key I'd dropped, and the soldiers all jumped away, tightening their grips on their weapons.

Carr said, "If you can open the door, do it!"

"If we open the door, he'll attack us, and we'll have to kill him."

I said, "He won't attack you. We're walking out of here, all of us."

Carr said, "Call off the ship."

"Let us out and I will."

My key turned in the lock, but the door didn't open.

"Mia, we don't have time. Call it off now!"

"Then you better do it quickly."

Carr yelled, "Open the fucking doors!"

The soldier beside Jack said, "His cell has the auto locking feature. All of the cells on this side do. As soon as the alarm sounded, the mechanism engaged, and it can't be overridden from in here."

21

Carr said, "Please, Mia! If that ship takes off, people will see it. Just give me five minutes! Please!"

I said, "Molly, come with me. We'll come back for them, I promise. One of you assholes give her your fucking shirt!" I grabbed Molly's arm as Carr began removing his shirt.

She resisted me, and the man in the cell waved her away. "Go. Get out if you can. I love you. Please go!"

I ran for the elevator. She'd either follow or not. I didn't have time to worry about her. Carr chased after me followed by three of the soldiers.

"If one hair on her head is harmed, I'll fucking destroy Olympus!"

Carr said, "She won't be harmed. We haven't hurt her. This is a secure facility meant to hold Hifis spies."

"Shut up! And get this thing moving."

Carr punched buttons with shaking hands. "You shouldn't have been brought down here. If you let me have the phone, I can call and get the jammers turned off so that you can speak to your ship."

Molly ran down the hall. I held my hand out to stop the door from closing so she could reach us and hugged her quickly when she did.

"Give me the guns," I said as the elevator began to move.

Carr removed his shirt and handed it to Molly. "Give her the weapons."

Jack said, "We can't do that. We shouldn't even be letting it leave."

"If you don't, she'll send her ship back to Geromi for reinforcements. We're going to let her step outside to order the ship to remain where it is."

"It's on the moon by now and you aren't giving me orders. You have thirty minutes before Whiroon begins its attack. You can kill me and then it will proceed to our last resort."

Carr said to the soldiers, "Your standing orders allow for the delivery of prisoners to the offices upstairs. I want you to call in to get your new orders, which I'm certain will be to do whatever she tells us to do. This hasn't escalated to a no-win scenario. It was a misunderstanding that we can work it out if everyone remains sensible."

I said, "I want them all released and that isn't negotiable. I'm done playing your games."

The door to the elevator opened onto the same hall I'd left minutes ago but now the hall was full of armed men. Car stepped into the hallway with his hands lifted.

A soldier stepped forward and offered him a cell phone. "The jammers have been turned off. The phone will work. General Bradly has ordered us to escort Recruit Sutton to him." He eyed me doubtfully, his gaze traveling my bloody legs and then swinging to Molly who held the back of my shirt.

I said, "What time is it?"

"Sixteen forty-two," Carr said after glancing at his watch.

"Then we can wait right here for ten minutes."

I took Molly's hand, pulled her into the nearest exam room, and closed the door.

She ran for the sink.

I said, "I have no idea who to call for help."

She drank deeply for a minute and when she backed away, I drank as she said, "Thank you, but I'm not helping you either."

I snorted, moving away so she could drink again.

"I'm not an alien. I'm as human as you. I just have a grot form and believe me when I say you don't want one. I thought it would turn me to dust to use it. How many of us do they have down there?"

"Thirty or so."

"We're they all hiding in the service?"

"I don't think so. Alex and I were. We thought it would be safer for them and us. We should have run..."

"I hear that..."

"What are we going to do?"

"Make them let us go. I have no idea where we can go... I have to get my pack back. Did they bring anyone down there recently?"

"No. You're the first one in weeks."

"Jesus, how long were you down there?"

24

She began to cry again, and I awkwardly patted her back.

"That fucker!" I said angrily as she leaned over the sink to vomit.

"He deserved everything he got! Don't you dare feel bad about him!" I left her vomiting in the sink to search the room. There was nothing we could use as clothing or as weapons.

The sirens shut off, and I ran to the window to look outside but couldn't see anything, except another building like the one I was in and a group of armed men forming up to the right.

"What are we waiting for?" she asked.

"My coms to come back online."

"Will they?"

"Maybe."

She joined me at the window. "I'm fast but not faster than a speeding bullet."

"I don't think we can run," I agreed. "I have a cat shape and it's really fast, but they know I do. Our only hope is my ship. If I can call it, they'll have to stand down, but they know that..."

"Then your coms aren't coming back online..."

I grimaced. "Not if they can help it, but I was the one who turned them off, so maybe they didn't have time to finish whatever it was they planned to do to stop us from calling."

She gave me an incredulous look as if she couldn't believe anyone would be that stupid.

"How do you have two shapes?"

"You might be able to have two shapes. Is all you need is fresh blood, the will to transform into the shape, and the ability to metabolize HGTRF. You haven't happened to eat raw tiger lately, have you?"

She snorted with nervous laughter, and I said, "Don't try a new shape until I can check your HGTRF levels unless it's life or death. You might have enough, but it might dust you."

The men outside stood in neat rows and were facing away. I wasn't sure what they were doing or if they were involved in this.

I said, "I'm not sure what I should do now. Whiroon will fight for me but it can be destroyed, and we really need the information it has although maybe they figure they have all they need from it..." My voice broke and I was suddenly crying. "I think they killed them. God, I can't believe how stupid I was."

She said, "I have to agree. Turning yourself in was really stupid."

The men in the hall began to talk loudly.

I angrily wiped my eyes to put my ear to the door.

"*Uh oh*, they're ordering them out."

Lines appeared by Molly's eyes. She bit her lip, her glance darting to the window and the door.

26

I knew she was debating if she should run or try to go back for Alex.

"Will they burn the building?" she asked.

"Maybe, but I can call my ship in just a few more minutes and there's men right outside. I don't think they'll bomb it with them so close."

She said, "They can burn the cells individually."

"Fuckers," I muttered, and she laughed an angry laugh that changed to tears. "Make them let him out."

"I will but I have no way other than Whiroon to do that." But I yanked the door open and said, "I want Alex..."

"Petrov," Molly said.

"Alex Petrov brought to me!"

Carr said, "I have General Bradly on the line—"

"I have nothing to say to him!"

"Mr. Lewis would like to speak with you urgently. I've told him your coms are still down but..."

I ran into the hall to snatch the phone from Carr.

"Adan?"

"This is General Bradly. What the hell is going on there?"

"Don't bother, General. That bird has flown. Get me Adan or so help me God..."

"Mia, I really have no idea. Carr called me in hysterics. Bauer called to say the ship has closed its hatches. The ship blew the flagpole in front of my building and then scorched a line in the pavement. Adan called threatening to destroy my base if you weren't brought to him pronto. No one seems to know what caused this rapid escalation. I thought we had an agreement?"

"You thought you had me trapped! What is wrong with you people? Why the hell would you do this? She's just a girl with a disease!"

"You're not making any sense!"

I was so furious that I stuttered as I yelled, "Kn-kn-kn-ock it the f-f-fuck off! I've seen your s-s-secret labs here and what you have in st-store for me! Get me my pack and do it right f-f-fucking now!"

"The labs... Do you mean the holding cells there? You shouldn't have been sent to a cell."

"Damn right I shouldn't have been! You sh-sh-should've assured I was neutralized first, but you fucked up and every fucking lie from your mouth is making me angrier!"

"Mia, I assure you—"

"Save it! Your assurance means nothing! Nothing! You assured me the infected, the people in your custody, were receiving the best, most humane treatment possible. You assured me I'd be free to continue my training. You assured me my Hifis needs would be met and my pack safe, that we wouldn't be separated, and then you tricked me into turning off my coms and threw me into a cell. Well, I assure you, you're going to regret it! If I don't have every single one of the people that you're fucking torturing brought to me within thirty minutes, I'll let Whiroon do whatever the fuck it wants—and that's on you!

"Shoot it down. Murder me. Do whatever the fuck you're going to do, but the loss of everything that ship might have done for humankind is on your head, you lying sack of shit!"

Molly's eyes had widened during my tirade. She gaped at me.

Carr said, "The men and women downstairs were apprehended on military bases and are being held for questioning. Mia, you've seen how well Geromi can infiltrate and the distasteful methods we sometimes need to employ to get their cooperation."

"Fuck you! She's a human girl just like I am and raping and torturing her isn't going to do a damned thing to help us! You're a sick fuck who gets off on humiliating us."

Molly said, "I've never met him."

Carr nodded, spreading his hands and shaking his head with such an overdone sad expression that I laughed. "It won't work. Save your manipulation for someone who's buying."

"Mia!" Adan shouted from the end of the hall.

I dropped the phone to run to him.

He caught me in a hard embrace, saying angrily, "Whiroon, continue program- I say it three times."

"Acknowledged," Whiroon said from Adan's x-com.

"What the fuck did you do to her?" he asked as he examined me.

"They locked me up with a psychotic guard." I examined my bloody shirt and legs. "Most of this is her blood though."

"Most of it..." His expression darkened and he opened his mouth to say something, and I laid a hand over it. "Don't order Zeus to do anything until we have them all somewhere safe. Where's Luke?"

"Going to the ship."

"I'm fine," Luke said from Adan's x-coms.

"How did you get away?"

"We weren't caught."

I frowned and stepped farther back to examine him. He wore BDU and looked angry but not disheveled.

Carr said, "See, we weren't trying anything. It was all a misunderstanding."

"Fuck you!"

Adan looked shocked for a moment and then hugged me, reaching a hand to Molly.

"They're coming with me."

Molly said, "I can't go without Alex."

"Her pack," I whispered, as Adan said, "Are you hurt?"

I wasn't sure if he meant me or her.

I said, "I think we're okay. Grot is disgusting. Don't do it unless you have to. I couldn't have gotten away without it though. We need a monkey."

He kissed the top of my head.

Molly said, "I'm okay..." she began to cry. "I'm not okay. I'm scared to death. I just want out of here! This place is a nightmare!"

I said, "The feed parts of her to her boyfriend to make her cooperate."

"We never..." Carr's indignant shout trailed off when Molly collapsed at our feet crying. Adan released me to pull her up and swing her into his arms. His gaze darted from Carr to the men at the end of the hall.

Carr cleared his throat. "I can see there was some misconduct here, but I assure you—"

"Shut the fuck up! Your assurance means shit to me! What's taking so fucking long to get Alex up here?"

The men at the end of the corridor began to exit. Adan grabbed my hand, but we hadn't taken two steps when Bradly entered. He'd come alone and was unarmed but the hair on my arms remained standing. I figured he'd sacrifice himself to stop Whiroon.

Luke said, "Troops withdrawing. I don't like this, Adan."

Adan said, "Are you with the ship?"

"I'm at the hanger but they won't let me in. They're checking my clearance."

Bradly said, "He'll be allowed through any moment."

I said, "We have moments!"

I tugged Adan to the room we'd just exited.

Neither Bradly or Carr attempted to stop us. I covered my face with my arm and jumped through the glass. Adan and Molly followed me.

A few men hollered but distance and my heart beating in my ears made them unintelligible.

I said, "She has a dog shape. I don't know if she can be small."

"Not really," Molly said. "I can't leave him!"

She was standing on her own again, looking pale and shaky.

Adan said, "He'd want you safe. We'll go back for him. I promise."

"Luke?" I asked.

Luke said, "I don't know. There's lots of movement but I'm not sure what's related to us. They really locked you up?"

Adan said, "They hurt her. She's all bloody and half naked."

Molly began to cry again, and she stumbled, falling to her hands and knees. "He was going to rape her and feed me her tongue. Oh god. Oh god."

She began to vomit, and I squatted to put my arms around her.

"Did he..." Adan trailed off, hugged us both a second, then tried to pull us up.

He said, "We need to get out of here."

Luke said, "Bradly is saying it was a mistake. A misunderstanding and that he didn't know."

"Fuck them!" I snarled.

Luke said, "I just meant, maybe he didn't know."

"He should have known! These are his men on his base!"

"I'm not arguing that. I just mean maybe you're safe now."

Adan said, "We'll never be safe."

Molly was crying hard and shivering. Her skin felt cold and clammy. I didn't think she'd be able to run long, if at all.

"Molly!" Alex called, and she collapsed completely as he ran up to us.

"Thank you," he said to me as he knelt to pick her up. "They fucking tortured her. They're the animals! We should fucking kill them all."

"He's dead," I said. "I'll do my best to see they all pay but we're not safe here."

Luke said, "Bradly said to tell you that he's having the Hifis all brought to the auditorium were we see the exhibits and that you can go there to speak to them or he can patch in a feed from there to wherever we want. I'm in the ship with Jay."

"Jesus, I forgot all about my damned crew."

Jay said, "That's understandable but not very reassuring. You're our only protection too."

"How do I make them safe, Jay?"

"I don't think you can."

I said, "Luke, patch the general through to me."

Bradly said stiffly, "Mia, thank you for speaking to us."

I said, "My nation has just gotten bigger. I'm asking for an embassy with all of the same rights that any embassy has. I want a signed treaty with the United States saying that every one of my citizens, which includes every single Hifis main grown human on this planet, or any other planet, is now a citizen of the nation Whiroon.

"You can locate our embassy wherever you like or even have a few locations, but all embassies must remain in contact with Zeus. My citizens will be allowed to live in my embassy without interference from anyone. It's sovereign ground of Whiroon. If you want to speak with anyone, you'll use the same channels you'd use for any other embassy."

Bradly said, "I'd like to cooperate. I *will* cooperate, but some Hifis are very dangerous."

"That's my problem, not yours."

"It's my problem if they leave your custody. It's my problem if your embassy is attacked and your citizens are used as hostages."

"Then you better make sure that doesn't happen. Give them a safe place to live and let them live in peace. They can apply for a visa if they want to leave the embassy, and you can deny it or not. I won't stop them from leaving but I won't lock them up and treat them like animals either. The things they did to her... you should be ashamed!"

"I *am* ashamed and angry. I'd like to speak with her to apologize but also to find out who else was involved. Luke has replayed the conversation, and I'm horrified. I really had no idea, and before you say it, I know that isn't an excuse. I've ordered every person who works in this facility held for questioning. I'll get to the bottom of this, and she'll have justice."

"Speaking of justice, Nimons deserved everything he got. We were fighting for our lives. I didn't attack him until he attacked me. I know I can't prove it because he's dead and you don't believe her, but it's true, and I'm not letting you pull her in for any reason. She's the victim here, and I'll protect her with all the force I can."

"I'll speak with our lawyers and see what I can do to arrange things as you'd like."

"Is Jacobs really dead?"

Bradly's voice softened. "Yes. I'm sorry, Mia. I wish it were a ploy, but he's really dead."

"Well don't send me Captain Newels. He's an ass and he hates me already."

"Where will you be?"

"I have no idea. Luke, where should we go?"

"Come to me. Zeus will see if any aircraft come in range, and it can shoot down missiles or we can run from here."

I said, "They'll be trying to figure out ways to disarm Zeus. I think we should move the ship."

Adan said, "I agree. We should move it and deactivate all coms and fire all crew."

Bradly said, "We really do need access.'"

"Then you'll just have to work with us."

Alex laughed bitterly. "You can ask the animals for help." He kissed the top of Molly's head and said, "She needs somewhere warm and quiet."

Adan said, "Jay, get us some blankets. You're in charge of our crew now and our Visa officer. Decide who gets to stay working with Zeus and who doesn't. We'll be staying with the ship until further notice, so we'll need supplies brought in, and I hope I don't need to say this, General, but the first inkling that you're not working in good faith with us means we'll declare war.

"I believe you mistakenly sent her to the cells, but it's opened my eyes to how ruthless you'll be with us.

I'm damned sorry, Jay, that it took this to do it. I should've done this the minute I met you. Actually, the minute I knew we could use Whiroon, but I was trying to be normal." He laughed bitterly. "I was hiding, even from myself, I think."

Jay said, "I'd have hidden it too. No hard feelings, commander. Do I have your permission to arrange for x-coms for spouses and dependents of Hifis main grown human?"

"You do. Do whatever you think best to arrange for their safety. Don't hesitate to call us. Luke, work with Jay on whatever programs he thinks we need to have as a backup. General, I'm aware our situation is precarious and that it rests solely on the power of that ship, but I'd like to change that. If you'll help us, I mean really help us, we could show the world that we can be treated just like anyone else. We still want to help the United States win the coming war.

Bradly said, "Let me discuss this with legal counsel."

I said, "Tell Carr someone from Whiroon will be in touch shortly to see about resettling his slaves. Disconnect from them."

"All clear," Luke said a moment later.

I said, "I'm not convinced it was an accident. And I don't think it matters. We can't trust them."

Adan said, "We'll be stronger now with more people. It will be harder for them to silence us all before Zeus notices."

I said, "Should I call for an ambulance for her?"

Luke said, "I'll arrange a car. Stay there until it arrives. How the hell will we handle dangerous Hifis though?"

"The same way we handle dangerous people. Anyone would be dangerous if they were locked up like that. If they have no criminal record, they can just go."

Jay said, "Some of them really are dangerous. They can't control themselves at all."

"Then they'll know that, right? I mean, if I were prone to attacking everyone I saw, I'd want someone to confine me, and I wouldn't object to that confinement unless it was scary. Couldn't we just give them a nice house to stay in with people they like and won't attack?"

"Sure, but where do we get this house?"

Adan said, "Let's see how many we're talking about first. I'm sure whatever building they give us will be a very secure building. Use whatever existing crew you need to figure out how many of our new citizens would be dangerous if released. I don't see any reason why they couldn't just put the Hifis up like they do crew."

I said, "There was no reason for them to take her from training and throw her into a cell."

Luke said, "Actually we don't know why they threw her into a cell. Maybe there was. Maybe she was working with the Chinese or something."

I rubbed my suddenly throbbing head. I'd forgotten about the quislings and hadn't told the boys about them. It was possible that she'd been arrested for working with the enemy. I'd acted on impulse because she could have been me.

Alex said indignantly, "She isn't a criminal! We were just recruits like you!"

I said, "How'd you get caught?"

"We'd sneak out when we could to be together. Not for sex just to be together although sometimes... he trailed off, clearing his throat.

Molly said, "You called him my pack and I guess he is although I never thought about it like that."

I squatted beside her to feel her forehead. She was still cold and clammy and very pale.

I said, "I want to be with them all the time, so I understand. It's relaxing to sleep together, and I don't mean sex either."

Alex shrugged uncomfortably. "We'd shift and play a bit if we could, but there wasn't much space to run. We can be smaller but not by much. I guess we got cocky because we fell asleep and someone stumbled on us."

Moly said, "We didn't mean to hurt him."

"Did he die?" Adan asked.

"I don't know. I think so."

She began to cry again, and Alex glared at Adan.

Adan shrugged at him, saying, "They should've known to let sleeping dogs lie."

I let out a surprised bark of horrified laughter.

Adan said, "If we weren't terrified, we wouldn't attack when startled!"

Alex said, "They're not going to keep their word to us! You know that, right?"

Adan said, "I'll make them keep it."

Alex picked Molly up and said, "I don't care if you're aliens or not. You're nicer than they are."

"We're not aliens," Adan said.

Alex's expression said he didn't believe that, but it was clear that he didn't care either. He wanted her safe, and I could relate. I wanted my pack mates safe too. I also thought he was right and that the people in charge here wouldn't keep their word. I hoped Adan was right too and we could make them.

3

My head ached with the worse stress headache of my life. Whiroon's hanger was crowded. Hifis crew that Adan and I had made had jammed into the room and were arguing over what we should do. Molly and Alex were the only Hifis from the lab here. All the rest of them had been brought to the auditorium where we watched exhibitions, except for a group of ten who were going through the offices there.

Five of them were crew and five I'd picked at random from the Hifis incarcerated there. I'd given them x-coms and they were scanning every document with the simple expedient of looking at it and the document was sent to Zeus who was cross-checking all names in the files to be sure we had them all. The humans had been locked out of the building. So far we'd been given access to every room and file.

More Hifis were being brought in from other labs but most were still in whatever cells they'd been in. Now we were trying to figure out what to do with them all.

My crew was happily employed and didn't feel the need for protection that the incarcerated Hifis did. I thought if I wasn't being so adamant about freeing them that most of them would be fine leaving their fellows in the labs.

Molly sat beside me on the floor and leaned against the wall. She wore a borrowed gray sweatsuit like I did and hugged herself as though she was cold.

"What are we going to do?" she asked.

I took her hand. "Whatever we have to do."

Her gaze stayed on Alex who was talking to Luke and Jay.

I said, "You can have a normal life. I mean as much as anyone can now. You and Alex can decide where you want to go and what you want to do. No one will know you're Hifis unless you tell them. I'm insisting that all records be kept under our code names."

She pulled her hand from mine to rub her arms again.

"I'll help however I can," I said.

She said, "I believe you. I just don't know what to do. I thought we could make a life here and be useful. Our homes and families are gone. We were happy here or maybe not happy exactly, but we felt good about this, and honestly, I thought being Hifis here was sort of a good thing and that we'd be able to show ourselves eventually."

"That could still be true. I know they plan on asking me to infect combat specialists. Maybe you could apply for that job?"

"I don't trust them."

"Me either. I don't trust anyone but my pack. But that being said, I think their own rules will protect you now that you have us checking up on you."

"Thank you for that. Thanks for everything..."

"I should have done more sooner." I was going to say more but Luke and Alex approached, and Luke looked worried.

I stood and he gave me a hug.

"I have good news and bad news."

I sighed hard, and he said, "We're getting another fifty-three people delivered."

"Is that the good or the bad news?"

"I'm not sure. One of the people is Margaret Enfield."

"Goddamn Margaret Enfield..."

Luke laughed and Alex smiled uncertainly. My tone hadn't been angry but exasperated.

"Who's she?" Molly asked.

"My nemesis." I slashed my hand through the air. "It's nothing. Private joke. My life is a private joke..."

Luke slung his arm around me. "Let's get these guys coms and have their HGTRF checked and see if we can get them a better form."

Molly peered at us uncertainly.

Alex crouched to take her hand. "We should do it, Mol. A monkey form would be really useful."

I said, "There could be risk in it. It might dust you."

Luke shrugged one shoulder. "It's a really low chance."

"About three percent," I disagreed.

Molly said, "Are you going to do it?"

"Yeah. Speaking of that, where's Adan?"

"Don't get mad," Luke said hurriedly.

"Jesus! What now?"

I tapped the icon to connect me to Adan and got a message saying, *Unavailable by Request.*

I grunted in annoyance.

Luke said hurriedly, "I said don't get mad..."

"Just tell me, Luke."

"He and four others have gone into hiding and will remain in hiding, monitoring us until things are settled."

"What!"

"It was Jay's idea, and it's a good one. You're going to have to go to Washington to straighten this out. I'll stay here with Zeus, and Adan is our back up."

"I'll stay here. You go."

"No. I'm staying because I can work on programming, and you're going because you're the captain."

"This is ridiculous! And, oh my God, did he get a monkey shape without us?"

"He did, and the monkey is waiting for us."

"Jesus Fucking Christ!"

I stomped away but had to stop after ten feet because I had no idea where the monkey was.

Luke said, "She gets mad fast but calms quick too."

I stomped back to yell, "He didn't even say goodbye!"

"Because you'd never have agreed." He glanced at his wrist then waved me forward. "He'll check in on the hour and we should see that monkey first." He grabbed my shoulder to shake me lightly. "He left you a letter. I'll forward it. Don't be an ass and refuse to read it."

I huffed and tapped my foot. I wasn't angry, I was hurt. Luke's anxiety made me think this letter would be a dear John sort of letter, but anger was better than letting the pain of that thought take hold.

"Read it," Luke said again.

Molly and Alex trailed us to the far side of the hanger where a black curtain blocked a small cubicle that was filled with wire cages containing an assortment of animals.

Luke pointed to a chimp and said, "That one." He dragged an empty human-size cage out of the corner and opened the door.

I said, "We're doing this old school?"

"Yes." He gave me a hard hug and whispered, "I sent you a note too but don't read it unless it dusts me. It would just make you sad and there's no need to be sad. Promise me that you'll remember me with love and never regret our friendship, *mi amor*."

Tears clogged my throat. I nodded and kissed him.

He rested his forehead on mine a minute then knelt beside the chimp's cage. "Sorry, fella," he said as he offered a treat.

The chimp reached through the meal slot and Luke grabbed its arm and slashed a small cut that he ran his finger over then licked. I did the same.

Luke kissed me again and stepped into the cage, closing the door. Before I could say I love you, he'd shifted.

I sobbed once with relief.

"You okay?" I asked, and he nodded absently as he stretched out his arms and flexed his feet.

I turned away to read the email from Adan.

46

He'd recorded himself in front of the cage.

"*Mi amor*, don't be angry. It's better this way. I couldn't stand to see you attempt this and I don't want your last image of me to be dust on the floor. Remember how much I loved you and be happy. Take care of our Luke and yourself. You're the bravest person I've ever met, and I know you can survive this. I want you to fight hard for life and live it fully with love and children and happiness and hopefully me." His crooked grin made my eyes fill with tears. "Don't let Luke give up either, not on life or love. Make him be brave. And don't take any crap from anyone! Especially not your dad. You're perfect just like you are and don't need a persona to accomplish anything you set your mind to. I love you, *mi amor*."

I turned on my recorder and then turned it off. Everything I thought to say was too mushy or dramatic and I knew he'd save this recording—even if I lived.

Luke took off his pants and boots and let himself from the cage wearing blue boxers and a white t-shirt.

He said, "*I'm getting something to eat. Want anything?*"

"No thanks. I'm good."

He grew bigger to hug me then sauntered away and I giggled nervously.

"You're good?" Molly asked.

"He was talking on the coms."

Alex said, "We can get them too and we should before they're gone."

I winced at the reminder. Whiroon didn't have supplies to make unlimited coms. It was one of the things Jay was working out because it would be impossible to give them to every Hifis.

"Are they safe?" Molly asked.

Alex shrugged. "So far."

Alex pulled her away, and I turned my recorder back on. "When you ask, the answer will be yes." I sent it before I could change my mind. "Luke, there are no words for what you mean to me. Take care of each other. I love you both so much."

I sent that too then stepped into the cage, envisioning chimp paws as hard as I could.

The shift was quick and smooth. I hardly felt a whirl. It was more like a blink. My clothes hung on me, so I rolled up the legs and sleeves and stepped out of my boots. I made a mental note to try this in spandex. My paws and feet moved naturally, without me needing to concentrate, and I could feel textures. My skin felt thick and lacked the sensitivity of human skin.

I grabbed at the metal bar, laughing a chimp laugh of delight when I bent the metal.

I let myself out and scampered after Luke. Talking slowed and halted as I passed. Stares and whispers followed me across the room. I wondered how many of them hadn't realized they could have a second form.

I found Luke at the 'buffet' which was an assortment of packaged foods and metal chafing dishes with a random assortment of items. The base kitchens sent over fresh trays every two hours. Everyone was sharing without complaint, taking small servings to be sure everyone got something, which reminded me uncomfortably of the Hirsit. I laughed to myself that I'd have preferred them to hog the food and helped myself to a heaping plate and sat by the wall to eat it. When I was finished, I unrolled my pant cuffs and shifted back.

I said, "Alex and Molly want coms. I'm going to go handle that. See if you can find us somewhere to play a bit."

"We don't have time. Your ride will be here in just a few minutes."

I glanced doubtfully at my rumpled clothing.

Luke laughed a chimp laugh and people again stopped to stare.

"Jay is borrowing something from his wife."

"Awesome," I said dryly, and he laughed again.

I headed to Molly and Alex, and they followed me behind the screen that blocked the hatch.

"I'll authorize you as crew. Just put your hand on the orb there and it will authenticate you. Then I'll tell it to give you coms. A tentacle will touch you for a few seconds. It will knock you out for about ten minutes and give you the coms, but if you're thinking of getting another shape, do that first because we think it equates rank with how many forms you have.

"Mol?" Alex asked anxiously.

"I will if you want me to."

He bit his lip then nodded. "I want you to be able to escape."

I said, "I'll have Whiroon scan you and see if you can get another shape. Some Hifis can't. Let me go grab a monkey. Did you want a particular kind?"

"Chimp, I guess."

"I'll be right back. Don't cross the red line or its defenses will dust you." They both hastily stepped backward.

I rolled the chimp back to the ship inside its cage followed by stares, but no one questioned me.

"Ready?"

Alex nodded decisively.

I crossed my fingers.

"Authorize Molly Walters main grown human as crew."

"Authenticate," Whiroon said and I gestured her to place her hand on the orb.

"Authenticated."

"Examine Molly Walters to determine if she needs HGTRF."

"Levels adequate."

"Chances of unsuccessful acquisition of new DNA sequence?"

"Two point six three."

I turned away to say, "That's the same chance I have but it *is* a risk."

"Do me first," Alex said.

I introduced Alex, had *Whiroon* check him, and then administer the chimp DNA.

I said, "I envision the paws while imagining the sensations and there I am."

He nodded tightly, taking a deep breath.

"I love you so much," Molly said and burst into tears.

"I love you to and I hope to God this works so I can fight for us, but if it doesn't, I want you to fight, you hear me?"

She sniffled and nodded, and he expanded and was a chimp.

"You good?" I asked, belatedly thinking I should've grabbed a human cage but I didn't want the people in the hanger to know I was using the chimp to give them a second form although everyone who'd seen us enter probably suspected.

He nodded and I let out a relieved breath.

I said, "It's up to you, Molly, and you better live because I'll feel like complete shit if I dust you."

She laughed nervously, nodding quickly.

I said, "Whiroon administer chimp DNA to crew Molly Walters."

"Please God," I muttered.

I laughed in nervous relief when she became a chimp. My laugh changed to a startled scream as she leapt at me. Alex grabbed her as she bit my arm, tearing away a gob of flesh.

"Whiroon, administer radio dots to crew Molly Waters. Alex, get her hand on the orb there!

It took both of us to force her hand to the orb and she took another bite from my shoulder that was a sharp pain and then a feeling of warmth.

A tentacle whipped out from the wall, and she collapsed to the deck.

I said, "I need to shift, and we'll get her into a cage and then I'll get you coms."

Alex nodded and patted my cheek. His lips remained curled. I could tell by his body language that he was scared and unhappy.

I became the chimp again and rolled up her pants and shirt sleeves. My wounds had disappeared, but my shoulder was still bloody. I took off my bloody shirt and handed it to Alex.

'Stay here. I'll get it,' I said using my text to speech app.

It only took me a few minutes to bring the cage back. I set it before the screen and jumped around on it a minute and then pulled it behind the screen, which was the best I could do as camouflage. I made a mental note to have the cages and animals screened off so no one could see what was brought in and out.

I used my dirty shirt to wipe myself off. Whiroon had already cleaned the deck. Alex handed me his shirt and I shifted back to human.

"Ready for coms?"

He nodded and I had *Whiroon* apply the coms then dragged him into the cage with Molly.

I examined their dots thoughtfully. I might be able to get another one now that I'd taken a new form and if the dots did signify rank that would likely be helpful. "Whiroon, check my radio dots and ensure their working correctly and are up to date."

"Acknowledged."

I laid my hand on the orb and had time to think—*I should have told someone I was doing this*— before the world went black.

I woke to find Luke glaring at me from inches away. "Daffy," he said in exasperation.

"Yeah. I know. I thought of it a split second too late."

"You're okay?'

"Yeah. I'm hungry..."

He laughed and hugged me while muttering about how stupid I was.

Adan said, "Jeez I'm gone for like an hour and you replace me already."

I flushed as I tugged up the ripped shirt that I was no longer wearing but had been draped over me. Alex and Molly were awake but not paying any attention to us. They were huddled together, facing away. I tapped my video connection to Adan and was relieved to see him. He was in a bathroom somewhere staring into a mirror, grinning ear-to-ear.

"Thank god!" he said and then his eyes narrowed as he leaned forward. He leaned forward again, and I knew he was using high magnification to examine my new dots.

"What the fucking hell?"

Butterflies began to dance in my stomach. My dots had been replaced by two small dots, a larger one, and two even smaller ones to the left above that.

Luke said, "Whiroon what's the significance of the size and shape of the new arrangement of radio dots?"

Whiroon babbled a string of noise interspersed with a couple of English words.

I said, "Do the radio dots work the same way?"

"Affirmative. Range improvement, upgraded security protocol, Ship...class upgrade, command... hierarchy increased."

The pauses gave me pause because I knew Whiroon was using closest approximation meaning and not exact meaning.

Luke said, "Any new negative side effects?"

We exchanged uneasy glances over the delayed reply.

Whiroon finally said, "Unknown."

I said, "That doesn't sound good. It paused for like forever."

Luke said, "I'll figure it out. You go shower and change. You have a plane to catch."

"Which is stupid. They should just send their lawyer here to talk to ours."

"Well, you aren't meeting with a lawyer or not only a lawyer. Your meeting with the president."

I stopped to stare at him as Adan laughed.

"That better be a joke," I said.

"No joke, Daffy. Go get ready."

I walked slowly to the bathroom. "How the hell did this happen? What am I supposed to do?"

Adan said, "Just be yourself."

Which self, I thought crossly. I'd been playing so many roles I had no idea what I even wanted anymore.

4

"I can't believe I'm doing this," I whispered soundlessly as I stepped off of the private jet that'd been sent for me.

Secret service ushered me to a black sedan. They looked sharp in their suits. I was way underdressed, but I'd had no time over the last thirty hours to go shopping. I'd barely had time to eat and the only sleep I'd gotten was on the plane ride here and I hadn't had time to sleep long then either.

Someone was constantly calling on my coms. It seemed as if every human-hifis had their own ideas how things should be done and they were all calling me or Jay. Freeing them was a much more complex problem than I'd imagined, but I wasn't willing to compromise on it. If they wanted my ship's help, they'd free them all.

For lack of anything better to wear, I wore a pink pantsuit borrowed from Jay's wife. I'm sure I looked as ridiculous as I felt with my shaved head, ill-fitting clothes, and black combat boots. I wished now I'd worn my BDU although I had no more right to wear it.

That still hurt and pissed me off. I'd been working hard to achieve an unachievable goal, but leaving my friends with no word was what angered me most. I hated to think they'd hear some warped version of what had happened, but they might despise me even if they were told the truth.

"Adan?"

"*I'm fine, mi amor. You got this.*"

Senator Barnes, one of the four men who'd accompanied me here on the plane, got into the car with me. He pressed a button on his armrest to raise a glass barrier between us and the driver, and then he opened his laptop.

"That ship of yours is an amazing vehicle. Priceless really. And the Hifis... Imagine what people would pay to be able to reset themselves when they were sick?"

"This isn't about money."

"No, no, of course not. You want what's best for your friends. Perfectly understandable. We all have friends and family we'd like to help." His phone vibrated and he grunted in annoyance when he glanced at it. "The market is in an uproar and my broker is a maestro. I'd be happy to introduce you. I have lots of contacts that you might find useful."

He opened his laptop and typed a minute, angling the screen so I could see it.

My eyes widened at the amount of money displayed.

He closed it a moment later and said, "It's a tragedy that it's taken this to get us to work together, but imagine what we could do? You're in a unique but precarious position, but I'll do everything in my power to ensure you survive this and even prosper."

"*That son of a bitch,*" Adan snarled in my ear.

Jay said, "*Ignore him. Pretend you didn't understand.*"

My cheeks were burning. I doubted I could pull off ignorance, but I gave it my best try.

I faked a giggle, staring out the window, patting my chest and saying breathlessly, "The president himself will be there?"

"*A bit too thick,*" Luke said dryly.

Adan laughed an angry huff of sound.

Luke said, "*I'm tracking his cell and looking up that account.*"

Barnes said, "You've never visited Washington before?"

"I haven't been anywhere, really."

"I can arrange a tour of the city if you like.

"No way!" Adan said.

I said, "Thank you but I have to get back. My friends will be worried."

The driver lowered the glass to say. "We're arriving and your escort will see you in."

Barnes gestured dismissively. He opened his briefcase and removed a business card that he pressed into my sweaty hand. "If you need a friend, I'm a phone call away."

"Thank you. You've been very kind."

He nodded and smiled and hurried from the car as soon as it stopped.

A secret service agent opened my door, and another offered me his hand.

Luke said, *"We need witness protection."*

"I agree, but it can't be arranged by them."

"Ma'am?" the closest secret service agent said doubtfully.

I held up a finger and turned away.

"I have to go. Work on something but keep it legal. They claim they'll issue us visas. We can let those of us who want to go into hiding with their help do it."

Jay said, *"And what about those of us who don't?"*

"Then I suppose you'd have to break the law, forfeit the protection of the embassy, and live like a fugitive."

"Fair enough, I guess."

"I really wish that none of this was necessary, Jay."

"Ma'am," the agent said again.

I turned back and marched into the building.

I slid the foot-high stack of forms away and folded my hands. "It's amazing how fast you can do things when you want to."

I reminded myself of Gina Harper, which amused me for a moment—until I remembered that all of this had happened because Captain Jacobs had been murdered.

A wave of nausea followed that thought.

I really hoped my family had nothing to do with it, but I was really afraid they had.

Bradly said, "You don't sound happy about that."

I tapped the stack. "I could print up these forms with internet access and a secretary or two. How do I know they're even legal?"

"I guess you'll just have to take our word for it..."

I examined the angry faces of the men around the table. I figured most if not all of them would prefer to see me shot then to give me any legal standing whatsoever.

Hostility was thick in the room.

I said, "You people are going to cause an uncrossable rift between humans who have a disease and ones who don't. This hostility is entirely your making."

Bradly said, "We aren't hostile. We're prudent, and if you were sitting in my chair, you'd be doing the same thing."

"Maybe, but I plan to check up on all of my embassies to be sure no one in them is being abused."

Senator Lindau said, "Do the documents meet with your approval and satisfy your requirements or will you demand further compensation?"

I glowered at the speaker and then forced myself to take a deep calming breath.

"I haven't asked for any compensation, senator. All I've demanded is basic human rights for people you illegally incarcerated. I'm not doing this for money. I just want those of us who suffer from Hifis to be treated like the rest of Americans."

"You aren't like the rest of us. You have a disease that needs to be studied and *your* criminally selfish actions here today might very well have doomed all of humanity."

Bradly cleared his throat and Lindau sniffed in a superior way, smoothing the front of his jacket.

He said, "I suppose I miss-spoke. I should have said childishly selfish."

I laughed. "You're the childish one, pouting because you didn't get your own way. There are more Hifis volunteers then those who caught it on arrival. If you need some experimenting done, ask one of them, or you could come to the ship and I'll gladly infect you!"

The president stood, bracing his hands on the table. "Gentlemen, I think this is an eminently suitable approach to a troubling problem. One that might even further benefit us by appealing to Hifis who have eluded recognition. Perhaps they'll see that help is available and turn themselves in before our foreign enemies have time to locate them."

Lindau flicked his fingers. "The fate of a few Hifis is hardly a concern for this cabinet. Even if a Hifis were captured there isn't much that could be learned from it that isn't already public knowledge. Even assuming it was turned against us, they're hardly a threat."

The it comment made me flush with anger.

I said, "The *men and women* who have Hifis aren't a threat. Hifis isn't contagious. My concern is that they're being abused to find secrets that don't exist."

The president said, "We believe they aren't contagious on their own but it's too soon to say with any certainty that our science couldn't duplicate the contagion. I hate to contemplate the methods that might be employed to accomplish that. We've kept the infected sequestered for their own safety, to prevent just such a thing happening. What happened to recruit Molly Walters was a criminal offense and not sanctioned in any way by this cabinet."

I said, "Your attitude that we're animals sanctions it. The soldiers who serve under you and call us it"—I glared at Lindau—"have learned the terminology from their superiors. As long as you treat us as subhuman, people will feel free to treat us badly."

Lindau said, "She mauled a man to death. No—two men! She's a viscous animal hiding in a human shell. The most humane thing to do would be to put her down! Paying for her crimes by cooperating in minor medical procedures isn't too much to ask."

"And she wouldn't have mauled anyone if she wasn't frightened out of her mind over your so-called minor procedures! How would you like it if I chopped off your arm!"

The room erupted into yelling.

The president slapped his hand to the table. "Gentleman, please!"

The senator stood, knocking his chair to the ground. "I understand that we need to pacify this—girl, and I'll cooperate and sign the damned treaty, but I don't need to stay and listen to her ignorant ranting."

Two other men followed him from the room.

The president settled back into his chair. "You're right, the paperwork is legal and completely meaningless. Paper isn't going to keep you safe. You're a tiny population with one asset, but we have treaties and issue visas to many small weak countries, and we honor them because it's in our best interest to do so. America can't afford to break treaties when those treaties are all that keep complete anarchy at bay. We have many foreign nationals here working with us. Afar is the perfect place for you and we'd like you to return."

"He can't be serious."

Adan's tone in my head was both shocked and hopeful.

Bradly said, "If you want things to change you need to do that yourself by treating uninfected humans as you want them to treat you. If you lock yourself away, the general populace will assume there's a reason you do and you'll make it difficult for Hifis to mix with the general population. On the other hand, if you show Americans that you're willing to fight alongside of them..."

"We were willing, and you made it impossible. And I don't mean just me but the twelve other Hifis who tried to serve and were arrested for it."

"Not arrested. Detained and held for questioning."

"That's what I mean. You detained"—I made air quotes—"them for a disease they had no choice in getting. You ignored their basic American rights. Yes, they kept their condition secret, but there was no law against keeping it secret. American's have the right to medical privacy. You were in the wrong and twisting it to be any other way is just as wrong. I understand the reasoning for keeping Hifis humans secret, and even agree with it, but the way you're going about it is totally unacceptable."

"Hmph." Senator Madison's annoyed expression was mirrored by the men sitting beside him.

I made my own annoyed sound, crossing my arms. "You can't have your cake and eat it too. We're not toys that you can take out when you want to use and then throw into a box when you're done with us. We need the same protections any other person gets."

Bradly said, "I agree. But you're much more dangerous than an uninfected human. We have a proposal here." He opened his briefcase and withdrew another much smaller sheaf of papers.

I read them slowly to give everyone watching through my x-coms time to read it.

Luke whispered, *"No way,"* and a section of the page appeared highlighted.

I said, "No. We aren't agreeing to be incarcerated when off duty."

Senator Housman said, "Then you have to follow the same rules! You seem to be ignoring the facts.

Those Hifis were caught on a military installation where they had no right to be. We can't have you sneaking all over as the mood pleases you. Locking you up when not on duty seems like a sensible precaution."

"Again, you're trying to have your cake and eat it too. We have special abilities that you want to use, and those abilities come along with special needs. Hifis require time to assume their secondary shapes. The recruits you caught were mostly all caught doing that very thing. They had no choice in sneaking out to do it. If you give them time and a safe place to run or climb or sit with their pack mates, they'll have no need to break your rules. But if you persist in making it impossible for us to follow your rules, then we'll have no choice but to fight for the things we need."

Bradly said, "I don't think it necessary to lock them up or treat them differently. Melton, Lewis, and Sutton were exemplary recruits and there's no reason to believe anything will change in the future. They seemed able to work within the normal confines of our rules with very little adjustment. Those adjustments were easy to manage and very infrequent. I propose we go on as we have been but with the very minor exception of bunking Hifis pack mates in the same suites. What they do behind closed doors is none of our concern as long as they follow the rules."

"And their special privileges will be a sore point among the rest of our recruits!"

"A dorm policy of closed-door privacy is perfectly acceptable to me. I expect my soldiers to be on time, well rested, and fit for duty. I expect rooms to be kept to the same level of cleanliness, and for my future officers to show a certain level of decorum, which means no late night running around. I think it entirely possible to be discreet without deception.

"I intend to keep their status as Hifis as covert as I can, and I'll need their active cooperation to do that. Locking them up, denying them the same privileges that the other cadets receive isn't practical. They'd need to be housed and trained separately but for the best results they need to train with the people they'll be working with.

I frowned at the pages. Bradly was certain we'd join, and I hated that certainty. He knew we were weak and in no position to turn him down when the choice was comply or remain locked up in our embassies.

I tapped the symbol on my sleeve that asked for feedback from my council, which was Adan, Luke, Jay, and twenty other men and women who Jay had picked. I'd only spoken to them very briefly. The hurry to get these papers signed was both reassuring and alarming.

I thought the rush was to tie us down legally before we had a chance to really organize and it reassured me that they wanted to do it legally, but it made me nervous that I might sign something that screwed us all. But the president was right. It was just paper. Only our intentions mattered, and I intended to honor a fair deal. I hoped they did. I also hoped the American people would accept Hifis humans and support their rights.

Jay said, *"Make it clear it's completely voluntary."*

I said, "You're free to try to recruit any Hifis, and they're free to decline."

Bradly said, "Will you support my authority over them?"

"If they sign, they're yours unless you break your word to them, and by that I mean I expect you to actively ensure none of them are being abused. We're not expendable just because we're tough. I understand we'll be sent on hard missions, but I expect all efforts will be made that the mission is a survivable one."

Adan said, *"Tell him we'll be checking on fatalities."*

"Every fatality will be reported, and we'll be checking facts."

"Fair enough."

"Speaking of that, we'll need different medical care than usual, and something will need to be done to make sure injured Hifis aren't left behind for dead but approaching an injured one could lead to attack. We aren't animals but have animal instincts in our secondary forms that stress can heighten."

Jay said, "*I have some ideas on that, Mia. We need some time, training, and testing.*"

"Sergeant Bauer has some ideas on how to do that, but we'll need time, training, and testing."

Bradly said, "We have some ideas too and plan to gradually work Hifis abilities into the training."

I said, "Hifis in the military can refuse any medical test unless that test is also being given to uninfected humans as well, and they have the right to have the Hifis of their choice notified and brought to them. If we find out you're tricking us and claiming humans are undergoing the same tests, it will be a serious breach of contract."

The president said, "I agree and will put it in writing."

He nodded to the lawyer sitting beside him, and the man began to write.

I had no lawyer with me but three were with Luke and one with Adan. I didn't know where Adan was. He was our backup and it was like having a toothache. I could ignore the discomfort, but it worried me with sharp stabs of anxiety when I considered I had no idea how to find him.

The president said, "Introduce the cadets to the new Ranger-X team. Tell them we'll be recruiting more and that some are already classmates but that their identities are classified. Mr. Melton, I'd like you to see about getting us x-coms for non Hifis. Make that your priority, please.

Luke grunted in annoyance.

I said, "He said he'll get on that."

Luke grunted again, sounding amused and annoyed.

"Jay, how are we doing?"

"Polls look good. Eighty percent approval rating."

"So I should sign?"

"Yes. We're behind you."

"What if they kept some of us?"

"Then we declare war for breach of treaty, but they can keep all of the convicted prisoners. I'll send someone there to double check they really are all felons, but we don't want them. If they insist that we take them, tell them we plan to execute."

"Will we?"

"Maybe. But don't worry about it. They'll want them."

The seated men's expressions had grown irate as I spoke.

I said, "I'll sign. I understand that moving all of them will take time and we'll give you that time as long as we can remain in contact and see that an effort is being made to get them to our agreed upon housing. You can keep the convicted felons, but we'll be sending someone to check and ensure they really are felons."

"Housing," someone mumbled in the tone that said it was ridiculous.

I ignored it although it made my face flush with anger. They thought nothing of keeping us locked away, sucking us dry of knowledge, stripping our dignity and terrifying us. The costs for that had yet to be paid.

"Make them take the damned felons," Madison said snidely. "They should pay for the housing too."

I said, "I'd be happy too. It wouldn't take us any time at all to clean the dust from our deck. As to compensating the Hifis for their pain and suffering and illegal incarceration, that will be left to their discretion, but I assume you'll be hearing from their lawyers. We aren't charging you for the knowledge we're giving you, priceless knowledge, but I guess we can arrange a payment plan exchanging food and shelter for time with Zeus." His expression darkened and I continued smugly, "We'll happily arrange an hourly rate."

Jay snorted with laughter.

I was so angry that tears filled my eyes, which made me angrier.

The president said, "We'd prefer to keep the felons and are perfectly happy with the arrangements laid out. Housing is being readied as quickly as possible. I expect most will be in their new accommodations within two weeks."

I said, "I'm aware that you've recruited most of them to live on bases, and I don't need to know which bases, but I do need to be assured that they're safe, so Jay will be arranging inspections that will include a way for them to contact us. We have no intention of interfering with the issuing of visas, except that we be notified if one is rescinded."

"Agreed," the president said. "We'll notify your consulate if arrests are made or a Hifis is wanted for questioning in a crime."

"And we'll do our best to accommodate the apprehension of criminals, but our embassies are off limits for everyone, except us."

"Agreed."

"Then I guess we have a deal."

I began to sign my name to the mountains of paper.

When I'd finished, the president stood to shake my hand. I was surprised—and embarrassed—when a photographer entered and photographed us. My ill-fitting pink pant suit was a wrinkled mess after the hours I'd spent here shuffling papers.

Most of the seated men hurried from the room but a few stayed and spoke quietly among themselves. A waiter entered with a tray of drinks.

The president said, "Hifis humans couldn't have a better ambassador. I hope soon they won't need one but can instead be Hifis Americans again."

I said, "They can apply for citizenship whenever they like but I think they'd be crazy too."

The president took a champagne glass from the tray. "I did what I believed was necessary for America."

"I'm doing what I think is necessary for Hifis."

Bradly handed me a champagne glass. "Well, here's to Whiroon."

To my surprise the president smiled and clinked his glass to mine.

I lifted the glass but didn't drink it. I couldn't wait to get out of here. I wouldn't feel safe until I was with Luke and Adan. My throat felt constricted and I was glad no one else tried to speak with me. I knew this was a hollow victory and not real safety.

These men would do whatever they could get away with doing. Law, morals, even love appeared to be beyond them. I had no idea what motivated them and didn't want to know. I wanted nothing to do with them and their cold glances and shady deals.

With relief I left the room when an agent said my plane was ready.

Bradly and Trist joined me at the last minute.

I reluctantly returned my chair to an upright position.

Bradly said, "I was just informed that Senator Barnes tried to bribe you. Why didn't you report it?'

"I did report it, and who I report to is none of your business."

"I meant you should have said something immediately."

I shrugged.

Trist said, "I'd thought despite everything that you were concerned for all Americans."

"Don't be ridiculous. We all know there are worse them him working there. I bet you a bazillion dollars that half the men there weren't at all surprised he was involved with crooked dealings."

"Still, if we let them act unhindered..."

"Who said I was letting him act? My lawyers assure me that once he crosses into international waters, he's fair game."

"You're tracking him?"

"Yes. And I'm not breaking any laws to do it. I have no agents on the ground although it would make my life easier if I could have those agents, but we'll make do." I leaned back in my seat and kicked my feet up. I was almost asleep when Trist said. "You can't just execute him."

"Actually, I can. I'm a sovereign nation. If I capture him on international waters I have just as much right as any other nation to hold him for trial. A trial that will be held under my legal code. But you don't need to worry about him. I don't plan on doing a thing. He isn't my problem, he's yours.

"You shouldn't use Zeus for this," Bradly said with heavy disapproval.

"Why not?" I sat up to speak to Bradly.

"Its dangerous. Everything that ship learns it could be telling other ships. You're teaching it to hack us. It isn't something it needs to know."

"It already knew how to hack us. It's showing us what it knows, and before you ask me, I have no idea if that's being reported or not. I have no idea what contracts are still being honored between individual Hifis and the United States or even which hifis have asked for American citizenship. It's none of my business and I'm not going to ask. If you want to know, then I guess you could ask whoever your liaison is."

I was almost asleep again when Bradly said, "I'm very sorry about your friend. I had no idea she was being so mistreated."

I spoke without opening my eyes.

"She isn't my friend. Maybe someday, but I barely know her. Calling what happened to her mistreatment is such an inadequate description that it makes me feel sick. I suppose I feel it more because it could happen to me. It's wildly unlikely to happen to you because a captor would know that it would most likely kill you if they cut off parts of your arm or foot and fed it to your wife or cut out her tongue or breasts to feed to you so that she wouldn't say anything when she was raped. But if it could happen to you or her, you'd likely not be calling it mistreatment.

"That guard was cocky as hell. I wasn't the first person he tried to terrorize into submission and neither was she. That was a secure facility and I don't believe his crimes were unnoticed or even unsanctioned. I'm not saying you knew, but you should have known."

"I agree. I should have sent a trusted aide or went myself to check on the conditions of the prisoners in my care. My only excuse is that I was busy and was getting results. I was aware that harsh measure were being used and are still being used against our alien captives but hadn't realized they were being used against our human ones."

Adan said, "Leave her alone."

I flushed and muted him. "I'm fine. It's upsetting is all."

"They're hounding you and you're not fine. Your pulse is racing."

"I don't know how I can make them safe with people like that out there."

I was speaking to Adan, but Bradly answered. "Law. And a strong police force."

Trist said, "Your spot in the academy is waiting for you."

"I'm no longer an American."

Saying it made tears fill my eyes.

"Mia... mi amor... I hate them so much for hurting you."

"Dual citizenship," Trist said. "Or you could fight under your own flag. We really want to work this out. You must see that."

"She gives me nightmares. To put myself in your power again... I want to help. I can see how having Hifis would drastically improve the chances of mission success, especially against other Hifis, but it's a miracle I got away once."

"Not a miracle. We would've realized you'd been falsely imprisoned."

"Maybe, but not before he'd murdered me. I wouldn't have cooperated. He'd have had to kill me when he was done with me. And he wouldn't have been able to do that if I hadn't trusted you and turned off my coms. I've done battle drills where we had to maintain radio silence. I know it happens frequently and you're asking me to trust that it isn't a trap when I know you'd kill me if you could do it without losing Zeus. Eventually, you won't need my ship, but I don't know when that will be. Helping you is a roll of the dice that I'm not sure I want to take."

"Helping us helps you too."

"I know, but there are other ways I can help. I don't intend to sit idly by if the Geromi return."

"And we can't afford for you to lose our only working ship by fighting with no training."

Adan said, *"Unmute me, please."*

I sighed hard but unmuted him.

He said, "Stop pressuring her. We need some time to get this mess straightened out. You'll have other Hifis to train. There's a lot we can learn by textbooks and even private tutors, and maybe when we're a bit more organized we'll feel safer about working with you."

Bradly patted my knee. "Just stay open to the possibility. We have no reason to kill you or any other Hifis who isn't a criminal. I'm not sure why you're so certain we would. It's not like we order our special forces murdered when we don't need them anymore. Why would Hifis be any different? Think about it."

He left me alone, but nightmares kept waking me. I was cranky when we landed and grew crankier when Luke told me I had to meet him at the auditorium. I wanted to shuck the stupid pantsuit, shower, eat, and sleep, and instead I had to go make a speech as if anyone cared what I had to say.

5

I took the microphone from Luke and said, "I really have nothing to add to what you've already heard. You'll be released from here as soon as possible. I'm sorry about the crowding but there isn't anything I can do about it other than what we're already doing. The visa is meant for your protection as a way to check up on you and make sure you aren't locked away without your permission, but you can give up your Whiroon citizenship and apply for American citizenship and walk out that door any time you want to. Our consulate staff is working on a way to let you apply for citizenship in other countries but our treaty with the United States means all such requests need to go through them. All travel needs to go through them. Basically, we're a tiny landlocked nation in the middle of their territory."

I felt stupid talking to them with my synthesized voice. Black plastic had been hung in the amphitheater to make small rooms, none of which I could see into. Every effort was being made to give the Hifis privacy from each other, and they were cooperating for the most part.

Four men walked the narrow plastic corridors. It was their job to enforce order and bring anyone who left their cubicle to the cells here. A few other men and women in pink lab coats were in the corridors. They were our consulate. The pink was meant to identify them as such because I thought white lab coats would be scary. I'd never trust another white coat wearing person as long as I lived.

"We're keeping you sequestered from each other to protect your identities, but you can waive that protection whenever you want and join the public community, which as of this moment has twelve members."

I lowered the mic and shrugged at Luke. He shrugged back and we both laughed a moment. I gave him a hug and whispered, "This is nuts. I hope Jay has a handle on all this."

"I think he does."

I lifted the mic again and said, "Well, that's all folks."

Adan began laughing.

"She really is Daffy," Luke said.

I grinned and punched his shoulder.

I laid the mic down and headed for the door. Heat buffeted me. The sun was high. It was a scorching August afternoon. I stood for a moment to soak it in.

"Can you come home now?" I asked Adan plaintively.

"Not until Jay okays it."

I sighed hard, and he said, "I miss you too. Both of you."

Luke grunted in annoyance. "Where is our home?"

The capitol building," I said laughingly although it made me sad that we had no place.

"Mia!" Sutak called, and I halted in surprise.

She ran up and gave me a quick hug, examining me with laughing eyes.

A hot flush heated my cheeks.

"Where have you been?" she asked. "I was worried."

"I can't say. We're fine though."

"Will you be back?" She again examined me and this time her eyes were worried.

"I'm not sure. We haven't gotten orders yet. I'd love to talk but we're already late."

"For what? A rabbit's tea party? You look ridiculous."

My flush darkened and she laughed again and patted my cheek. "I meant that in the nicest way possible, but I'm not letting you go shopping without me in the future."

Luke snickered, and I glared at him.

"It's borrowed," I said tightly.

Luke tugged me forward, calling back, "It was good to see you! We'll be in touch even if we're assigned somewhere else."

I waited until she was out of earshot to say, "Will we?"

"Why not? They were friends. Why shouldn't we stay in touch with them?"

Adan said, "*Do you want to go back?*"

I said, "I'm sick of making this decision. I feel like we decide this every other day."

Luke said, "I'm on the fence. I see the advantages for us *and* for them, but I don't trust them."

I said, "I don't trust them either. But I think Jay's plan will keep them in check and I hope Americans will support us once they're told about us."

Adan said, "*I agree. But was that a yes or no?*"

"It was an I don't know. I think I need to talk to my dad."

"*Frank....*" Adan said worriedly.

"I don't think we should tell him, or at least not all the details, but I do think we need to feel him out. He's going to be pissed if we cross him, and I don't want him to hide Shea."

"Shea..." Luke said unhappily.

I said, "I think he needs to know Fen has resurfaced and is talking smack because she might go for Shea."

Adan said, *"You think she'd hurt her?"*

"I have no idea what she's capable of doing."

She'd been more than capable of hurting me... it had always amused her to make me cry but there was a world of difference from teasing your sister to really hurting them, still I didn't trust her at all.

Luke and I reached the hanger.

The guards outside waved us through.

The people inside were as busy as usual but a new partition blocked the workbenches from the ship. Another partition made a small room, our room, and I gratefully headed to it and flopped onto my hard camp cot.

Luke leaned down to kiss my forehead. "Get some sleep. I'll see about arranging travel visas for us."

Adan said, *"I can meet you there and we can talk in person after we settle with Frank."*

I said, "I want to attend the funeral tomorrow."

"I forgot about that. Maybe I should come back?"

Luke pushed me back down as I began to sit. "No, stay away, Adan, until Jay okays it. I'll go talk to him."

Luke grabbed the blanket from his cot, covered me, and kissed my cheek.

"Get some sleep, Daffy."

"*I love you, mi amor,*" Adan said.

"I love you too."

"*We'll all be together soon.*"

I squeezed my teary eyes closed. He'd been counting down the days and we'd only had a few left. It hurt that he hadn't told me the count now, but we all knew that none of us had any idea when it would be safe for all of us to be together again.

Luke left, and I let the murmur of sound lull me to sleep.

When I woke, I showered and put on BDU. I needed to make time to get some different clothing but was happy to shuck off the pink suit, which I bundled up to return to Jay.

His secretary glanced at my ID and waved me into his office. I didn't know the woman and wasn't sure if she knew that I was the captain. I had no idea who'd been told. It was one of things I planned to ask about.

Jay's office had thick glass walls that deadened the sound from the rest of the hanger. I wasn't sure if they were soundproof or not but doubted anyone could hear us unless they used some sort of listening device. *Firt* coms couldn't listen in like mine could. One radio dot meant the listener could hear when spoken to and reply, that's it. I'd had to issue special orders to let them call when they wanted to.

"Thank your wife for me," I said as I handed the pantsuit back.

"Did you get any rest? You still look tired."

"I'm good just hungry."

He said, "There's plenty at our buffet."

I wrinkled my nose. "Is it safe though?"

"Yes. They have no reason to poison us. I'm not saying things couldn't change but as of right now they're happy and we're happy."

Luke joined us and gave me a hug.

I said, "Is it safe for Adan to come back?"

Jay said, "I believe so. We have a team in constant contact with Zeus who's watching every crew member by x-com and Zeus will notify all of them if there are alert signs."

"Which brings me to my next question. Who knows about us?"

"If you mean Hifis in general, the list is really long and I'll send it to you. If you mean a Hifis in particular, we keep that information on a need-to-know basis. Every Hifis is assigned a code name and the real identity is locked in Zeus. We're supposed to inform the consulate when our real identity is breached, and the list of people who are aware of it is updated. You should be checking that list periodically to ensure it's up to date or put yourself in the public list."

Luke said, "About that, how public is that?"

Jay waggled his hand side-to-side. "It isn't like we're in the phonebook under infected but those Hifis are known to almost all the other Hifis and will be making themselves known on the bases once clearance is given, which I expect to happen any time now. The president is working on his speech to reveal us.

"I'm having two more embassies built, one in Chicago and one in Michigan, and he'll announce Hifis can go there for help."

"Will it hurt us to be so distinctly separate from other Americans? I'm worried about giving people ideas, making them prejudice against us."

"Maybe some but that's inevitable." He held up a finger and shuffled papers for a minute. "Whiroon, show Mia surveillance map twelve."

A map appeared before me. It appeared to be the sort of map you'd see on a GPS map app, except there were multiple red dots across it.

Jay said, "Senator Barnes. People he's spoken with or driven to see."

I said, "We're handling security ourselves?"

"Yes and no. I've forwarded the info but have no way of knowing if they're doing anything about it. There isn't a lot I can do about it without agents. Zeus can inform us of who he contacts though, and we can trace who they contact. The problem is that's a lot of potential suspects and we have no idea how much information Zeus can juggle before we start to overload him. I think we need a way to weed out the unimportant hits, but I have no idea how to do that. I think we need to recruit some Hifis with specialized training or hire some humans."

"What good would the information do us? It isn't like we could arrest them."

Luke said, "Our security would know to be on the lookout for them. One of the first places Barnes called when he exited the car was a pizza joint. They spoke for ten minutes, which makes me believe he wasn't ordering pizza. The employees there are now on our watch list and Zeus will notify us if any come near us. I'd like to narrow down the amount of people he's watching from there and we could likely do it easily if we had an agent who could go there and ask questions."

Jay said, "He called Senator Landau next and Landau's especially dangerous to us because he has access to official channels. It's possible he could infiltrate those channels and fool a Hifis with legitimate documents. If he did manage to nab some of us, any leads we had on who his contacts are would significantly increase our chance at rescue."

I said, "I'm sure he isn't the only shady man who'd sell us out to make a buck."

Jay grimaced and nodded. "We're doing everything possible, but it won't be enough if someone is ruthless enough. Which is why I plan to keep my identity as secret as I can. I have a family to worry about."

My expression must have revealed my unease when I thought of Fenris because he grimaced again. "Sorry. I didn't mean it like that. We all have family we're worried about."

Luke said, "We'll be on the lookout for Fen."

Jay said, "We need trained agents who can handle things like this."

I said, "Speak to whoever you need to, to see about recruiting some. I'd like to say we should hire some, but we have no income for it."

Jay grinned crookedly. "Actually, we do. I've instituted rates for time with Zeus. It's enough to support the embassies, not enough to pay for much of anything else.

"Our crew is still paid by their former employees too. We no longer need to pay federal taxes to America, but we could institute a tax for ourselves. We could use Zeus to make money by applying knowledge we get from him to develop marketable goods."

"I'd rather not do that, at least not without clearing it first. I think we should talk to whoever we talk to about these things and arrange for a budget and some guidelines. Maybe we can just get their agents to report to us?"

"I've sent in a request, but we really need our own. Their agents will be loyal to them. We need ones with undivided loyalties."

"Do whatever you think best."

Jay leaned back in his seat, rubbing his face. "Neither of us are qualified to run this. We need to find someone who is. We need a president."

"Mia's the president," Luke said.

"Mia is ... I don't know what she is. I guess she's the state. She needs a prime minister or whatever we want to call it to run the state. She could learn to run it but right now she has no experience or know-how."

"I don't want to run it."

Jay snorted. "Me either."

"Well, I'm not doing it," Luke said.

Jay said, "That's why we need to find someone."

I said, "I'm all for that as long as whoever we find doesn't try to exploit us or this situation to make a buck."

Jay closed his eyes, pinching the bridge of his nose. "That's the problem. Who do we trust?"

I said, "I trust you. I think you're stuck with this job. If you find someone more qualified who you can work with, they can have it."

Jay groaned.

Luke said, "Make a public announcement, to Hifis I mean, and ask for help."

I said, "You can ask the president for help. Maybe he knows someone who'd be willing to work here. I don't care if we hire humans or have human volunteers or whatever. I should have worked something out about money though so we could hire help. That was stupid of me, but I wasn't thinking about costs or anything."

"It was stupid of both of us, but I'll see what I can do to rectify it."

I said, "Well, you'll be on your own here for a while. We're going to visit my folks if we can get travel visas."

Jay said, "You have them already. You can go wherever you want."

Luke said, "What we don't have is money."

"My dad will pay for the tickets, I'm sure of that."

Jay said, "The consulate is working to recover our assets. If you had insurances or if your home wasn't destroyed, you might have some assets you could access."

Luke frowned. "I still need to arrange for a headstone for my mom. She might have had insurance, but it would go to my dad. I have some personal stuff in the apartment. It never occurred to me to see if it was still standing."

Jay shook his head. "I'm sorry, but it isn't."

Luke's expression didn't change but I knew he was really upset and not about the dumb apartment. He was keeping his feelings to himself because he knew the reminder of his mother would upset me too. We were both pretending we were okay by not mentioning her, but we needed to face it.

I said, "Jay, see about locating Gina Melton's remains. We need to bury her properly."

Luke's breath caught in a sob, which made me cry.

I sniffled and said, "Let's take a break and stop running and hiding and worrying and let ourselves be sad that we'll never see her again."

Tears began to trickle down his cheeks. I led him back to our room where we lay on the bed and cried ourselves to sleep.

6

Adan woke me with a kiss.

"Adan!" I said and burst into tears.

He laughed and groaned, laying beside me to hug me tightly while I shook and sobbed. It had been so close. I might have killed us all by turning off those coms. I might have sent him to his death, and the thought of it made me moan and cry harder.

He made comforting sounds until I stopped shaking and then just held me with his lips against mine.

We lay there a long time. Long enough for my arm beneath him to go numb.

"God, I'm sorry," I finally whispered.

"You have nothing to be sorry for," he said briskly as he sat.

Circulation returned to my arm with a shooting pain that faded quickly to numb discomfort.

He said, "Bradly sent over our dress uniforms with his compliments and assurances that we can wear them legally but with no strings to attend Jacobs' funeral."

"Is that safe?"

"Jay can order Zeus to attack or run."

"But will he?"

"Yes. There are four others who can order it if we lose contact with Zeus. And he knows if he doesn't, none of us are safe. They'd take him out next if our own people didn't."

"Are they our people?" I asked dryly.

He shrugged. "Not really. Most of them don't give a damn about anyone except themselves. A good portion of them are staying where they were voluntarily. We're sending inspectors to make sure they weren't coerced into it, but it does make me feel better about Bradly's assurances."

I said, "I'm certain Carr knew how awful the conditions were here. I'm not convinced I was sent there by mistake. What would've happened if they'd been able to terrorize me into submission?"

His expression darkened. "It makes me goddamned furious that they tried."

I said, "It would've worked but only if we let it work. If I ever call you and you think I'm acting under duress, don't give yourself up! Molly's situation gives me nightmares. They'd use us against each other, and we can't let them!"

He said, "Do you remember the Halloween dance at our school last year?"

The *non sequitur* made me frown, but I nodded.

"And do you remember the incident in the cafeteria?"

I nodded again, my frown growing.

"That incident will be one of our recognition phrases that verifies what we're saying is true."

"*Ahh*... okay. We can use that pizza place we liked with the crazy menu too."

"And our last date or where we sat at Luke's games."

"The posters on your bedroom walls. I wish you'd seen my room..."

"Me too. I wish we had more normal memories to share together." I shivered, and he added hurriedly, "We'll make tons of new memories."

But they won't be good ones, I didn't say.

He said, "Did you want to go to the funeral?"

"Yes. But see if we can get weapons."

He lifted an eyebrow, staring with wide eyes.

"I don't mean for Bradly, but Fen might show. This could be her plan... or his."

"Damn it," he muttered, hugging me again. "Right. I'll see what I can do and speak to Luke and Jay and maybe talk with Bradly. We'll need another liaison with him. I can't be calling directly, except for emergencies and this isn't one. I think this is us being paranoid but there *is* a slight chance it's a setup."

I grimaced and shrugged. "I know but the new lawyer hates me already."

Adan said, "I think it should be a Hifis anyway."

I said, "That would mean an extra step in communications. We tell them and they call his man. It would be better to skip that step."

"We could compromise. In fact, I think it's a necessary step. We should have a Hifis liaison officer who helps all Hifis who work in the service. Someone they can contact if they have a Hifis need. We can get a direct contact link as far up the chain as Bradly wants but we'll put all requests we can through our Hifis liaison."

"You want to go back, don't you?"

He grimaced and nodded.

I said, "I'm still thinking about it."

"Fair enough. Luke has arranged a ride for after the service today. We can be in Florida in a few hours and stay as long as we want."

"I don't want to stay long."

"Whatever you decide, Luke and I are behind you."

"That's what worries me. I keep screwing up and if I take you down with me..."

He chuckled, kissed my forehead, then strode for the curtain that was the door to our room. "Too late to worry about that now," he called back. "It's all for one and one for all."

I called back, "I'm not like most people, I can't stand pain—it hurts me!"

He opened the curtain to wink at me. "I'm keeping a sharp eye out for puddy tats."

"Get out of here loon and let me dress!"

We were both laughing, and I was pretty sure we were both faking it.

7

The sound of gunshots faded away and the crowd surrounding the grave began to break up.

Our entire platoon had come and our personal friends made their way toward us lead by Sutak.

I greeted her with a handshake.

I said, "I should've expected the Sutak Force."

Sutak said, "I'm sorry I made fun of the pantsuit. I hadn't realized your friend was killed."

Luke shook her hand and said, "How did you find out?"

"Garfield. She asked about you for us." Sutak glanced over her shoulder then leaned forward and lowered her voice. "Stephanie was being an insufferable ass saying you'd all been kicked out for fornicating."

A blush bloomed on Sutak's cheeks. She fussed with her gloves, clearly avoiding our eyes and just as clearly wondering if there was some truth in Stephanie's allegations.

Our friends were all flushed and avoiding our eyes.

Luke laughed a harsh bark of laughter. "She has no idea what she's talking about. I'm gay."

My mouth dropped open and I grabbed his arm.

He patted my hand. "I'm done hiding, Mia."

Sopon leaned past Sutak's shoulder to slap his. "Good for you. I'm gay too."

The rest of our friends began shaking our hands as Sutak said, "Garfield told us you were called away for a special assignment. I had an idea what it might be about but couldn't say anything. Reynold's asked Garfield to check up on you, and we were told your friend had died and you'd been given compassionate leave to attend the funeral, and we knew this funeral was going to be hard since you couldn't attend the funerals of your other friends, so here we are..."

"Thanks for this. It means more than you know."

Reynold's said, "That bitch is getting on my last nerve."

Tom Basile, a friend of Adan's and Luke's said, "Will you be back in time for commencement?"

Luke said, "I doubt it."

Adan squeezed his shoulder, and I realized Luke really wanted to attend too.

I linked my arm in his. "We'll be back when we can. Have they announced who made it yet?"

Sopon grimaced, and Tom laughed and slapped her shoulder. "You're a shoo in."

"I'm a gay woman in a man's world. Nothing is certain, except there'll be people who despise me because of it."

"*Ha*," Luke said, and Adan ruffled his hair.

Adan said, "I got your back, bro." He grinned and added, "I can't wait to see that bitch's face. Promise me I can be there when you tell her."

I laughed but shook my head. "He doesn't have to tell her or anyone. It's his own business." I frowned at Luke as I said, "But you need to grow a thicker skin about it. This isn't high school, and you can't let her name-calling get to you."

Luke kissed my cheek. "It gets to you more. I love that you worry about me, but you don't need to."

"*Ha!*" I said, in the same tone he had, and Sopon laughed.

While we'd been talking, the crowd had been passing us to pay their respects to Jacobs' elderly parents. I'd been watching them, hoping I'd spot Fen and dreading I would.

I said, "We have to go pay our respects if we're going to catch our plane."

"Is this about..." Sutak trailed off, biting her lip.

"This isn't but some stuff was, but I can't explain now. I will as soon as I get clearance to, I promise."

"For God's sake, be careful."

I gave her a quick hug, and they all stood at attention as we hurried away.

"Tom, *huh?*" Adan said musingly, and I was surprised to see Luke's flush.

"Is he gay?" I asked.

Adan shrugged, and Luke said, "Yeah."

Adan said, "You're a crafty one. I didn't once notice you sneaking away or even flirting."

"Because I didn't. Look can we talk about this never?"

I laughed then grimaced when the closest people glared. Their anger reminded me how tragic this was, and a hard ball of guilt suddenly made my throat tight. I really hoped it wasn't my fault.

I was quiet until we reached Jacobs' tear-streaked mother.

"Ma'am, your son was a good friend to me when I needed one..." I trailed off as my voice broke, the ball of guilt squeezing my throat closed, making my tears fall.

Adan nudged me aside to clasp Jacobs' mother's hand in his. "He meant a lot to all of us and we'll never forget him."

"I'm so sorry for your loss," Luke muttered, and Adan dragged us away.

"It isn't your fault!" he said forcefully once we were free of the crowd.

Luke hugged me. "So far it appears to be just a dumb accident."

I knew him well enough that I knew he didn't really believe it.

Adan snapped, "Let's just get this over with!"

The car that had brought us to the cemetery was waiting to take us to the airport. We'd be traveling on military transport and as far as I knew at military expense.

We were all quiet on the ride to airport. We passed through security with no problems and no noticeable differences from the other men and women waiting to board.

I said, "What are we going to do about money?"

Luke slapped his duffel bag. "I have some contracts in here for us to go over and we should do it on the plane before we speak to your dad. We have a few options."

I said, "We aren't taking money for our position. We need real jobs."

"I agree," Adan said.

Luke nodded. "Okay. I'm fine with that. It narrows our options a bit. I've got a copy of a proposed contract for us that Jay and the lawyers have vetted, and our visas are good for two years. We could work wherever we wanted. Our job placement office has a list of jobs all over the US that we would qualify for."

"I thought they were confining us to bases?"

"They are but there's bases all over and all sorts of jobs are available on them."

"I want to see the school contract."

Luke opened his duffle bag. "It's a good contract. The base pay doesn't look that great but that includes all living expenses and school supplies. We'll receive an additional stipend for uniforms and be issued experimental gear free of charge, and then there's the hazard pay, plus we can use military transport to travel, not that we'll be allowed to for eighteen months, but after that we can."

Adan said, "Where will we be stationed?

Luke handed him a flyer and said, "The housing is still being readjusted. It was a civilian school. Jay warned me that we'll probably be sharing rooms for at least a semester and maybe as long as the eighteen months while they finish construction and settle us in. But our contract lets us pick our roommate, and we'll get our own rooms at some point. Most of the dorms are two or four bedrooms, a shared bath, and a small common area. There will be a mess hall, and we can cook in our rooms.

"I assume we'll be in a four-man arrangement because the rule is we get to stay together. We're allowed visitors in our rooms and as long as we're discreet we can have, *um*, private time in them. We'll have roommates, so all nighters are probably out but lights out isn't until eleven."

"There's a list there of the rules and the general layout of the day. Jay can get us class schedules if we'd like to see them."

I said, "I want to see them."

I plucked the pamphlet from Adan. The front of the pamphlet was black with a rocket ship in a circle with Allied Forces Armed Responders Academy written on the bottom half of the circle and *Ad Astra* across a banner crossing the ship.

"To the stars," I said, laughing a small, surprised laugh. I hadn't known it was the school's motto. I hit my record app as I flipped through it and then handed it back.

Luke said, "I've begun my own security check of the surrounding grounds, and I'll demand we be let in to map the entire place or at least any place we might possibly be sent to insure our coms work perfectly."

"What about battle drills that need radio silence?"

"In drills we could just not use them, but I know you mean the real thing and that's the sticking point. I don't just mean com silence but the fear we have that they'll take advantage of it."

The announcer called for our plane to board.

Luke stopped speaking to gather his duffle.

Adan said, "Let's talk to Frank and think about it a bit more. We're all stressed and haven't gotten much sleep. A few good nights sleep will have us less paranoid."

I wrinkled my nose at him, and he tapped it.

"Well, it will have Luke and me less paranoid."

"*Ha,*" I said, grinning at him. "I don't call him Wile E. for nothing you know. My nickname should have been the Roadrunner."

"That's Jay's nickname. You're our Daffy." Luke gave me a quick one armed hug as Adan took my hand and whispered, "And *mi amor.*"

8

Luke destroyed all the paperwork before we exited the plane. None of us had said it, but we all knew we were debating what to tell my parents.

My mom and Shea were waiting for us and both got teary when they hugged us.

"Your beautiful hair!" Shea said unhappily.

People passing us were staring, some even lingering. I bet we were the first AFAR they'd ever seen. We still wore our dress uniforms, which were black and silvery gray but otherwise identical to Army dress uniforms.

"You look good, Mia, very modern and fit."

Mom gave Shea a warning glance, and Shea pursed her lips, then rolled her eyes at me.

I said, "It's just hair and will grow back. I don't mind it though. Most of us wear it really short. Our BDU—battle dress uniform, is a one piece jumper sort of like what the astronauts wear. They're training us to get ready for space and hair will get in the way of our helmets."

"Have you been to space?" she asked in amazement.

"No. But someday, I hope."

The men and women who'd been eavesdropping on our greeting began to shuffle away.

I wasn't worried about the eavesdroppers. I'd have halted too. AFAR was new and seldom spoken of on the news according to the report I'd read that Jay had sent me.

I put my arm around my mother, and Luke took Shea's hand.

She beamed up at him.

I made a mental note to take her aside to tell her that he was gay before her infatuation grew strong enough to break her heart.

Adan took my duffel bag, which only had my borrowed sweats in it.

I said, "We need to do some shopping. I have no civilian clothes at all.

Mom said, "There's some really nice stores here."

Shea said, "I got to decorate my room myself and pick out most of my own clothes."

Adan said, "Maybe you could pick me some? I hate shopping."

"Sure." She grinned happily at him.

Mom said, "Will you be staying long? I was worried. Your last call was so hurried and cryptic, but you look okay if a bit tired and strained."

"I wanted to talk to you and Dad about that."

Shea glared, yanking her hand from Luke to cross her arms.

I laughed, ruffling her hair. "It's nothing you can't know, bugs, or anything you need to worry about. I was upset because a friend of mine was killed in a car accident. I wanted to talk to Mom and Dad about my options because Afar is offering compassionate leave to us if we've lost family, and we might take it. Luke and Adan still haven't buried their moms, but leave will make us late for the start of school."

"Oh..." She grabbed Luke around the waist. "I'm sorry. Your mom, momsy..."

She began crying, and Luke squatted to hug her.

Mom said, "We can certainly arrange whatever they'd like to do. You're all welcome to stay as long as you like."

I released her to put an arm around Adan.

I said, "I never even asked if you had other family. Aunts or uncles or grandparents maybe who we should call and visit?"

"It's just me."

I shook my head. "It's just us."

Shea sniffled and wiped her face to take Luke's hand again. We were getting more curious stares now.

Shea said, "It's all of us. We're your family now."

Her expression lightened and she gave me a watery smile. "Do you have a ring?

Adan said, "Not yet.

"Shea," Mom said warningly, and Shea rolled her eyes again.

He laughed and slung my bag atop of his to take Shea's hand. "Maybe you could help with that too. I'll need a beautiful one. I was waiting to officially ask her until we could have a nice romantic dinner and romance in basic is impossible."

We'd reached the exit and the boys kept hold of Shea's hands, making her laugh as they exited in a chain.

Mom and I crossed a crosswalk ahead of them. She glanced over her shoulder before saying, "Is everything really okay?"

"I'm not sure. We need to talk privately."

"Shea won't leave tonight but tomorrow she will, especially if she thinks you'll all be sleeping in."

I nodded and said, "It can wait until tomorrow, I think."

Mom's lips tightened, and she said, "You think?"

"It's about Fen."

Her lips tightened even more, and she said, "We'll talk tonight downstairs after Shea goes to sleep. I hate to do it, but I'll give her a Tylenol PM."

I nodded, turning back at the elevator that led up in the parking garage. Her smile was bright but little lines bracketed her eyes now. I knew the smile was a lie and that she was really worried.

Luke and Adan sat in back with Shea, joking and laughing like normal while my stomach twisted and flipped.

A soft chime played in my head. I tapped the icon to accept Jay's recorded message. *"Don't miss the news tonight.*

Luke said, "We heard on the way here that's there another big news brief planned for tonight at six."

Mom said, "We'll make it home in plenty of time. How's pizza sound for dinner?'

"Sounds great," Adan said.

"Was the food there bad?" Shea asked.

"No. It was fine. Not as good as I can make but—"

Shea laughed, and I said, "He's an amazing cook. Maybe you can make us dinner one night?"

"If your mom doesn't mind, I'll make us all breakfast."

Mom said, "By all means. You can take my car if you need to run out and there's a grocery delivery service I use."

Shea said, "That's pretty cool. I get to put whatever I want on the list although sometimes she makes me wait to get it."

Mom snorted. "No one needs three bags of different types of chips in a week."

"You're going to get fat," I said teasingly.

"Am not! Hey, maybe you can come to the skatepark with me?"

"Sounds fun, but I have no board."

Her face flushed, and she cast Luke a guilty glance.

I said hastily, "I can probably rent one though."

I kept the smile on my face although I was cringing internally. I'd forgotten my own damned birthday, and by her guilty excitement I was in for a surprise party.

9

My father greeted us all with hugs.

Lines appeared on his forehead as my mother hugged him. They smoothed instantly and if I hadn't been looking for a tell I wouldn't have noticed.

"You guys look spiffy," he said.

Adan grinned, saying, "We're doing very well, sir."

"None of this sir stuff. We're family. Call me Frank."

Mom took the pizzas from Luke that we'd picked up on the way home and headed to the kitchen. The house was nice and very similar to the one I remembered from my youth. It stilled smelled of fresh paint. I took the time to examine the furnishings and colors my mom had picked, realizing how difficult it must have been for her to hide herself so completely in our shabby apartment.

Shea dragged me upstairs, calling over her shoulder, "Your room is right down the hall!"

"Look," she said as she threw open a bedroom door. "I picked out your stuff. Isn't it cool? We have our own rooms now. Mines right through there. We share that bathroom."

"It's great. I doubt I'll get much time to stay here though."

She'd chosen a dark purple color for my walls and bright orange and white bedding. A bright blue rug was on the hardwood floor beside the bed and curtains with orange and blue stripes on the windows.

"You don't like it," she said in a hurt tone, and I realized tears had filled my eyes.

"No, I love it. It just makes me sad that I can't be here in it with you."

One of Shea's hobbies, a hobby that she'd hidden from everyone except me, was design. She'd loved to pour over magazines and design her dream house. I'd offer my opinions and play along and she'd obviously remembered the colors and styles I'd liked, but this nice room was too late for us.

I was suddenly angry.

She said, "Come see mine," and ran through the bathroom to reach hers.

Hers was the same colors as mine but the walls were orange and the bedding purple. Hers also had knickknacks and other furniture, a desk, a bookcase, a comfortable looking chair, and a television.

"Mom said I had to wait to see what sort of furniture you wanted but we can get you ones just like mine."

"I'm good. You did a really great job, Shea. This looks great!"

It did look great, comfortable and safe. It eased my heart a bit to see her so happy here. I examined the pictures on her wall while she happily told me about her new friends and the places in the pictures.

"Girls, come and eat!" Mom called.

"I'll show you my new clothes after dinner," she promised as she ran down the stairs.

I followed slowly. It was clear she was happy here. I hoped I wasn't the harbinger of destruction to her new happy life.

We ate the pizza while watching the news. A banner ran along the bottom of the screen warning the live broadcast would be interrupted by a presidential address.

Shea said, "I hate when they do that."

I said, "If it was an emergency, they wouldn't make us wait for the news. It's just an announcement."

"Yeah, maybe they're announcing the aliens are returning..."

I shook my head.

Adan said, "No they'd tell us that immediately. It's probably something to do with politics."

Luke said, "I wouldn't worry too much about it, Shea. There's bound to be tons of announcements and speeches."

She shrugged.

It made me sad and angry that she was so scared, but there wasn't anything I could do about that. We were all scared of the damned aliens returning.

The expected interruption didn't happen until the end of the hour and the timing eased both my parents and Shea.

The president sat at his desk. My breath caught when I recognized the man beside him as a Ranger-X. Captain Hendricks wore a one-piece spandex suit very similar to our BDU, except it was short sleeved with shorts.

The president said, "My fellow Americans, we've put a name to the aliens and now know they call themselves Geromi. The Geromi have manufactured a way, a type of virus, which they call hifis, that can remake the body into a different more useful shape for a task at hand. They can merge with each other to accomplish tasks that a single being couldn't. They call these lesser pieces of themselves segments. We aren't certain exactly how they do it.

"The Geromi's knowledge of biochemistry is impressive and we can learn a lot from them. This virus that they call Hifis can remake a segment as good as new. Their segments seem less intelligent than humans, but that too is being tested. There appears to be two distinct types of aliens. The Geromi, that we know very little about, and the Hirsit who seem to be enslaved by them. Like Earth, Hirsit has an abundance of wildlife, and the Geromi have made it possible for Hirsit to shift into some of the animal shapes to use as extensions of themselves. They're attempting to do the same with humans."

He nodded grimly, saying, "That's just as dire as it sounds.

"You've all been hearing rumors of alien plague, humans abducted, and animals strangely deformed. We've assured you that there is no danger of contacting an alien disease and this is only partly true.

The aliens have used germ warfare on us and are likely to again. Research is being done around the world. Our best and brightest scientist have made it our top priority. Hifis can't be spread by any means we know of. That alien ship dusted us with the pathogen when it flew over and that dust infects the subject immediately and either kills them instantly or doesn't. It has a zero shelf-life.

On average, a bit over half the people exposed to the dust will die."

My sister moaned softly and I said, "You have to be exposed, bugs, and we can hide from it."

The president said, "Captain Hendricks here suffers from Hifis. There are many adaptations to this disease. Some people who've contracted it can go on to live a normal happy life while others aren't so fortunate.

"The rumors of malformed animals are true. It effects any vertebrae animal it touches. Animals who contract the disease can make themselves smaller and in some case bigger when frightened. They're no more dangerous than any animal, excepting in proportion to their size, but they remain animals without the means to attack in any way other than with tooth and claw.

"Humans affected by Hifis, on the other hand, posses intellect and they can use the disease to help themselves.

"Do they get bigger?" Shea asked me.

"*Shh,*" my father said.

The president said, "I'm sure there are people out there who are suffering with this disease and are afraid to seek help. Your differences will make you fear that you'll be held against your will and that *was* true. We did gather as many of these people as we could. We needed to be sure they couldn't spread it and we want to find a cure.

"Most of the infected are working with us voluntarily and continue to work with us even though we've released them as they pose no threat whatsoever to the rest of us. We're opening two embassies. The phone numbers and locations and websites will be shown after this. If you're suffering from Hifis, you can contact an embassy and the people there will help you manage your disease, including helping you find a safe place to live. While living there, you'll be asked to submit to some testing but can refuse.

"Our nation's medical laws prohibit the sort of testing that might be done elsewhere, and I'm certain fear of testing has kept some of you hidden. We'd like you to come forward. A place will be made for you, but we also need you. Afar will need your special skills.

"Captain Hendricks..." the president gestured, and Hendricks took a step forward.

"I'm one of a few infected who are training with Afar. We live under tight security for our own protection and you can live there too."

Shea screamed when he shifted.

I put my arm around her.

The chimp on the television said, "I've adapted fully to Hifis and am in total control of this form and myself." His uniform hid his x-com and it was difficult to tell if he was typing or using prerecorded messages but it sounded and looked as if he was speaking.

"As a chimpanzee I can make myself smaller or larger." He shifted sizes as he spoke and then resumed his original size. "I'm stronger and faster and can eat things I wouldn't touch as a man."

Adan let out a bark of laughter, and Luke grimaced.

"*Eww*," Shea said, and I nodded.

"They eat bugs, don't they? Like maggots and stuff?"

"I sincerely hope not," I said, and my father pursed his lips.

I gave him a fake smile, saying, "I work with the captain and it would gross me out to see it."

"How many are there," Shea asked.

"I can't tell you. That's classified information, but not enough. We need more if we're going to win."

"*Shh*," my father said again.

As we were speaking, Hendricks had been demonstrating. He could use his feet to hold a gun and use his hands to hold a pen and he was able to do both at once.

The president said, "Captain Hendricks has control of himself, but unfortunately some people suffering from Hifis don't. They become confused when they shift to their animal form and will attack if frightened, which is one of the reasons that we need this embassy.

If you're suffering from Hifis, you can go there and your particular needs will be accommodated. The facilities are inspected and monitored to ensure that your rights will be upheld, even if you're unable to ask for those rights."

"Some are stuck," my father said grimly.

I nodded.

Mom gasped with dismay, reaching for my hand.

Shea said, "Stuck?"

I said, "They can't shift back."

"Ohh... that's horrible..." she sniffled, wiping her eyes.

I didn't know if she was afraid for herself or feeling bad for them—it was infuriating either way.

"I hate them for coming here..." I said as Luke hugged her.

The president said, "The aliens posses this ability. They can shift their forms and some of the forms would be more dangerous than others. There will be further announcements when we have more information about that. Stay tuned for the special report following this address to hear what we know now. I'm making this public plea for you to come forward if you have Hifis or even if your pet does. There are so few of you, and you're our only hope of fighting fire with fire."

Hendricks resumed his human form.

The president said, "You have my assurances of amnesty but that only applies to this date." He tapped his desk emphatically. "If you commit a crime because of your Hifis impulses after this, you'll be charged as mentally competent and be held accountable. Get yourself the help you need."

Hendricks said, "Get yourself the friends you need. Service life isn't for everyone, but for those who love it like I do, there's no closer camaraderie. We're adrift now and those of you who've lost your families, homes, friends, and jobs will be feeling very adrift, but there is a place for you. Afar can be your new home."

The president said, "Let me leave you with these final words. Fear has always divided us, and the aliens know that. This weapon is intended to weaken us and make us slaves. Don't let them win. Don't let fear make you prejudice against those who are different from you but still human—still Americans in their hearts. They have a disease and it's one you might contract when the aliens return. In some ways this disease is a blessing. Hifis like Captain Hendricks have increased strength, stamina, and agility, but the intent of it is not. The intent to change us into their image is evil. The death rate of this contagion is horrific. Luckily, we can avoid the dusting ships and our recommendations on what to do in the event another ship appears will be following this broadcast.

"God bless you all and good night."

I said, "They've already managed to lower the casualty rate. We might even make a cure."

My father said, "How sure are you that it can be avoided?"

"Very. The dust becomes inactive after ten minutes. You can see it too as a yellowish pollen-like substance but only one tiny, microscopic spec needs to touch you."

Mom shook her head, giving Shae a meaningful glance, and I added hastily, "It would be fast and painless. But some live through it and you should see them. Some of them are damned cool looking. One of my friends is a pit bull. You'd like her a lot, but I can't tell anyone her name or anything. There's so few of them that they keep their identities hidden. They train with us because they can live through damage that would kill us."

"That sounds horrible."

"They say they don't feel pain like we do, and injuries disappear when they shift again. They're actually pretty normal. We have another friend who's a golden retriever, and you should see him play frisbee."

Shea laughed and Mom said, "They're certain it's not contagious?"

"A hundred percent sure. They're trying hard to spread it. They want to give it to the soldiers because they know the aliens can do it and it's a huge advantage for them when it makes them so hard to kill."

"If this disease is so great, then why do they hide?" Shea asked.

Adan said, "Because they're scared of the medical tests that the government wants to do, but the testing has mostly stopped. They have enough volunteers for it now."

My father said, "They must have quite a few if the dust infected everyone around the ship."

"I'm sure there were but then the Chinese killed them... only a few were out of the blast area. The army was trying to evacuate them, but it was hard to do with all the civil unrest and they had no way to even make announcements really, although I'm not sure if they would have if they could. They wanted to keep them secret, but then they decided to put them in Afar and have them work with the international soldiers."

As we were talking, the reporter on the television was introducing a slew of specialists, two of which were my crew.

My father shushed us again as Doctor Banks began to speak.

"Same old, same old," Shea said.

I grinned at her and stood. "You heard about one alien invasion, you heard about them all. Let's go upstairs, and you can show me your new clothes, and we can raid mom's closet for something for me. I want to shower."

I kissed Adan and Luke on the top of their heads and followed Shea upstairs.

10

While I showered, she sat on the bathroom counter and asked me endless questions and then showed me her new things while I lounged in her bed.

Mom came up and gave us cookies and milk and we sat in Shea's bed together eating it while I described my first few days and new friends. She fell asleep while I was telling her about our first hike. I covered her and tiptoed from the room.

Mom was alone downstairs, making a tray of nachos.

She said, "The boys are downstairs. We have a small game room that we're planning to make airtight. You're sure about how long the virus is active?"

"Positive. But that doesn't mean they won't have other ones. They used another type of biological—I was going to say weapon, but it isn't really a weapon. It's more of a repair agent. Our experts don't think it was intended to be used but was just fallout from the ships, but Geromi will have seen what sort of devastation it caused and can use it against us. There's a million theories, but the one that's gaining prominence is the one that says we're the first intelligent species they've run into. The Hirsit have no buildings manufactured with synthesized materials. They build but with sticks and rocks. They're animals with implants."

"Like cyborgs?"

"I have no idea... Some of the shapes they can take seem manufactured, so I guess they could have machine parts in them. We've just begun studying it, and it will likely all be classified."

"Help me bring this downstairs."

She handed me a tray, and I followed her.

The downstairs room was small with a low ceiling, a couch, and a television. Shelves holding all sorts of canned goods lined all the walls.

My father said, "So—they know about you?"

"Yes, but they don't know you knew. We told them we thought you might have suspected."

Adan said, "We lost that game, and we're lucky we didn't lose our lives. I'm done playing games now. I'm no good at it, and we don't need to do it. They offered us a real contract that we can live with and I think we're going to accept it."

He lifted an eyebrow at me, and I nodded.

"I appreciate everything you've done for us—more than appreciate it. You saved our lives. We've been hearing real horror stories about the first few weeks in detention for Hifis, but they've been treating us fairly and they really do need us."

I said, "Fen is going to be a problem. I'm under surveillance, every Hifis is, and she snuck onto the base." I told my father what Fen had said and that the security on base had heard it all and was looking for her.

Mom said, "You can't believe that, Mia."

I said, "I believe it's based on truth, but I don't believe her concern was genuine. The very next day, my Hifis contact there was killed in a car accident."

"*Ahh*, the phone call," my father said.

I nodded. "She spooked me. I'll admit it crossed my mind that you'd done it, but you have no motive. I don't know if she did it, but they're investigating."

Mom said, "That's a hell of a coincidence..."

126

Luke said, "We don't think it was a coincidence. We think she did it then on purpose to make Frank look guilty to Mia and maybe the authorities."

I said, "I was told pointedly that humans are actively helping the aliens."

Mom paled, lifting a trembling hand to my father. He clasped her hand, pursing his lips at us.

Adan said, "No one thinks you or Fenris are working with them, but it *was* mentioned. I'd assume I was being watched if I were you."

Mom said, "Will you tell us if you hear anything more?"

I said, "Of course, but we also mean to honor our contracts, including the confidentiality agreements. I assume they'd believe I'd tell my parents if they were going to arrest you or something, so I doubt I'll be told anything of any importance."

My father said, "It worries me that Fenris has a new partner. She has a history of picking bad men. Henley was a privileged asshole and on his way to being a very bad man like his father. Your mother and I thought she was grooming him as an asset, but he was grooming her. I think his car accident was meant for his father, but I can't prove it. Henley Senior was a lawyer with some very scary clients. We warned Fen she was playing with sharks..."

My father took my mom's hand. "We thought she was a patsy, but maybe we were wrong. Maybe she's better at this than we thought."

Mom frowned. "You think she didn't really need rescuing?"

"I hate to think it."

Tears filled my mother's eyes.

My father cleared his throat. "We might have been chumps."

"No," Mom said firmly. "Fen is a lot of things, but not a murderer. She'd lie, but she did love us."

I said, "She sounded pretty angry to me...."

"She was furious when we refused to help her. She had a plan to take a big—"

My father shook his head, squeezing Mom's leg. "You don't need details. Suffice it to say that we and Fenris had different views as to the types of scams we'd pull. Your mother and I didn't need money. We had more than enough to live the lifestyle we wanted. We worked for the fun of it. We picked jobs that amused us and were careful to leave the playing field undisturbed, which meant we didn't leave corpses or angry victims running around. Sure, we pissed people off, but that's part of the fun. We were really careful they didn't know it was us."

He winked at Mom and she giggled.

My father said, "One of our favorite pastimes is stealing art from forgers and other thieves. We sell some and return some, depending on who the original owner was. We have a Botticelli right now that we plan to return to the Louvre, although, I suppose now with the heat on we should drop it a bit closer. I can give you names and dates of other works of art that we've returned but they could be faked. But this will happen within the next month.

Mom said, "It won't prove we're telling the truth about everything, but it should prove that we're good at what we do and we have no need to run the sort of scams that Fenris was involved with."

Luke said, "You never told us what that was."

My father said, "I *will* tell you, but do you really want to know? Most of the people involved are dead but they were all also mostly important people in active crime syndicates. They'll have family holding grudges, and if you go looking for them, you could stir up a world of shit."

"All the more reason we should know," Adan said. "If Fenris is stirring up trouble, we need to know who could be involved."

My father examined me a moment then nodded decisively. "Henley's father was in the middle of a big trial. His client, Gus Ester, had been arrested for the murder of Abelino Acho. Acho was a big deal with the Matta in South America.

"Gus worked for the same outfit but a different—division. He was in charge of shipments over the border. This is all common knowledge. The feds knew it but could never pin anything on him. Henley Senior was trying to make the case that this was a frame. Acho, had just been subpoenaed to speak before a grand jury, and Henley's contention was the feds had killed him to shut him up.

"An entire shipment of hot off the presses TEC-9s had gone missing while in federal hands and the accusations were flying fast and furiously. The feds said Acho had stolen the guns while Acho claimed the feds themselves had sold them to rebels"—he made air quotes on the word rebels—"in their country. Honduras was having real problems, and it's a fact the US sent them military aid, and it's a fact that some of that aid was top secret, black ops stuff.

"I have no idea who was lying, but I know money was changing hands. Henley Junior was a courier, and Fen stole over two million from him.

"He knew it, and I still have no idea how he found out, but he showed up here furious. I thought he'd kill her, so I gave him the money. I had to sell every visible asset we had, but I was able to come up with enough that he could cover the difference. I moved your mother and you girls and went looking for Fen, and she can thank her lucky stars that I did.

"Henley had already been murdered. He'd been in his father's car and the breaks had been cut. Real amateur work. If your sister had had the sense to disappear right then, she'd have been fine, but instead she made a try for the old man.

"I don't know what ploy she used, seduction, threats, guilt, but whatever it was it didn't work. Celia and I think she'd meant to steal the replacement payoff. She knew who the couriers were and the house where the deals went down.

"So, I show up at senior's house and he tells me he hasn't seen her since the funeral, but I know that's a lie because one of his housekeepers was wearing the hat that Fenris had worn to the funeral.

So I left and came back later that same night to search the place and I find a high powered meeting of thugs going on and Fen tied in the garage already sitting on a roll of plastic.

But she was convinced she could still grab that money, and she thought we could take the guns and drugs they were talking about in the house. We probably could have, but I wanted no part of that crap. So, I knocked her out, tried to make it look as if she'd released herself, and got her out of there. I kept her locked up for three weeks while I tried to clean her trail."

Mom said, "She wasn't happy with us and wouldn't help. She wouldn't even tell us how she'd ended up in that garage. Henley Senior showed up looking for her—"

My father said, "She means his men showed up."

Mom nodded. "Men came looking for Fenris, but we were nobody and they left us alone. Henley was killed in a shooting on the courthouse steps before his case came to trial. The gunman was a member of a Chinese gang. He was caught during that altercation, admitted to the murder, but never said why, and is doing time, although maybe he's been executed now. But anyway, Fenris shows back up, and she's all hot to act on her information. Everything she knows will become worthless when they change the routes and contacts, which they were going to do any second since the old man was dead."

My father said, "We told her she was nuts and to leave it alone. I was seriously pissed. The cartel is powerful and they'd have no qualms about killing all of us if they thought for a second we were involved with any of their losses. During my attempt at cleaning her trail, I'd found out that more than that one shipment had gone missing. Fen denied involvement and pointed out how easy it would be to make a huge score if we timed it right.

"I turned her down cold. She'd already cost me almost two million and while I had other assets, I couldn't expose them because those men might notice. I had to be sure they didn't think we were involved with them and here's Fen, getting us involved every time I turn around. So I told her that we were through and if she showed her face I'd hand her over to them myself. I meant it at the time, and I regret that. I'm glad I didn't do it, but she came so damned close to getting us all killed."

Mom said, "I knew it was going to come down to that, so we hid. She's right that we just fudged some records a little bit. Enough that a record search wouldn't show us but that we could still use our names. It didn't matter if the neighbors called me Celia Sutton as long as the phone company called me Cecily Button. We changed every single official document and it worked. She lost us."

"Those letters..." I said.

I don't know why the confirmation hurt but it did.

"Complete fakes and I'm sorry for it but we had no choice."

My father grunted in annoyance. "It has been a complete pain in the ass putting us back into the records. Lots of them were destroyed but some remain.

I'd begun changing them days after I knew you'd been infected. I figured our past would need to be sparkling clean, and it's a good thing I did because I'm sure they're looking now."

"I'm sorry, Dad."

He waved dismissively.

Mom said, "Fen isn't your fault or responsibility."

I said, "They told me they'd keep me informed, and if I hear anything, I'll tell you, but I'm not sure how I can do that."

He said, "Celia and I will discuss it and work out some code phrases. I was shocked they let you come home..."

"They promised it to me when they took me to the ship."

"The ship..." he trailed off invitingly, and I shrugged.

We were both playing a game. I knew he wanted the info he was pretending disinterest in, and he knew I was going to lie about it.

Adan said, "We've signed nondisclosure agreements, and if word leaks and it's traced back to us, we're in a world of shit. This better remain between us."

Luke inhaled sharply, saying, "I thought we'd agreed..."

Adan said, "We owe them the truth."

I crossed my arms and said, "It's your funeral."

My father said stiffly, "I'm not demanding answers."

I snorted, uncrossing my arms to grab a handful of nachos that no one had touched yet.

I said, "I have no idea which of you are telling the truth. I'm sure your story will check out if I looked, which I'm not going to bother to do. I don't really care. What I care about is surviving the coming war. I don't trust anyone, except them." I pointed at Luke and winked at Adan. "If he thinks we should tell you, then here it is. The ship will talk to me, but it talks mostly gibberish that a ream of experts are trying to figure out. It talks to lots of the Hifis, so I'm nothing too special, but all of the Hifis are being trained because they hope we can talk to other ships of theirs if we can catch them, and maybe if we have enough time we could learn to turn them on or off or even to use them."

My father grinned at me, scooping up a handful of chips. "I'm sure that was all perfectly true," he said with his mouth full.

I grinned back, nodding. Mom sighed hard. She glared at us both a moment and said, "So how much danger are you in and will it blow back on us?"

"I'd say the usual amount and probably. I have no idea when they'll reveal us at the academy, but I'm certain every nation on Earth will be looking for us because we have the best chance of subverting alien tech. We have good security and are getting training.

Our government has to be aware that we can be manipulated by threats to our families, but thanks to the Chinese most of them have none, so I'm a weak link in that department..."

"We're a weak link," Luke said firmly.

"I assume they'll keep security tight around you. I can ask them about it. I can tell them we haven't told you or that we have, whichever you want us to do. What I'm not going to do is give you any particulars about where the ship is, who's working on it, or what they're learning. The less you know, the safer you'll be."

Mom said, "We might need to stage a spat or two."

"Shea," I said unhappily.

"Exactly. We need to protect her. I'd rather have her think you don't love her then have her hurt."

I winced at my father, and he reached over to take my hand. "Love is hard sometimes." He patted my hand then released it. "We can tell her you're not allowed to talk to her and let her think everything is fine. She doesn't need to know if we're having pretend arguments. But that might not be a smart play either. We need to think about it a bit."

Mom stood to begin gathering the dirty glasses. "It's late and you should get some sleep. You look exhausted. We can talk more tomorrow."

I said, "I *am* exhausted. I've been running around all over working on this Hifis embassy thing. I could sleep for a week."

Adan laughed, saying, "Well, we're off duty now, so go ahead."

I knew by my father's none-reaction that he'd heard I'd been traveling, but he didn't ask for details. I wasn't sure if I would lie or not and was glad I didn't need to make that decision.

I said, "I need to get a taser and a cattle prod and we need somewhere we can use it."

"For what?" Mom asked.

"Apparently, we can acclimate to it, which we should do before going back."

Luke sighed hard.

"Those goddamn bastards!" Adan snarled.

I said, "I don't think it will hurt much if we do it slowly."

My father said, "I can get what you need, and you can use this room just make sure Shea won't catch you."

Mom said, "Are you sure it's necessary?"

"Unfortunately, I am. I'm beat and it's nothing that we really need to talk about."

I kissed Adan goodnight and headed to my room where I tossed and turned for an hour before sneaking down the hall and into the boy's room.

I stood in the dark room debating which of them to wake. I really wanted Adan, but my mother would freak, especially if Shea woke and saw us.

I wouldn't stay long, I finally decided and released my sheet, letting it drift to the floor.

The isle between their beds was narrow and I moved slowly so as not to bump anything.

I could see perfectly in the dark and I knew I'd woken Adan before I even touched him.

He reached to lay his hand on my cheek as he pulled his sheet off.

He'd gone to bed wearing basketball shorts and I gratefully lay beside him.

"You okay?" he whispered.

"Better now."

"I couldn't sleep either."

I kissed him to silence him and we lay with our lips touching for a long time. I knew he was aroused. I was too but neither of us let our hands wander.

Our lack of privacy was beginning to seriously annoy me.

I snuggled my face against his neck, trying to relax.

Luke surprised me by putting his hand on my shoulder.

I grabbed it hard. I wished we could all snuggle together but that would likely be awkward for them, not to mention irritate my mother. I bit back my groan.

I should return to my bed, but I didn't want to. My muscles were finally unclenching.

I lay there holding Luke's hand and clutching Adan until the first tendrils of gray morning light filled the room.

Adan sat when I did. I kissed Luke's hand, wincing apologetically.

His smile was sad and sweet, and I hated that I was the cause of his worry.

I needed to work harder at making them happy.

11

Adan tossed the taser to the floor, glaring at Luke.

I said, "I'm not doing that. It looks stupid as shit!"

Luke reached for the taser, and Adan kicked it away.

"Enough, already! Just pretend to zap her. Who the hell knows what kind of damage it's doing to us on that setting? Just because we can't feel it doesn't mean it isn't hurting us." He turned his glare on me. "Just fake it already! He isn't wrong and who cares what it looks like? The entire point of this is to save our lives and that means we need to be convincing that being tased really is hurting us."

Luke said, "They'll tase you, and while you're out, they'll reach for restraints or whatever it is they have planned. You need to look convincingly neutralized and choose your moment."

Adan said, "Let's watch a few more videos. We should have recorded the first attempts."

Luke said, "What we should do is shoot each other a few times."

Adan turned from the laptop he'd just opened to glare at Luke again. "We aren't doing that."

I said, "I think we should too."

"You guys are crazy! What if we miss and the shot kills you? A gun shot will be real damage, not nerve endings being abused—but holes. It's dumb to even think about doing it. I swear to god, if you two sneak off to shoot each other, I'm going to be seriously pissed!"

"About what?" Shea asked as she entered.

I winced as I glanced at the alarm pad beside the door that was still blinking and that I hadn't been paying any attention too.

Luke said, "Oh good, you're home. I have a favor to ask." He slung his arm around her shoulder and turned her back to the door.

Shea called back, "Dinner will be ready in ten minutes! Mom brought enough Chinese food for twenty people!"

"Think she heard us?" Adan whispered as the door closed.

He grabbed the taser, holding out his hand for the cattle prod, which was laying in plain sight on the coffee table.

"My father is going to be pissed if she did," I muttered. "I can't believe I didn't notice the lights. I'm relying on Zeus way too much."

"We should've locked the door."

He lifted a shelf on the bottom of the bookcase and dropped the taser into the space revealed. I tossed in the cattle prod and he let the shelf back down then spent a few seconds straightening out the games stacked on it.

I opened the game on the top of the stack and slid the dice back to the center.

Adan said, "I bet he has ten other ways to tell if anyone opened it. I bet this entire house is bugged."

I shrugged.

Adan's lips quirked in a rueful grin. "I wouldn't care either but I'd like some real alone time with you..."

I sighed wistfully and grabbed him by the t-shirt to pull him closer. Our kiss was interrupted by my sister yelling that dinner was getting cold.

I said, "I'm looking forward to school more and more," and he laughed.

I paused in the doorway to straighten my clothes.

"Do I look okay?"

You look beautiful." His eyes darkened and he leaned in to kiss me again.

"I meant do I look too mussed for the brighter upstairs lights? If this is going to be a surprise party, I don't want to look like we were rolling around on the floor."

He winced, smoothing his t-shirt.

I said, "You look fine. Better than fine."

His smile returned.

I'd have kissed him again but Shea hollered, "You guys coming or what?"

I braced myself to hear them all yell surprise but they were just sitting at the table.

Adan chuckled as he pulled out my chair.

I shot him a dirty glance and he winked at me.

Mom handed out the cartons of food as my father said, "I'm afraid I have some bad news, Adan. Your mother's remains haven't been located. That entire block was totally consumed by fire. I've checked every avenue I could think of and the only information I was able to get was that six bodies were recovered from the building. Four of the retrieved were women. All six were burned beyond recognition and sent to the local crematorium and then were buried at Oak Lawn along with twelve thousand others. I think it very likely she was one of the women but there's no way to know which box holds which remains. She's on the official list of the dead but they wouldn't give us permission to exhume her even if we knew which box held her ashes. Im truly sorry, son."

I said, "I'm so sorry. I wish there was something I could do."

Mom said, "I'm glad we didn't stay there or we'd be dead too. Your mother would be glad you escaped, I'm sure of that."

My father said, "I've arranged for a stone to be put up here right beside Gina."

Shea said, "We'll visit her and bring them flowers. I'll take good care of her for you."

My father reached over to clasp her hand.

Adan said, "Thanks, Shea. It will ease my mind to know she wasn't forgotten. I'd been worrying about it. Her birthday is in November and she loved the purple mums. If you could bring her one for me..."

Shea jumped up and ran to hug him. "Of course. Momsy liked the pink ones. She loved all pink flowers."

Mom said, "We'll plant a memorial garden for all of our friends we lost. I've applied for permission to search the phone records. If you'd like me to search any of your mom's friends to see if they had any pictures of her stored in their clouds, I'd be happy to look."

"It never occurred to me," Luke said excitedly. "I'd thought all of our pictures were lost but maybe some are on her cloud?"

Mom said, "They're letting anyone who had friends or family in the quarantine zones apply. I'll email you the link."

My father said, "I found your father, Luke, and told him you were well and staying with us. I think you should call and speak with him."

"And say what?"

Mom said, "That we're going to be holding a memorial for your mother..."

She trailed off, biting her lip as my father shook his head.

My father said, "He knows. I told him. I even offered him a plane ticket or to hold the ceremony in Illinois. He said he'd already said his goodbyes and it was morbid to keep burying her. But that doesn't mean he doesn't care, Luke. People mourn in different ways and some people just can't face it."

"Did he ask for my number?"

My father hesitated and then shook his head. "It might just have been a bad time for me to reach out to him. Shock does crazy things to people, Luke."

Mom said, "Call him, honey. Don't let this worry you. Give him a chance to make things right between you. I'm sure he feels really bad and guilt can make us do things we regret."

My father stood to hand Luke a slip of paper. To my surprise Luke reached for his phone and called it.

We all laid our forks down.

Luke stood as he said, "Dad?"

He turned away, stopping with his back to us in the doorway as he listened for a minute.

I could've listened if I'd wanted to. My coms would've easily picked up the conversation but I purposefully dialed them down. I didn't want to hear Harvey's lame excuses. Hearing the pain in Luke's voice was bad enough.

I thought Adan was listening though. His expression grew angrier before Luke said, "I'm not coming back. I'm going to school. No, this isn't about money. I have a scholarship, remember? Mom gave me a college account." His shoulders tensed and I knew whatever Harvey was saying was making him angry.

"Then put it fucking back! I don't care if you thought I was dead. You had no right to it!" he listened for another minute then said, "You know what, Dad? Never mind. Just keep it. It's all you ever really wanted from her anyway. I don't need it and I don't want anything from you. Not the fake interest or to hear your lies about how much you loved her. Let's just cut to the bottom line. I'm never going to be a professional ball player and I have better things to do than be a toady for some mobster."

He turned to face us again as he listened. By his angry expression, I knew Harvey was still being an ass.

Harvey talked for a good five minutes before Luke finally said, "Well good for you. I'm glad you're happy there. I don't need a job, but even if I did I wouldn't work for those assholes. I'm going to school until it's time to do my service. If you want to talk to me, I guess you can call Frank seeing as how you never asked for my number."

He set his phone down and resumed his seat.

Adan said, "We could go see him in person."

"There's no way I want Mia anywhere near him. He's such an ass. I mean, he's talking about the babes I could score there as if I hadn't called to talk about his wife's funeral!"

Mom leaned over the table to pat his hand. "I'm sure he was speaking like that to connect to you. He probably thought it a good way to entice you to come to him."

"What kind of man wants his kid to hang out with mobsters? It's just ridiculous. He doesn't know me at all...."

He stabbed his food with his fork. I remained quiet. His father might not know him, but I did. I could see how much he was hurting and how much he didn't want us to know it. He'd wanted his father's approval for as long as I'd known him. It's what had kept him so deeply in the closet.

I was really worried, but I picked up my fork and said, "We'll need to get our uniforms cleaned if we're going to wear them."

Adan said, "As much as I hate to say this, I want to go shopping tomorrow."

Luke's shoulders relaxed as Shea and Adan began talking about where to shop. I had to resist taking his hand. The rest of them chatted while Luke and I pretended to eat.

When Mom finally stood to begin clearing the table, Shea jumped up and said excitedly, "Can I show them the video, Mom?"

"Yes. Your dad and I will clear the table."

Luke took my hand as we followed Shea to the living room where we sat on the loveseat. Adan tucked a throw blanket over us and kissed both of our foreheads before sitting at my feet.

Shea said, "Mom and I have been working on it. Dad says it's good to remember them, that being sad is better than pretending to yourself that you don't miss them or care. He says if you pretend that you don't care for too long then you'll forget how much they meant to you. They'd want to be remembered. I know I would. I'd want my friends to cry but to also be happy. I wouldn't want them to pretend I'd never existed to save themselves a few tears."

I was braced for it after that speech but seeing our high school still brought a lump to my throat. I gripped Luke's hand hard as we said goodbye to our old life.

12

My mother zipped up my garment bag and laid it over my now full duffel bag.

"I hate that your leaving us on this sad note."

I said, "I'd like to stay longer but I don't want to fall too far behind. Every minute might count."

"I know but..." She hugged me tightly and when she pulled away she had tears in her eyes. "I'm a terrible mother with so many regrets. If I could do things over again... My biggest regret is that I know that in some tiny corner of your heart you doubt my love for you. You can't know how sorry I am that I did this to us. I love you, Mia. There will never be a moment in time when I don't. I love Shea too, and she needs me more right now, but don't think I'd choose her over you. You'll always be welcome, no matter the circumstances."

I said, "I don't doubt that you love me, and I want Shea to come first. Do whatever you need to do to protect her. I have my pack and she has you. I know you love Frank, and I love him too in my own way, but I don't trust him, and you need to be smart about him. I'm not saying that he doesn't love you and Shea, but he loves the game too and I'm not sure what he'll risk while playing it. Take care of my sister—both of them."

"You're so like him... I hope you have some of me in there too and can learn to forgive and trust again."

Shea ran down the stairs dragging my other garment bag. Tears had left tracks across her cheeks, but she smiled at me.

"The boys are still dressing. They look so handsome."

Mom said, "I better make sure the car is ready. I'll bring these bags out." She smiled her worried smile and hurried outside.

I smoothed Shea's hair and kissed her brow, leaning down to whisper, "Can you keep a secret? A real secret that no one can know I told you?"

"Yes, but I already know you have that disease."

My heart began to thud hard and tingles raced over me. I peered around to be sure no one could hear us, shaking her shoulder lightly as I said, "You can never tell anyone you know. Not anyone! Not even Mom and Dad. It would be so dangerous for all of you."

"I haven't and I won't, I promise."

"How did you find out?"

"I'm not stupid," she said indignantly. "I was there when you got home, remember? It didn't take a genius to figure it out after listening to that speech."

"Shea, if you love me, you'll never tell."

"You're scaring me, Mia."

"Good. You should be terrified. Never let on you suspect!"

She put her hands on her hips, tapping her foot impatiently.

The mannerism was Luke's that he'd learned from his mother. Gina had done the same thing whenever she thought we were stalling, and despite my worry, it made me smile.

She said, "So, what's this big secret then?"

"I probably shouldn't tell you. I want to, but it isn't really my secret to tell. As soon as I can tell you, I will, but you should know that Luke really loves you. It isn't just words for him. He thinks of you as his little sister and what you think of him really matters to him—to both of us."

She sighed hard, saying, "You're really really bad at keeping secrets. I've known he was gay for ages."

My mouth dropped open, and she laughed then hugged me tightly.

"How..."

She flushed, staring down at her feet. "Mom and Momsy. They worried about it all the time because he never told them." She looked up to glare at me. "No one tells me anything either."

"I'm sorry. I hate it when people kept secrets from me too. The only thing I can say in my defense is that I'm not supposed to tell anyone at all that I have Hifis. It scares me to death that someone might hurt you to find out my secrets. If anyone asks you, we were all in Humboldt. Never tell anyone any different."

She nodded.

I debated a minute and then whispered, "I have one more secret, and I'm not sure I should tell you or not. I'm afraid to tell you and afraid not to."

I debated another moment, but she had to know to be safe.

I said, "Fenris came to see me and she scared me. She said some scary stuff about Mom and Dad. I don't know how she knew that Dad and I have issues but she was for sure trying to cause a deeper rift. Her and Dad are fighting, and I don't want either of us to get in the middle of it." I glanced at the stairs where I could hear the boys coming. "She broke onto my base, and the police are looking for her because they're worried she meant to try to blackmail me or scare me into giving her Afar secrets. If she contacts you, tell me or Mom right away, and no matter what Fenris says, never go anywhere with her."

Shea said, "I hate all of this. You should run away and come home!"

"I can't."

"I know. I just miss you so much."

She hugged me until the boys joined us and then she hugged Luke. "I love this house and all but I'd rather be home with Momsy right upstairs..." She began to cry, and Luke leaned down to rest his cheek on her hair.

My father opened the front door and said, "Our ride is here."

Adan and I went to the rented limo and sat beside my mother who took my hand. Luke and Shea got in and my father spoke to the driver for a minute before joining us.

Mom said, "Gina was probably the best friend I ever had or will ever have, and I wish I'd done more to help her. I was trying to be Celia the nurse when I should have just been myself and helped her whether she wanted the help or not. Not that she really needed help, but I knew your father's debts weighed on her and I could have helped her with that. I think she was much stronger than you imagined her to be. She loved her job and her friends, but you were her life.

"I debated telling you any of this, but if I were to die, I'd want my children to know, really know, how much I love them and to settle our differences. I'm so sorry, Luke. She'd be so proud of you."

She opened her purse and handed Luke a picture that Harvey had taken of the five of us at the lake. Luke and I were running into the water hand-in-hand while Shea was building a sandcastle and Mom and Gina sat arm-and-arm on a beach blanket toasting something. I'd seen it a million times but hadn't realized Mom had managed to save it and it brought tears to my eyes.

Mom said, "You keep this. I made a copy for myself, but you should read the back."

I leaned over Luke's shoulder to read it. *Silly Celia, I know our children will never marry despite the love they share but we will always be sisters, G.*

Mom patted Luke's hand. "She adored you—and she truly saw you. We spoke of our worries frequently and she hoped that when you were ready, you'd speak to us too. I know I can't replace her, but when you need a mother, I'm here for you."

Luke turned away and his shoulders shook. I knew he was crying but I also knew it would embarrass him if I made a big deal of it. I lay my hand on his leg and Adan hugged him.

Luke sobbed once and then began to cry quietly on Adan's shoulder.

Adan said, "We'll make the fuckers pay, Luke. We'll make them pay!"

13

My bags made an awkward armful. Adan nudged me aside to use his key card on the door. He carried more bags then I did. All three of us had garment bags and our duffle bags, which were jammed now with three sets of clothing all chosen to be somewhat similar and three exact duplicate sets including sneakers that we could hide on campus.

We all also carried skateboards and protective gear that my mom had insisted we buy, which I doubted we'd bother with. My birthday party had actually been fun because Mom had gotten us all new skateboards, the model I'd wanted, and she'd had them custom painted with our Loony Tunes characters.

We'd only used them once, but I couldn't wait to do it again. Hifis made me much more agile, and I wasn't worried about injuries. I was going to be able to nail stunts I hadn't been able to pull off before.

Besides his skateboard, duffel, and garment bag, Adan was also juggling two bags of groceries. I was pulling a suitcase that held toiletries, including a theater makeup kit that we'd all practiced using, and strategically chosen underwear.

My mom had helped me pick out underthings, Spandex boy shorts and bras in a bunch of colors, one-piece shape-wear, camisoles, and bathing suits that could be mistaken for clothing that I could wear as a squirrel if I remained big enough and would protect my modesty if I shifted to human. I hadn't told her I now had a monkey shape, but I think she suspected we did. She'd bought the boys new underclothes too that would, hopefully, stay on when they shifted.

She'd bought us bathrobes and slippers and had insisted that I buy a few dresses, heels, and an expensive black pantsuit with dress shoes, which made me wonder if she'd seen the pink pantsuit.

I nodded my thanks to Adan as he held the door with his foot, and stepped inside, stopping when I heard Sutak.

"—care. This is my room and I want you the hell out of it!"

Stephanie said, "Jeez. Chill already. I was just—"

"I don't care what the fuck you thought you were doing! Her things are none of your damned business!"

"Oh please. They were cut and aren't coming back. I was just putting a goodbye note in her bag so when they sent it on, she'd get it."

Luke said, "I'm so not in the mood for this."

I exchanged worried glances with Adan. Luke hadn't said more than a few words since we'd left the cemetery.

I said loudly, "No need. I wasn't cut."

Sutak exited the room grinning and Stephanie glowering.

Her glower faded like magic when she spied Luke.

He ignored everyone, dropping his bags to use his key card on his bedroom door and closed it behind himself.

I grabbed Stephanie's arm and pulled her to a halt. "Leave him the hell alone!"

Adan said, "Put these away and I'll check on him."

I dropped my bags to take the groceries.

Stephanie said, "I can help you unpack."

Sutak said, "For crying out loud! take a hint already! He doesn't want your help. Can't you see he was upset?" She grabbed my bags and said, "We're roomies."

Stephanie said, "No way he got cut and you made it."

I sighed in exasperation. "None of us got cut. We just got back from burying his mom. Give him a damned minute!"

"Oh..." Sutak said, "I'm so sorry."

I grimaced at the closed door. "We probably should've stayed away longer but we didn't want to miss the start of school. Adan lost his mom too and we couldn't locate the body. Luke's mom had been buried and we had her moved and a new stone put up. It's been a tough couple of days..."

Sutak dropped my bags inside the door of our room and began to help me unpack the groceries.

She said, "The groceries at our commissary are pretty lame but we can't go into town. Did you see the fencing?"

I nodded.

"We aren't allowed passed it. This is a one-horse town anyway. It probably doesn't have a much bigger store. The bar is so old it might as well have word saloon over it. I don't think we're missing much, although I saw some really spectacular blooms in the old cemetery we passed on the way in. I'd like to get a sample for my book, but maybe I can find some on the trails here..."

Most of the cabinets were empty and the refrigerator only held condiments and drinks. Stephanie frowned at us as we unpacked the food.

I said, "Adan likes to cook and wanted to make us dinner but..."

Sutak said, "I'm an okay cook and can whip something up if you're hungry, or we can go to the snack bar."

"I'm not hungry. Who's in the other room?"

Stephanie said, "Lana rooms with me and it's just bullshit they're cramming us in like this. Sinclair and Felipe have the room next to Luke's. These rooms are meant for four not eight."

Sutak said, "They're plenty big enough to share."

I headed for our room. "I'm going to unpack and take a nap."

Sutak followed and closed the door in Stephanie's face. She grimaced, leaning against it.

"I caught her going through your things. I'd left the door open while I was in the bathroom and that's the second time I caught her in here. I was in Sinclair's room for like a minute and she was in here. She's a snoop and a slob. There's a lock box in the closet and our top desk doors lock. Make sure you lock up anything you don't want her to see or steal."

"Did she take anything?"

"Not that I noticed, but Lana was yelling last night about Stephanie using all of her shampoo and taking her notes without asking, and it sounded like a familiar argument."

"Which side is mine?"

"Any side you like. My stuff is in the left side, but I don't care which side I have and can move it."

I headed to the empty dresser on the right and began unpacking my clothes.

"I guess I'll lock this then. I have nothing to hide, but I don't want her poking around in my underwear either."

Sutak grabbed my garment bag and headed to the closet. Our room held two twin beds, one on either side of a window. There was a small nightstand beneath the window with a lamp on it, two desks with shelves built in at the foot of the beds, and two narrow dressers bracketing the closet door. The closet was long and narrow with our footlockers stacked in the back.

"Your uniforms are in the back half. My stuff is up front. I figured because you're smaller than me, it be easier for you to squeeze by."

I nodded.

The room had obviously been a single because there wasn't much floor space, but I was grateful we weren't in bunk beds.

Sutak said, "I brought all your gear."

"Thanks."

"I'd have made your bed but regs call for leaving the bedding folded like that if the bed is unoccupied."

I began making the bed.

She held out one of my garment bags. "Want me to empty this or just hang it?"

"Either."

It didn't take us long to unpack. I flopped onto my freshly made bed.

Sutak said, "We'll be inspected tonight, so make sure your drawers are tidy. They won't look in the footlocker, but if you've been issued a weapon, they'll ask to see it and you better have it locked in there and not under the bed or anything.

"It's okay if the bed is mussed on snap inspections but not announced ones. It always has to be made, and we can't have food or clothing on the floor. We can have food and drinks in our room but no food wrappers in our garbage in here or old food laying around. That all has to be in the kitchen garbage, and garbage can never be higher than the rim.

"The bathroom floor is supposed to be kept clean and dry but Stephanie always leaves a puddle after she showers. I'm tempted to leave it but I'm afraid that bitch could weasel out of punishment detail and we'll be doing it without her.

"We're also supposed to keep our showers under five minutes. We can shower whenever we want, and there are other showers at the gym, and we have a locker there. I see you got your keycard, but did they give you your locker numbers? We get another one at the classroom, which they haven't showed us yet."

"I was given locker numbers. How much of the tour did I miss?"

"I can show you guys tomorrow. We get free time after dinner and we can leave our bunks at five a.m. to get gym time or anything we want to do before reveille. But we all need to be in the days uniform and in the field out front for that and then we go eat and then to class. We have to be back in our rooms by nine p.m. and it's lights out at eleven.

"We can have anyone we want in our rooms before lights out and even close the doors. We were told this campus has a closed door don't ask don't tell policy but getting someone pregnant was grounds for dismissal for both parties. If you'd done your stint, you'd just be dishonorably discharged but if you hadn't, you'd be in a world of shit."

I stood and smoothed my covers. "Thanks for making it."

"It's no problem."

She bit her lip, looking worried.

I said, "I'm going to go check on him. I don't mean to be rude, but he's really upset, and I'm all the family he has now."

"Sure. Of course. Go ahead. Stay as long as you want. I'm no snitch. If you want to bunk in there or anything, I won't say a word."

"Thanks." I hesitated at the door and turned back. "Luke and I are used to the rumors that we're lovers. I never cared but now there's Adan's feelings to consider and I'm not sure how to handle it. He and Luke are best friends, and Adan knew I was Luke's cover girlfriend, but it's bound to be weird for them if rumors circulate about Luke and me here, and yet, he doesn't need any more stress. I don't want to out him or turn my back on him, but I don't want to make Adan uncomfortable either. I sort of wish they weren't roommates because then I could just ask their roommate to give us a few minutes, but now..."

"Well, I could run interference for you..."

"No. That's all I need, making you uncomfortable too. It's my problem and I'll handle it—just if you see Adan or Luke worrying alone, let me know."

Sutak winced as loud music and laughter erupted right outside our door.

"That girl... Honestly she's the most self-absorbed person I've ever met." Sutak jumped to her feet and brushed past me to yank the door open.

14

"Keep it down, clowns. People are resting."

Sinclair said, "Oh, hey, Mia! I didn't know you'd gotten back from leave. Welcome home."

Sutak flipped the radio to low, and he frowned and reached for it.

She slapped her hand down on it. "Not right now. Adan and Luke just got in too and they're beat. Let them have some peace and quiet."

I said, "We cut our compassionate leave short to make it back for the start of the semester. They both lost their moms and this was the first chance they had to get memorials for them."

"Oh, man, I didn't know. That's a real bummer. Sure, we can keep it down."

Stephanie slid off the kitchen table where she'd been sitting and said, "Let's get out of here."

Sinclair hesitated, frowning at her and then their closed door.

She said, "We'll go get them some snacks since they missed chow."

Sinclair's expression lightened and he nodded. "Good idea. Let me just leave a note for Felipe."

"Where is he anyway?'

"He and Lana went grocery shopping."

Stephanie made a face and opened the door between our rooms, revealing a small half bath. She messed with her hair until Sinclair was ready and then gave us an airy wave.

"He's an idiot," Sutak mumbled as the door closed.

I laughed an agreement.

She opened the door across from the bath to show me two shower stalls. Both were small. I thought it had recently been a bigger single bath because it looked freshly tiled but oddly proportioned. Each shower had a tiny, curtained alcove and hooks to leave clothing and towels. A full-length mirror hung on the back of the door. An open shelving unit to the right of the door held eight small baskets and some cleaning supplies. All the baskets were full.

167

Sutak said, "I'll remind them they need to share the space. I have no idea whose is whose. This green one here is mine.You can use anything you like in it. You can pick up toiletries at our commissary.

"The toilet is across the room and we're supposed to be sharing the drawers there. There are three drawers, and we added a shelf above the mirror, but I plan on getting a mirror for our room and fixing my hair there."

I laughed, and she grinned at me.

"We haven't split the space in the main room although we probably should give everyone some cabinet space of their own."

Our main room was small, a refrigerator, a two-burner stove, a sink, and a wall-oven microwave combo with a counter and cabinets along one wall. The table was a decent size with four, office-type chairs that did double duty as seating for watching the television that hung on the wall in a built in shelving unit. Books partially filled the shelves.

Sutak grabbed one as she said, "That's Felipe's game console but he doesn't care if you use it. Your books are on the shelf below mine and Adan and Luke's are the next shelves over. Our campus store is closed while they remodel it or restock it or whatever it is they're doing to it. You're supposed to check to see if you got the right books and report to our platoon leader. That's Sopon by the way, and she's one floor down.

"They gave her back her rank. She's a lieutenant now and taking graduate courses. There's a big common room at the end of the hall on every floor that any of us can use, and there's a few study rooms that we can book if we need to meet and have private space for projects or whatever. The rumor has it those rooms are for the animals."

"The animals?"

Her choice of words made me uneasy.

"Oh, maybe you didn't hear? We have some human-hifis attending. They showed us a demonstration and those men are tough as shit. Real animals."

She'd said it admiringly, but I didn't like it.

I said, "They don't mind being called animals?"

"They didn't seem to but maybe..." She sat at the table, frowning down at her book. "I never really thought about it, and I guess it could be a problem, but I think it's too late to change their nickname. The entire school was there and cheering and talking smack about pitting our animals against theirs."

I said, "I guess it will work itself out."

I headed to the bathroom to call Adan.

"Can I come in?" I whispered on my x-com.

"Yes, but I think he just fell asleep."

"I'm an idiot. I should have insisted we stay a few more days. God, I'm so sorry. I feel like an insensitive ass for rushing you guys back here."

"We wanted to come back and it's good to be busy to take our minds off it. I think it just hit him now and it really upset him that his father is making himself so scarce."

"I used to be jealous of Luke. I thought his dad loved him. Harv was always an ass, but I really did think he loved him..."

"Are you okay?"

"I'm fine. Sutak has been filling me in, and she offered to give us a tour tomorrow during our free period. I'll let Luke sleep. You should catch a nap too. I'd come kiss you goodnight, but I don't want to wake him. We have an inspection tonight. I'll wake you both an hour before."

"Call me if you need me."

I thought he'd disconnected, but a moment later he said. *"This is sort of awkward. I don't want to leave the room and wake him, and honestly, I don't want to leave him, but I feel like I'm ignoring you and I don't want that either."*

"I'm good, getting the lay of the land. I might go nap too. Sutak is guarding your door. She'll keep Stephanie from knocking."

"We need to do something about that bitch."

"I know. But don't worry about it now. Get some rest. I love you."

"Love you to."

I washed my hands and face and rejoined Sutak.

"Can I ask a favor?"

"Sure."

"I'm beat and could use a nap too. If you're going to be here, could you make sure Stephanie lets them sleep? You can wake me if you leave and I'll guard the door."

"No problem. I won't let her bother anyone. I was looking things up and we have a counseling service here and religious services, which I'm sure have clergy that could talk with him."

"Thanks. I'll tell him, but he's a really solitary worrier. I think he's been repressing her death. We knew she was dead but... I think it just really hit him."

Sutak stood to give me a hug.

"I think it just hit you too. Go catch a nap and maybe speak to one of those counselors yourself."

"Gina, his mom, was a really nice lady. She used to babysit me and my sister, Shea. Luke and I spent as much time with her as we did with my own mom. Shea and I called her momsy."

Tears had begun to trickle down my cheeks as I spoke, and I angrily rubbed them.

Sutak said, "Let yourself grieve for her, Mia. I get you want to be strong for him, but you need to let yourself be sad."

"There's so many to be sad for... Wake me an hour before inspection, please."

She nodded, biting her lip.

I plodded into my room, flopped on my bed, and cried myself to sleep.

Reynold's woke me by sitting beside me and rubbing my head.

"Hey," I said as greeting.

She surprised me by kissing my cheek.

"Sutak filled us in. I'm really sorry for your losses, all of them. Did you get to see your family?"

"Yeah, you?'

"I did. It was weird having to say everything is classified. They had like a bazillion questions, and I was embarrassed that I had no answers so kept saying, sorry, classified. But it was nice to see them. They already have a nice shelter in place. My gram is old-school and we have a big garden and always had all sorts of canned goods. She's teaching all of my cousins now... This is so weird. I feel like we're devolving in lots of ways.

"My uncle's farm is busy again. They're fixing up the old cabins that his migrant workers used to use and building new ones. His business had been steadily shrinking and now it's booming. Our entire town is busy. We were just a small farming community that was dying out, but we've got this huge influx of people and they're all learning to farm... And then there's the animals... The aliens are trying to de-evolve us... we're building holes in the ground to live in like we're cavemen again. It's terrifying..."

"We just need to adapt. I think we're smarter than them and can use their tech against them."

"God, I hope so. I've been studying hard on the Hirsit and I have some ideas that I was hoping you could speak to your friend Dawe about."

"I will but he isn't really my friend. I've only met him a few times. He worked in our evac center and was the one who showed us the aliens there."

"Sutak told us she'd met you there and there was some stuff that she couldn't talk about. Whatever it was both scared her and made her hopeful." Reynolds stood and headed to the door, speaking with her back turned. "I won't ask about things you can't talk about. It reassures me that we have people like you and Sutak on our side who are afraid but still following orders."

My breath caught hard and tingles raced through my blood. The sudden surge of adrenaline left me breathless. I was sure Reynolds suspected I was Hifis and thought Sutak was too. Her people like you comment would have alarmed me if she hadn't kissed me and I realized I was projecting prejudice where there was none.

I was still worried about the animal comments because I could see how that could be twisted into an insult, and one we could hardly refute. We were animals in all but our thought processes and even those were impaired, sometimes impaired so greatly that for all intents and purposes we *were* animals.

"Great," I groaned and flopped back to my bed. "Now I can worry about prejudice too."

Sutak said, "We haven't told a soul about him, and we won't."

I jerked up in alarm, and she made a face at me. "Sorry, I didn't mean to intrude."

"*Meh*, you caught me talking to myself. I do it a lot...."

She laughed and said, "Me too. Luckily, I haven't begun to answer myself yet. I just came in to tell you that you need to be in BDU for planned inspections. You can wear civvies when officially off duty, but we're on duty most of the time—well all of the time, actually. They won't announce our leave schedule for another month but since we can't actually go anywhere..."

She trailed off, and I huffed a short laugh as I headed to our closet.

She glanced over her shoulder, lowering her voice to say, "All of our roommates are back, and she tried twice to flank me, but I think she's given up."

I said, "I just don't get her persistence. I mean, Luke is cute and all but it's like she's obsessed with him."

"Maybe she is. It happens."

I snorted. "If she knew she could get him, she wouldn't want him."

"Maybe she just wants what she thinks you have."

"I used to think that but then I began dating Adan and she never makes a serious play for him like she does with Luke."

"Maybe she does and he just doesn't say anything. I hate to say this, but I've seen him flirt with her."

"He's trying to distract her from Luke."

"If you say so."

I winced, turning away to exchange my red t-shirt for the approved gray one. Our BDU was a different color and a bit nicer than the ones we'd worn in boot camp. It was shades of black with a silvery gray camouflage pattern. We had a long sleeved and short sleeved version with shorts the same as Captain Hendricks had worn. We could wear a charcoal gray T-shirt, a sleeveless white one, or a thermal one beneath it.

Sutak said, "They're talking about issuing us new uniforms. Word has it that the material is some new, alien inspired, high tech fabric. I'm hoping it isn't too difficult to get into and out of when I've got to pee."

"Any word on actual spacesuits?"

"I know their working on flight suits, but I haven't heard anything official."

Sutak neatened my bed and began checking her drawers as I finished dressing.

I said, "I'm going to go wake the guys. Thanks for waking me."

"Nash, Short, and Sopon dropped in to say hello. We'll see them tomorrow."

She followed me from the room and sat at the table. Everyone's door was open except Adan's and Luke's. Stephanie entered the common room when I knocked on their door.

Adan answered in boxers and a flush rose to my cheeks. I wanted to kiss him badly. Really kiss him, not a quick peck or a comforting hug.

He waved me in and closed the door.

I regretfully turned away from him to hug Luke who was half sitting in his bed.

"Sorry to wake you. Are you feeling any better?"

"I don't think I'll ever feel better about it."

Adan winced and sat beside me, putting his hand on my neck. The small gesture made my flush deepen.

I said, "Honestly, I hate thinking about her and that makes me feel bad, but I don't want to think about it..."

Luke hugged me and his voice was muffled in my neck when he said, "She loved you too."

"I wish I could go back in time..."

He snorted, pushing away to go to his heaped bags.

I stood to help him unpack. "BDU for planned inspections and neat beds and drawers. You guys dress. I'll get you all unpacked." I began unpacking Luke's bags. "Sutak warned me that Stephanie is a snooper. I think we should buy laptop locks."

Adan said, "Don't use the school laptop for anything except classwork."

"I was going to use it to talk to Shea too if I got clearance. You think I shouldn't?"

Luke said, "I'll talk to Jay about it."

Adan dressed quickly and picked up the laptop from the desk. It was still in a cardboard box on top of a small carton labeled school supplies. I hadn't opened mine or read any of the papers that accompanied it. He flipped through them while I finished unpacking Luke.

"Well?" Luke asked as he remade their beds.

Adan placed the papers back on the desk. "Mostly information and a few forms we need to fill out. I sent copies of them to Jay."

He began unpacking his bags and had everything unpacked in no time. Adan began going through the carton, putting the office supplies in his desk. They'd given us all the usual office supplies and a stack of printer paper.

"I didn't see a printer," I said as I leaned over his shoulder to examine the supplies.

"Must be one around here." He opened a slim box at the bottom of the carton and took out a shiny gray, hard-shelled, plastic case with a gray carrying strap with his name on it. "For the laptop, I'm assuming. It locks and it looks like you can charge it while it's locked."

Luke was reading the paperwork that had accompanied the supplies and he said, "You better get yours and go plug it in. It's on the inspection list."

I said, "As soon as I open this door, she's going to come over. I'm surprised she hasn't knocked already..."

"Whatever," he said angrily.

I hesitated then shrugged and turned to kiss Adan. I'd meant it to be a short kiss but his lips on mine sent a delicious thrill through me. I deepened the kiss, running my hands over his back and pressing hard against him.

His soft surprised exhale made my stomach muscles clench in anticipation. He deepened the kiss, and I would have kept kissing him, but someone tapped on the door.

Luke went to answer it as I reluctantly stepped away.

15

Sinclair greeted Luke happily, and I stepped closer to Adan, straightening his already straight collar just for an excuse to touch him again.

"Damn it," I whispered. "We never get a damned minute."

"I want more than a minute," he said.

My gaze flicked to his bed.

"Soon?"

"It can't be soon enough," he said in a laughing annoyed tone.

I kissed him again and warmth spread through me from the hand he placed on my neck.

Someone cleared their throat loudly, and I jumped away.

I hurried to go unpack my school supplies and plug in the laptop while Adan joined the others in the main room.

Sutak stood in our doorway and held out a wrapped sandwich. "Want one? They aren't bad at all." She gestured with the sandwich she held. "That can wait. It's on the list of things to be inspected but they gave use four days to get our school supplies in order. It won't be checked until the next inspection, which is scheduled for this same time next week, although we could get one anytime, I guess, but you'd still have another day."

"I'm almost done."

I stared at my wrist and my smart coms appeared. I had fifteen minutes until inspection.

I said, "I'd love a sandwich. Who should I thank for it?"

"God, I suppose." She giggled and said, "Stephanie and Sinclair brought a bunch back. We're discussing kitchen chores now."

I joined her in the main room where they were discussing the best way to share the space.

I said, "Sutak, if it's okay with you, it's fine with me if we share a shelf in the refrigerator with Adan and

Luke, then Sinclair and Felipe can have one, and Steph and Lana can have the other."

"Sounds good. I think we can agree to share the condiments and keep them on the door. Freezer space will be a bit tricky. It's too small to hold much,"

Luke said, "Maybe we can vote on frozen snacks? Or take turns and buy eight of whatever we pick?"

We all agreed to that. I ate my sandwich as they divided up the cupboard space and agreed to the cleaning schedule and rules.

Adan said, "Let's get a whiteboard to leave each other notes here, and if you're planning on cooking, you can write it here with your time slot and leave a note asking if we want in or telling us it's just for you. I like to cook but we don't have a lot of fridge space, so I'll need to know in advance how many I'm cooking for."

Sutak said, "We're supposed to eat in the mess and were told that starting Monday we can't use the burners without permission, but we can use the fridge. I think they mean to use cooking in the rooms as a reward for keeping up in the classes, but I like your idea."

Lana said, "Let's not knock on each other's doors unless we need to inform each other about work related stuff. If you don't mind drop in's, leave your door a bit ajar, and if you have guests here, keep it down if doors are closed."

"Agreed," I said, with the others.

Adan said, "We have printer paper but where's the printer?"

Sutak said, "There's one in the common room down the hall. We could chip in for one here if you want. I think there's room on top of the fridge for one. And speaking of that, can we get a toaster and leave it on the counter? I'll buy it."

"It's fine with me," I said as the others agreed.

Luke said, "We can probably fit two more chairs at the table but eight aren't going to fit unless we change these out for stools or something."

I said, "I'm fine with a first come first serve system. We can always drag two desk chairs in if we want to watch a movie together or something."

Sutak said, "We can have a television in our rooms too. Felipe brought this one but if he wants to move it to his room, we could chip in for another one."

Felipe said, "We already have another in our room. This one is for everyone as is the game system. I have a bunch of games we can all play if you get your own controllers."

Sutak grinned. "I asked my mom to send mine and my games. Not that I think we'll have lots of time to play, but I have some really good flight simulation games."

Luke said, "Three minutes until inspection. We should buy an alarm clock for this room."

Adan laughed and then flushed.

Luke rolled his eyes at him then shrugged at me. Sinclair smiled as if he got the joke or maybe he just thought women were always late. We'd need to be careful not to expose our coms.

"Good idea," Sutak said as she began wiping the counter.

I tossed my sandwich wrapper and helped push the chairs in.

Sutak said, "I'm the squad leader in our rooms right now, so I get the door. It works just like in basic. I say attention and we stand before our desks. Our assignments will be changing, and we're supposed to check our orders every morning just like in basic. Pay attention to the inspector because we'll have to do it at some point."

I headed to my room while wondering why, if Sutak was the squad leader, she didn't just order Stephanie to clean the bathroom or put her on report for entering uninvited.

A girl I didn't know was our inspector. She wore dress uniform and ran her hand over our furniture, opened our closet and drawers, but didn't look through our things just glanced in to make sure they were neat. When she was finished with our room, she inspected us, grinning and tapping the silver wings on Sutak's collar.

"Congratulations, Cadet!" she shook Sutak's hand and said, "Carry on."

We saluted, and I waited in our room while Sutak waited by the door to the hall.

It only took the inspector a few minutes to check every room. Sutak opened the door for her to leave. The inspector said, "Cadets Lane and Bushinque are restricted to quarters until the next inspection."

"Yes, ma'am," Sutak said, saluting again.

The inspector returned her salute and marched away while Sutak closed the door.

"That bitch!" Stephanie said as she stomped from her room.

Sutak said, "If you have a problem with a superior officer, follow proper procedure. Insubordination will be reported in daily logs. We're friends here and these are our quarters but we're also on duty. Treat everyone as you would a coworker, which means no outbursts against the boss. If you'd like help or advice on how to pass the next inspection, we'd be happy to help."

Lana said, "Thanks, but we can fix it. We just need to cut down on our civilian clothing."

Adan's eyes laughed into mine. Lana's tight-lipped glare at Stephanie told me it was her who'd gotten them into trouble. I was just glad we all hadn't been confined to barracks.

I said, "What's the procedure for leaving early? I was thinking of going for a run in the morning."

Sutak said, "No procedure. Just use your card to swipe yourself in and out. If you miss reveille or roll call you'd be in trouble but other than that you can come and go as your schedule permits."

"When's roll call?"

"Twenty-one hundred and that's the squad leader's job. I report if we're all present and accounted for. Reveille is at 6:30 and we can leave here at five."

Stephanie said, "It's stupid that we all need to report then if our classes don't start until later."

Sutak shrugged. "Well, stupid or not, it's orders. We'll be doing PE before breakfast but some of us have early morning classes, speaking of which, Mia, they're offering us a lot of electives and one of them is learning to fly helicopters. I'm an instructor and that class is at my discretion. I still have some spaces available and I can take it up at five if we have no other free time that meshes."

"That would be awesome."

"Just don't wake us," Stephanie snapped and stomped back into her room.

Everyone else asked Sutak for lessons too and she went to get her laptop to see what time slots she had left.

I pulled mine out to examine my schedule and we all brought them into the main room to compare them.

Sutak tapped her lower lip as she examined my schedule. "You're scheduled for Lab Three while I'm in the flight hanger and my hour allotted to lessons is already full there. I think it's going to have to be the zero five-hundred thirty slot, unless we want to cut into our hour after evening mess, but that one is my planned catch up for homework and extra study. I figure I'll have some time there but not a lot, so it would take longer to finish the mandatory hours."

"I'm in no hurry but I don't want to take your free time either."

She said, "We all get four hours Saturday. I can ask for permission to teach you as a group and then take you up individually if you're all willing to commit to forty-five minutes of your free time Saturday for instruction and wait your turns for airtime. Sinclair and I share a free spot here we could use, and Felipe can go right after class Saturday. The rest of you can split the morning and night one and if I can't make it, I'll leave a note on the board, and if you can't make it, ask one of the others if they want your slot or text me or leave a note on the board."

"You sure it isn't too much?"

She grinned at me. "Not at all. I've been flying all my life. Both my parents are pilots. My dad is a Navy pilot and my mom commercial. We have a few small planes and a one-seater mini that we built ourselves. I've been flying since I was a kid and I love it. I want all the hours I can get. We'll be starting off small, but I'll have you in a Blackhawk in no time."

"Then I accept," I said happily, offering my hand for her to shake.

She shook our hands, but I thought Sinclair would bow out. He hadn't looked at all thrilled at the time slots.

I examined my schedule again then pulled Adan's laptop closer to examine his. Luke leaned over my shoulder, pointing at the screen. "We have the same class hours but different battle drill and lab hours."

"Not much free time at all," Adan said unhappily.

Sutak said, "We get Sunday's off completely, assuming you don't have makeup work. I'm hoping they go easy on homework and we can relax until lights out, but I think we better prepare ourselves for lots of cram sessions."

Felipe said, "I hope I have the stamina for this. I know we need to hurry but this sort of pace could burn us out."

I said, "What we're learning is interesting though, which makes it more bearable."

"If by interesting you mean terrifying."

Sinclair said, "I hope they issue us full hazmat suits soon. It gives the cold shivers to see those fucking animals, especially now that I know they can do that to humans. I almost hope I'm one of the ones who'd turn to dust. I hate to even think about being absorbed and regurgitated as some sort of freakish human extension of one those blobs."

I said, "There's no evidence that that's possible."

"Hifis humans retain their free will," Luke said.

"Do they really? Maybe they think they do or maybe they just claim to. Maybe the infected are already under Geromi control and just don't know it. The Hirsit don't seem to realize they're being controlled. Hell, I don't think they even know they're animals."

Adan said, "We're all animals when you get right down to it. The Hirsit we have here aren't animals anymore. The chips that enhance their intelligence made them more than animals."

"And that's fucking disturbing."

"I agree," I said. "Those poor things must be terrified. They're smarter than nature intended but with animal impulses and instincts that make it really difficult to use that intelligence to help themselves."

Sutak said, "You think the Geromi could dial them up?"

"No. If they could do that, they wouldn't need us. I think there's a limit on what an animal can do even when it understands what is wanted from it. It lacks the innate ability to reason and just responds by rote like a trained dog. You can teach a dog to sit on command by verbal cues or gestures and even in situations like at feeding time, but that dog can't teach itself how to feed itself. At most it could break into a bag of food that it has seen or scented but it can't teach itself to go buy more food. If you gave a dog a Giftrikl, the dog could be taught to drive a car, but it couldn't think past the training. It could get food by hunting because that's a dog instinct, but it wouldn't know how to use the tools except in ways it was trained to.

Luke said, "Intelligence isn't static. Some animals are smarter than others just like some humans are. It might be possible to teach a smart dog how to open a door and that same dog with a learning implant might be able to use that intelligence to apply solutions to his problems using skills that it's been taught, but problems by definition would incite a dog's instinctual behavior. It would be a tough instinct to overcome."

Adan said, "A dog with a chip in its head is still a dog. It worries me that the Geromi are making other chips to dumb us down."

Luke said, "It's obviously still in the development stage or they wouldn't have been taking test subjects."

Sutak inhaled sharply, and Luke grimaced.

"Sorry, I shouldn't have said anything."

Sinclair said, "We all figured they'd been taking us for years..."

Luke said, "Our best estimate is eighty-two years. I can't talk about how we reached that number, but I can say I think the date and hypotheses are sound. This is class A info that I'm not certain they'll reveal source material for so I won't go into that but we know a ship was here eighty-two years ago and that the ship took at least three thousand humans aboard. It might have left agents behind.

"We also know that in that eighty-two-year interim they developed a different technique or strand or whatever we want to call it of Hifis. Chicago was dusted with both strands, and Michigan just the one. Geromi gathered some test subjects that we've retrieved and from that we know the results weren't what they'd hoped for.

"A new version of the Giftrikl was being tested on them and it wasn't working. I don't think they'll return in force until it *is* working. We have no idea if the eighty-two years was travel time, research time, or a combination. We do know they have active ships here. Three of the small ships spotted when they arrived haven't been found. Maybe the ships have already returned wherever they came from or maybe they're in hiding.

"We know they can communicate with Hirsit but have no idea where that is. They could be here, on the moon, or a billion light years away."

I said, "Actually we don't know that last for a fact. We assume it from confiscated tools but maybe they have no functioning ships, and even if they do, maybe they have no live Geromi to use it."

Adan said, "Someone has a way to order the Hirsit or they wouldn't have tried to infiltrate us."

Luke said, "It could be a human working with them."

Sinclair said, "They should shoot the fuckers who work with those filthy animals!"

Lana nodded agreement. "The humanoid looking ones are the worst. I bet our so called human Hifis are tentacled monsters under their skin too. They fucking give me the creeps. I get why we have to work with them, but yuck."

Sutak said, "That's a prejudice you'll need to get over even if it's true. We need them and I don't just mean because of their hand-to-hand combat skill. Here's some more class A info for you. I'm working with a few of them because Geromi made a big mistake. Their ships recognize Hifis. There's a chance human

Hifis can take control of their ships if we can get one on board."

"For real?" Felipe asked hopefully. His scowl faded and his eyes widened.

Sutak grinned and nodded. "You can expect them in your combat classes and all of our battle drills."

"Jesus, we might really have a chance!"

Lana said, "Don't get too excited. We can't have many of them and they're strong but not indestructible. And we'd have to reach the ship and who knows where it would be."

Sutak said, "Which is why we're practicing drops in all sorts of locations. I was in the hanger yesterday and there was a big group from NASA there. We'll be training in their simulators and going up in the weightless wonder. I think they're working on shuttles to get us into space. My entire division received handbooks to learn to fly the things. I assume we'll be bringing combat specialists wherever they're needed."

Sinclair said, "That's nuts. I mean, we saw how they could shoot from those little ships. They'd blast us right out of the air."

Felipe said, "It is nuts but what's our option? If it costs a million casualties to take one of their big ships, don't we have to do it?"

"Those casualties will be us! It would be smarter to shoot it down."

"In the short term but not the long. Imagine if we could get a working ship under our control!"

Lana sniffed and said, "It wouldn't be under our control if it takes a Hifis to do it."

Sutak glanced at her watch and stood. "Thirty minutes to lights out and I'm beat. We meet Saturday and start learning to fly."

"I'm in," I said and stood too, giving Adan a hopeful glance.

He grimaced, flicking a glance at Sinclair who was still glowering.

Lana headed to her room, and I knew it would be awkward for everyone if I went to Adan's, so I said, "Night all," and went to my own room.

"*I love you, mi amor,*" whispered in my head.

I knew by the slight robotic tone it was a recording. I waved over my shoulder and he waved back.

This hectic schedule would tear us apart if I let it. Recorded messages of love could become our spoken sentiments and the words would become as emotionless as the machine that uttered them.

I snatched sweats from my drawer and began removing my BDU. Sutak was undressing too. I waited for her to enter the closet to hang her uniform to switch my t-shirt for a sweatshirt and whispered, "I love you. Good night."

I glanced at Luke's icon and whispered, "Night Wile E. Don't dream up any crazy plans!"

"*Night, Daffy,*" he said.

I waited but Adan didn't reply. It made my heart feel heavy.

Sutak and I got ready for bed, and I lay in the dark for twenty minutes before Adan said, "*Sorry, Sinclair was talking my ear off wanting to know the deal between Luke and Stephanie.*"

Luke said, "*I'll fix it tomorrow.*"

I winced because Adan and I still weren't speaking privately.

Adan said, "*Wake me when you get up.*"

I didn't know if he meant me or Luke.

Luke said, "*If you mean me, then you're out of luck. I'm not a morning person. Daffy is though. She'll wake us both. Let's get up and go for a run at five.*"

"Will, do. Night, boys."

"*Love you,*" Adan said.

"*Me too,*" Luke said.

I sighed hard and closed my eyes.

16

Sutak didn't stir when I grabbed my clothes and let myself from the room. I used the shower and her soap and shampoo. I had my own but there wasn't anywhere to put them, and it seemed stupid to have all these bottles.

I called Adan as I dressed.

"I'm up but sleep if you want."

"I'm up and I'll wake Luke."

"He won't get up unless you leave a light on or something."

In the main room I helped myself to a heaping bowl of our cereal. We'd need to figure out a way to replace it unseen.

Adan exited his room a few minutes later and joined me at the counter. He'd dressed in BDU too.

He said, "Maybe tomorrow you can wake me before you shower..."

I laughed and pushed him away. "Not on your life. I don't have that kind of willpower, and I'm not getting caught in there."

He heaved a long dramatic sigh and headed to the bathroom.

I poured another bowl of cereal and took out two more bowls for them.

Luke joined me and had finished his first bowl before Aden exited.

He said, "I'll ask our Hifis liaison what we're supposed to do about hiding food intake. If he okays it, Adan and I can hide food in our footlockers, but I don't think it would be too difficult to sneak in full boxes of cereal and replace the empties.

He headed to the bathroom when Adan exited, and I handed a bowl to Adan. "Luke is on top of the food."

Adan said, "Want to bring the skateboards?"

"Not today. Let's just go for a quick run to get a feel for the place."

"Fine by me."

It was still dark out when we let ourselves from the building. Lights were on in a few of the more distant buildings, but we appeared to be the only ones up and about near the dorm. The air was fresh and clean, laden with the scents of sun-seared vegetation and fresh earth.

Machinery rumbled in the distance and the whir of a helicopter made us all crane our heads. For a moment I spied nothing, but the dark sky gained clarity. Colors weren't as vibrant as mid-day and everything appeared a bit flat, an effect I thought was caused by the lack of shadows.

"How's does night vision work?" I asked as we started off at a slow jog.

Luke said, "It's still being researched. Is all we know is generalities of what must be happening but not how it's happening."

"It's damn cool," I said, and Adan laughed.

I stared at the approaching helicopter and could make out the writing on the man's shirt who was leaning from the open side door. Swinging my gaze away caused a moment of disorientation as my eyes refocused but they refocused instantly when I glanced back.

I said, "The seem to be focusing faster now but maybe that's my imagination or I'm just used to them."

"Focusing?" Luke asked as Adan said, "Which way do you want to go?"

"You pick."

He headed left.

I said, "Maybe mine are broken. My rat couldn't see for crap. There's a slight delay when I stare at something before I can see it clearly."

Luke grabbed my arm, pulling me to a halt.

"How slight and is it only at night or all the time? We should get your eyes checked."

Adan said worriedly, "Maybe you should shift.

"It's like a second or so and I don't really remember when I first noticed it. I don't really try to see things far away that much."

"It's just your distant vision? You can see me okay?" Adan asked anxiously.

"Yes... you're worrying me."

He gave me a hug, and I realized Luke had walked a few steps away and was speaking to Jay, I presumed.

I pulled Adan's head down for a kiss that he returned perfunctorily.

He laughed an unhappy laugh at my annoyed sigh.

"Sorry, I'm worried and we're in uniform in the middle of the street."

I flushed, stepping away from him.

Luke said, "Jay is arranging for our vision to get tested. He wants to know if we'd agree to baseline testing eyesight, hearing, strength, stamina, and pain tolerance.

"I don't like that last one," I said.

Luke said, "I'd be there when they administer it and will make them stop when you tap out and they'll tell us what they're planning and we can say no. I think we should do it."

Adan said, "I don't like it either. I think we should fake that one. There's no good reason for them to know our pain threshold."

Luke nodded agreement. "I'm fine with tapping out early just be consistent."

"Fine," I said.

Luke whispered on his coms another minute then said, "It will show in our orders."

I said, "Let's finish our run."

We jogged down the street past classrooms and some obviously new signs pointing us to a rifle range, drill fields, and flight hanger three back the way we'd come. Twelve-foot-high chain link fence that was covered with black material bordered the road as far as I could see. The fence was taller as it curved around the front of the buildings with wheeled gates guarded by soldiers blocking the exit roads. Prefab metal buildings filled a parking lot with narrow paths between them. A line of helicopters in various sizes were parked between the buildings and the fence.

Luke said, "There's signs out front saying the school is closed and under construction, but the air traffic is going to give us away."

Adan said, "Maybe not. Maybe the locals think this is intended as a new Army base?"

Another group of four people were jogging in the distance. We caught up with them when they stopped to read an obviously new group of signs. They carried maps that they were examining with puzzled expressions. My coms would project a map onto my retinas if I chose to by tapping my wrist while folding three fingers over my thumb. The map looked exactly as if I was looking at a computer screen unless I choose a paper version and then it appeared to me as if a paper was floating in the air in front of me. There was also a version more like a computer game that that was opaque enough I could see my surroundings through it. All of the maps would expand or shrink if I focused on it and I could give voice commands to adjust it. Whiroon had thoroughly mapped a five-mile-wide corridor leading from Chicago to North Dakota and down to Texas. It seemed to map anywhere it passed without prompting, but I'd set it to mapping all of Texas.

If we had to run, I wanted it to be able to help us.

Adan said, "You lost?"

"No just confused." He held the map out to Adan.

Names tags had appeared over their heads when we'd stopped. I texted to Luke, *'Did you start the name plates or is that automatic?'*

Luke texted back, *'Automatic if we pause for more than a few seconds but you can turn it off. It will always show the dangerous ones though,* as Carrick O' Conner, one of the cadets, said, "It's probably a fitness medal."

I peered over Adan's shoulder to read it. It said, *Five-minute Desk Run.*

I typed to Luke, *'I don't see the red for Stephanie and Lana anymore.'*

He snorted, and O'Connor said, "You can get a citation for it. I thought it would be interoffice but that sign says desk trail and it's clearly going up that hill."

Luke said, *'We don't need the reminder with them.'*

Adan shrugged and handed the map back.

I said, "We can make it before reveille."

"Not today. Maybe tomorrow. I want time to shower."

I sighed wistfully, and he laughed, giving me a heated glance that set my pulse racing.

We all jogged back to the dorm together, introducing ourselves as we jogged.

More people were out and about although it was still dark.

O'Connor said, "I bet it's hot as blazes here once the sun comes up. I plan to practice the run in the mornings.

Jim Hershey said, "I'm in. I went by the gym, such as it is, yesterday, and we're going to need to get weights or something for our room. There's hardly any equipment yet."

O'Conner said, "According to the map, there's a big obstacle course on Hancock Hill with climbing walls and ropes that we can use anytime and a smaller one by building four. And there's four boxing rings in hanger seven."

I said, "With this busy schedule, I don't think exercise is going to be a problem. We'll be running all over."

He winked at me and said, "You can never have too much exercise."

Adan said, "We get all the exercise we need."

Luke said hurriedly, "Dibs on the shower," and ran away.

I followed him, cringing when I heard them laughing.

Adan caught up with me in the hallway. "God, I'm sorry, Mia. I didn't mean it like it came out. I just wanted them to know you were my girl and it wasn't like I could just say that or kiss you or hold your hand. I meant it to be a subtle signal, not an insult."

"It's okay. I'm not mad," I lied.

He followed me into our main room, and I hurried for my own room. "I need to get my stuff put away. See you in a few."

"I really am sorry!" he called after me.

I waved airily.

Sutak was up and dressed and reading at her desk.

I made my bed and put my sweats away while she read her orders to me. I checked my laptop for mine and said, "Mine's almost the same but I have a checkup at medical instead of PE after lunch. It's marked wait time unknown EA.

"Excused absence," Sutak said. "I did mine two days ago, and it took three hours."

"Jesus, why so long?"

"The tests were pretty quick, but the wait was long. And there were lots of them. They test everything, hearing, eyesight, even taste, and if you have a problem with one, they send you to wait in another line."

"Did you have a problem?"

"I have 20-15 vision but a mild hearing loss in my left ear. I have to go back for that test every two weeks. I don't notice the loss at all. It's probably from all the engine noise but it could just be allergies or earwax. I was proscribed really gross drops to put in my ears when I shower that make my ears fizz. I was also told I cut my toenails wrong and have an appointment at a podiatrist next week to learn to do it right."

"Jeez..."

"I know, right? So you might be there a while but they'll mark your file as excused."

Adan stuck his head in the open door. "Can we talk a minute, Mia?"

"Sure," I gathered my gear and followed him to his room.

He closed the door and leaned against it. "I feel really bad about earlier."

"There's no need to."

"Don't lie to me, okay? I know you're mad and you have a right to be. Just because I didn't mean to embarrass you doesn't mean you weren't embarrassed."

"Can we just drop this please? You're making it a big deal and it wasn't."

"I... If you say so." He left the room before I could think of a response. I sat at the kitchen table to put the case on my laptop and then stared at the blank screen while I debated what to do. Felipe and Sinclair were at the kitchen counter, dressed for the day and pouring bowls of cereal.

"Want some?" Felipe asked. "Chow might suck and it's a long time until lunch."

"No thanks."

He shrugged and sat to eat.

Luke exited the shower as Stephanie entered the main room.

"Morning," she said.

She wore a silk robe with nothing underneath and had barely tied it closed. The edges gaped wider as she sauntered past, leaving little to the imagination. I wondered if she'd slept in her makeup or had applied it before showering just for this short walk to the shower.

Luke said, "Adan's in the shower but he'll be out in a minute."

"There's two stalls," she said to me, shrugging off the robe as she entered the shower.

Luke pursed his lips, shaking his head at me.

"What? I didn't do a damned thing!" I snapped.

"You were thinking it though."

"Are you a mind reader now?"

"Problems?" Sutak asked as she entered.

Lana exited her room and headed to the shower.

"Showers are full," I said.

Lana nodded and changed direction for the bathroom.

"No problems," Luke said, and I knew he was talking to me.

I ignored him, pretending to read my computer screen again. I knew my face was red and it grew hotter as I grew angrier. Sinclair snickered, and Felipe stared at his bowl of cereal as a red flush climbed up his cheeks. I wondered if he was pissed at her or embarrassed for me.

Adan stepped into the main room soaking wet and glowering, wearing a towel around his waist and with his clothes thrown over his shoulder.

"We're supposed to be fucking adults here. The next person who steps into the same shower I'm in is getting punched in the fucking face!"

He stomped from the room, and Sutak sighed hard, pinching the bridge of her nose.

Felipe stood, and Sutak said, "No. We're going to the parade ground as a group." She yanked open the door to the shower and snapped, "Cadet, get your ass out here!"

She banged on Adan's door and said, "Everyone in the main room!"

Lana exited the bathroom a minute later. She'd done her hair and makeup but still wore her sweats.

Sutak kept her gaze on her watch, looking irritated.

"Attention!" she barked, and I jumped to my feet as Adan exited his bedroom. He'd dressed but still looked pissed, and he was avoiding my eyes, which made my stomach flip unpleasantly.

Sutak banged on the shower door and hollered, "I mean right now, cadet!"

Stephanie stepped out a moment later and Sutak's eyes narrowed.

Stephanie still hadn't tied the robe although she was holding it closed. The silk was now see-through and stuck to her wet breasts. She'd tied her towel around her waist and was letting her hair drip. The pose, the way she was biting her lip and clenching the robe and casting pathetic glances at Luke told me she knew exactly what she was doing.

I really wanted to hit her.

Sutak snapped, "Sexual harassment won't be tolerated. This is the only warning you're getting. There are two showers and both have curtains. If I hear of anyone opening one when someone else is inside, that person is going on report and can expect to be expelled. If the curtain is closed, don't open it. Ask if someone is in there! Lane, that bathrobe is entirely inappropriate. I never want to see it again. Have I made myself clear?"

"Yes, ma'am," Stephanie said tightly.

Sutak said, "Everyone will wear a robe that closes completely or clothing, no towels or naked dashes to your rooms. If someone does behave inappropriately, in any way, be it inappropriate sexual advances, stealing, making a mess, or just being obnoxious, bring it your squad leader's attention. Threats won't be tolerated either. We're leaving in five minutes, no exceptions."

She glared at us all a moment and then said, "As you were."

Luke said, "Stephanie, just to be clear, I'm not interested. I'll never be interested. We can be friends but that's all there will ever be between us."

"Whatever." She stomped to her door then turned back to say, "How come he can talk to me like that? Isn't that sexual harassment? I didn't even say a word to him."

Sutak said, "If you'd like to report it, you can, but it's going to be investigated. I didn't consider it particular harassing more like a statement of fact, but we can send it to our provost."

Adan said, "Great. Let's do that. Then I can tell you exactly what I think of you."

Stephanie turned red.

I had to bite back my laugh.

Sutak said, "Balls in your court, Lane."

Stephanie glared at me then whirled and ran into her room and slammed the door.

Lana said, "This is awkward."

Sutak glanced at her watch. I thought Stephanie would sulk and make Sutak report her, but she exited her room three minutes later dressed in BDU with her hair pulled back in a tight bun.

She said, "I need to apologize. I'm sorry if I offended you, Adan, it wasn't my intent. It won't happen again. I hope you can forgive me and we can be friends again. You guys mean a lot to me and I'm overcompensating a bit because I don't want to lose you too." Her eyes filled with tears when she looked at Luke. "I'm really sorry that I hurt your feelings. We've been good friends for years and I'd do it over if I could. I'm not really great with relationships and I'm trying too hard, but it means so much to me..."

Luke said, "We can be friends."

Adan glared at Luke, "Bullshit! You don't have to put up with her pawing you because you don't want to hurt her feelings." He turned the glare on Stephanie. "You need to learn some boundaries, Stephanie, if we're going to be friends. You make him really uncomfortable when you hang on him, and he's too polite to tell you to fuck off, so I'm saying it for him. If you want to be friends, then treat us like friends! Give us both personal space."

I couldn't decide if this was an act or sincere regret on her part. I could tell Luke was genuinely upset and everyone could tell Adan was pissed.

Sutak said, "Let's get going. Everyone needs to cool off. Let's all think about how we can make our roommates more comfortable. We all need to learn to get along with people in tight spaces. I'm not saying you couldn't ask for a transfer if you just can't bear being roommates, but asking is going to send up red flags in the personnel department for all of us. So really think about it and if you need help or advice, go speak with our counselors."

We walked out in a silent group to join the rest of the cadets heading for our parade ground.

Adan laid his hand on my cheek, clearing his throat when he dropped it.

He took my hand and pressed it to his heart. "Five minutes."

We'd fallen behind the others but weren't alone and we were getting some irritated and speculative glances.

"We'll make time tonight," I said as I pulled my hand from his grasp and ran for the stairs.

17

All of my roommates were in my first class, Security and Information Management, which was a prerequisite for everyone.

The lecture hall was full. Cadets settled into the blue office chairs and set their laptops on the desk that curved the length of the row, forming semi-circles in front of a podium.

Lana sat on one side of me and Sutak on the other. I was debating asking Sutak to switch seats with Luke so he wouldn't have to sit beside Stephanie when Lana said, "Steph was ordered to medical. I have to report after this class."

I said, "Luke and I report after lunch."

The lights dimmed and we all stood as the teacher entered.

He said, "Take your seats. I'm Major Grant and this is an introductory class on safety although probably not like you're thinking."

He set his briefcase on the podium, using a remote to turn on a projector.

"Every minute of every day technology changes and that's true now more than ever. The element of surprise will win battles. It's crucial that we keep our plans and abilities secret, but with recording devices the size of a pea made of materials that we can't scan for, devices that can listen and hear accurately up to half a mile away, beings that can shift their shape and enter rooms unnoticed—keeping our secrets secure is becoming more and more difficult."

He pointed at the screen where a small gold bead lay beside a dime on a piece of black felt.

"We call that an x-com. It can transmit and receive from anywhere on Earth and a good long ways beyond."

He changed the picture to show a row of four dots.

"Those are also x-coms. With four dots you could hear a mouse fart in the basement and an acorn fall two blocks away. You could hear a heartbeat and tell by the rhythm and tone if the person was excited, asleep, or injured."

He changed the picture again to a show Marie and Alfred. I knew it was them despite the fact they were a gelatinous grey mound because they were the only Geromi of that size that we had in captivity. He clicked the remote to zoom in on a row of golden dots of varying sizes that were embedded just beneath the outer layer of the jelly-like substance that was a Geromi's skin.

"Twenty-seven dots. Imagine what it can tell from them? So, how do we keep our secrets secure?

"The most important thing we do is use our common sense. We keep our mouths shut and our eyes open. Since we have no real idea how well they can hack us, we keep our files on paper and we lock them up."

He changed the picture again to show the testing kit that they'd found on the grot that had tried to infiltrate our camp.

"That is an alien device that's used to steal a blood sample that we believe the Geromi can use to clone us. It's possible that I'm an imposter or the man sitting beside you is. We figure it's very likely they have spies here, not to mention regular human operatives. Knowledge is power, and power is money, and there are people who will sell their souls for either."

The crowd stirred restively, and I turned to scan my neighbors who were all looking grim and a bit overwhelmed.

Grant said, "I say, let them try. We have technology too. We'll catch them and end up knowing more than they stole. The grot operatives who were caught with this kit were a windfall of information."

He pointed at the screen. "Memorize what it looks like and if you see anyone with one, you'll know they're an operative. The most important thing you need to know if you suspect your classmate is a spy is not to let on that you do. You'll report it in person to your commander and treat the suspect the same as always because a spy whose cover is blown but who remains unaware of it is a treasure trove of information.

"That doesn't mean let them harm someone or sabotage something. Keep using your common sense. Weigh the situation and if you deem that you can't take the time to report in person, call it in at once. I expect we'll get our share of false alarms. We expect it and it's better to be safe than sorry, but if we find you were pranking a friend, you're going to be in a world of shit.

"Base security is no laughing matter and I expect you all to act professionally about it. Now, let's talk about some of the ways an infiltrator could give themselves away."

He lectured us for an hour about things we should be looking for and what to do if we spotted them. They were all mostly common sense. He didn't mention eye shine at all, but we were warned to look for piles of dust.

I exchanged an anxious glance with Luke.

Grant said, "We have Hifis humans among us who will be making themselves known to you in due time. They've been ordered to remain hidden. I'll be interested to see how many of them you can spot. I expect those reports to be made discreetly to your platoon leader. If the Hifis you report notifies us that you're onto them, that sighting won't count for you. The cadet who spots the most Hifis on campus will receive a bump in pay grade. The Hifis who remain undiscovered will also receive that same bump."

He changed the picture behind himself again to show a side-by-side picture of a middle-aged woman with light brown hair.

He said, "Look closely at the woman's face when she smiles and frowns. In the picture on the right, you can see the faintest hint of wrinkles on her brow between her eyes and see how the grooves are deeper? The image on the left is an alien wearing her face. The new face doesn't have the weight of years behind it. It's an exact replica but the skin is new and doesn't bend and fold in the same ways. The effect will be most noticeable on the hands, wrists and facial muscles, but varicose veins, the small thin types, will also disappear. They might have a way to add them back after the fact but until they realize that it's a problem, we can compare before and after images.

"Scars will also disappear. They rebuild the visible ones. They don't generally redo the ones hidden by our clothing, probably because they don't know of them. Tattoos make it difficult for them as well. I predict the local tattoo parlor will have a brisk business. If you're considering getting a tattoo, speak to your platoon leader who will discreetly update your file. We recommend a small hidden one somewhere. If you opt for a visible one, fancy calligraphy, colors, and intricate designs are harder for them to duplicate, especially if only part of it is visible as a general rule.

"We've caught two imposters who had the word 'other' not Mother tattooed on their upper arms.

"Tomorrow we'll talk about how to run a scan on your computer to see if anyone has tried to log in and the basic safety precautions you should all be taking. I want you all to read the first three chapters in the textbook. There's a code in it, and if you can find it, you'll get an automatic A on the next quiz. Let the games begin."

He snapped his briefcase closed and strode from the room. The cadets began to rise and gather their things.

Luke sighed hard and stood slowly.

I wrinkled my nose at him. "I bet I can find it before you. I'm really much better at math now."

He heaved an even deeper sigh. "I already found it and reported it last night..."

Sutak laughed and punched his shoulder. "Good for you. How about a hint?"

"It's between pages one and thirty-six."

Adan huffed and Sutak laughed again.

I forced a laugh and slung my arm around Luke's shoulders. I knew he was upset that the entire campus would be looking for us. I wasn't sure how I felt about it. On one hand, I didn't think it really mattered all that much if we were found out because we planned on revealing ourselves eventually anyway. On the other hand, I hated the idea that we'd be thought of as different—or diseased.

I said, "We got this... There isn't by any chance another cipher in our Introductory to Computer text is there? It's okay to tell us now before the class actually starts."

I batted my eyes at him and snickered as he shook his head, making a zipping motion over his mouth and pretending to throw away the key.

"There is," Sutak said excitedly.

I snorted, punching Luke's arm, and he grinned at me.

"No there isn't," I said assuredly.

Adan glanced between us, his eyes narrowing. "I don't know, Mia, he looks awful smug."

"I know. He can't fool me for a second."

Luke laughed, grabbing me in a headlock to rub my head.

His laughter had sounded real and it loosened my shoulders that I hadn't even realized were tense.

I guess I was more scared then I wanted to admit to myself of being outed.

18

Luke and I waited together for our medical exams. I sort of wished Adan was waiting with me instead so we could talk but I was happy it was Luke in case they found anything embarrassing. And I didn't want Adan to see how much they still frightened me. Every time the door opened, I jumped. Their damned white coats made my pulse pound. The irony of being more afraid of the lab techs then aliens didn't escape me.

On my coms, Jay said, "*You okay, Mia?*"

"I'm just nervous."

"Can I watch from here? You're making me twitchy with all these sudden heart rate surges."

"Yes."

I was surprised Adan hadn't called if Jay was concerned but then realized he was already watching us remotely.

I typed to him, *'I'm fine just nervous. I'm turning off your surveillance. Jay is watching and it won't be as weird for me if I have to cut him hurriedly for privacy. Besides, you should be paying attention to the class.'*

He said, *"I could do this with my eyes closed. It's fun though. I think you'll like it. There's a special ops team showing us how they cross walls and enter rooms. This course is huge with a ton of different sections. Check out the link I sent. There's a house area to simulate urban fighting that we only ran through but there was another group there scaling walls."*

"Sounds fun," I agreed.

He said, *"I'll turn off visual but not the health monitor or sound. I promise not to make a peep or get angry or even question you if you want to speak to the doctor privately and turn me off. You aren't the only one who's nervous about you two being there."*

I hesitated, worried now that he was upset that I'd chosen Luke to accompany me, but I hadn't really given it a lot of thought. This was Luke's sort of thing. He'd accompanied me to every doctor appointment I had in the past, mostly because he'd been present when I'd gotten hurt. I was used to him with me.

Luke said, "At least neither of us is bleeding. It's an improvement."

I said, "I was just thinking that."

I typed to Adan, *'You don't need to worry. We're fine. I used to have to call and say that to my mom all the time and she'd be down to the emergency room before I hung up. Momsy would fuss and worry and my mom would lecture. I hope Shea doesn't need as many stitches as we did while learning to skateboard. Luke is surprisingly clumsy.'* I inserted a smiling emoji and then a heart.

He said, *"Save your free time tonight for me, please. We really need to talk."*

'I know we do, and I will. I don't want you worrying though. You mean everything to me.'

The waiting room door opened. *'Sorry, I have to go.'*

The interruption relieved me. I still wasn't sure what to say about this morning and now this doctor visit.

The woman who opened the door smiled and offered her hand. She was young with her long brown hair pulled back in a ponytail. She wore scrubs with cats on them, not a white coat. I wondered if they'd picked her to be our doctor because she looked sweet and harmless.

She said, "I'm Doctor Jasmine Monty. You can call me Jasmine or Doc. I've been working on this project since the event but have just recently been reassigned to human patients. My bedside skills will be a little rusty."

Luke said, "Were you at Statesville?"

Statesville was where all of the hifis infected animals had been sent. I was surprised someone so young had been sent there to work.

"Yes. It was truly fascinating work."

"Do you have a medical degree for humans too?" I asked.

"I only have a medical degree for humans, but I almost have enough credits to get my second doctorate in veterinary science, and I've already begun writing my dissertation." She gestured us inside as she continued, "My parents are both veterinarians and my mom was a big believer in pet therapy. I'm sure you've heard of that. You know, where they bring animals to hospitals and shut-ins and let them pet them and whatnot. It's a proven fact that doing so lowers blood pressure and stress chemicals in the brain and releases pleasure endorphins.

"I'd intended to have a dual major and was working in a lab at Yale measuring the varied results of stroking different types of fur to see what the correlations were." She gestured to an open exam room. "Right in here and I'll begin. I'm going to be doing some eye exams first. These machines look scary but they're not at all painful.

One of you sit on the stool there and keep your chin in the little cup and move as I tell you."

She sat on a rolling stool and fussed with the machine as she continued, "Where was I? Oh yeah, so my contention was and still is that different sorts of fur texture produce differing responses in the body. The human body, you understand, not the fur owner.

"We were running experiments that involved blind tests on people who claimed to have no real contact with animals in the past. They'd seen them of course and maybe petted them but had no pets or prolonged exposer."

She shifted her stool and had Luke turn his head.

"Our results are conclusive, cat fur, specifically domestic felines, will lower blood pressure and raise Oxytocin levels. Fur from a dead animal has no effect or negative effects. Even if that animal is presented in such a way as to seem alive."

"How the hell do you do that?" I asked.

"Hot water bottles wrapped in fur mostly. We can mimic breathing by manipulating the water. A subject is asked to pet the caged animal. The lighting is kept low and the simulacrum really did appear to be real. It felt real but had zero effect on our subjects. Petting an anesthetized cat would raise adrenaline levels slightly in the same subject while touching an animal that the subject knew was dead would rise them much higher.

The findings are consistent enough across a broad range of people to be significant. Some people respond to other animals without fur to the same degree but there's very few who don't respond at all to fur. Even when the subject professes to dislike animals or shows fear of them, if presented with a friendly specimen, petting will affect Oxytocin levels."

She stopped speaking again to bring Luke to another machine, warned him about puffs of air in his face and arranged him as she continued speaking.

"What that all means we really don't know other than the crazy cat ladies might be onto something and likely suffer from severe depression caused by chemical imbalances in their brains. The really interesting bit is that humans also experience surges of Oxytocin on first view of human family members even if they dislike the member. We'd just begun studying the effects of mixed groups with animals when the Geromi arrived."

She sat back, gesturing to Luke that he could straighten as she continued. "That was a crucial juncture in our experiment. I wanted to know if sharing the attention of a cat affected the levels, but I needed to know if the effect was caused by the people or the cat. In other words, are the positive effects negated by negative ones when the cat you were petting to relax jumps from your lap and into someone else's?

"Family dynamics, bonding, has been studied in the past. Chemical essays have been done that prove that a child affects the mother in ways it doesn't a father. Chemically speaking, I mean. A crying child can affect a mother's entire body chemistry. The really interesting thing is if the child is not her own child, the effects reverse almost instantly even when the woman doesn't consciously recognize the sounds aren't from her child. She'll still display the signs of worry but the chemicals causing it aren't being produced and she'll calm very quickly if told the child is being cared for.

"The effect fades as the child ages but rarely fades entirely even if the mother and child have been separated for years.

She slid her stool back to the original machine, "Have a seat, please."

She arranged me as she continued, "There's mountains of data and I'd been studying all of it as part of my research. We actually aren't that different than the Geromi. They seem to have mastered whatever triggers the chemical compounds that cause even humans to respond to family units. I don't want to say offspring because the effect is broader than that.

"Geromi manipulate the bonds that tie us together and those bonds exist outside of any affection we might feel. Humans can intentionally break those bonds and most of us feel badly when we do so. Gene mapping can show how closely related you are to someone, and I have a colleague who was examining a theory that you'd be more likely to consider a person a friend who shares familial genes with you. His findings were interesting but by no means conclusive, although, I think given time we'd find he's completely correct.

Luke said, "What did he find?"

"What everyone already knows." She adjusted the tilt of my head and messed with her machine a minute then grinned at Luke. "Cultural perception of race, how we look on the outside, how we speak, and even how we dress can be more easily affected by others who look and speak like us. Bonding with people who look differently is more difficult than bonding with someone who looks very similar. We all know racism is a real thing. We're just beginning to scratch the surface as to why.

"Sure, lots of what we think about people is taught to us. We might be raised to dislike any clearly identified racial group, but our body chemistry predisposes us to like more closely aligned groups although the word like is imprecise, even wrong really. Protect might be a better choice of word although that too isn't quite right. Accept, or adopt might be closer." She nodded at me when I inhaled sharply.

"Precisely. The very words that define the meaning of Hirsit. Put two Italians in a room and they'll befriend each other before befriending an Oriental in the same room. Coincidence? Conditioning? Fear of rejection? Or are our genes working on our bodies in ways we can't measure? I'm not saying we can't form tight bonds with people who are very dissimilar to ourselves. We can and our bodies will produce the chemicals that prove that the acceptance is real. I'm speaking about our initial impulses and the body's reaction."

She'd sat back and was speaking to us directly.

"Everyone reacts when confronting another person. We can tell by the release of chemicals if that person is a family member. My research at Statesville has proved animals feel the same. Our research there has made it possible to say with certainty that you will have no choice in how your body reacts when in the presence of family. Zeus has confirmed it and we're busily mapping previously unknown compounds our body's make. Humans can ignore the body's reactions and often do. Animals will respond instinctively. They don't possess the intellect to do otherwise and the chemical reactions they deal with are much stronger.

"Hirsit are animals and we believe Hifis intentionally magnifies the release of those chemicals to bond them together. Hirsit have been chemically conditioned to support each other. Hifis humans also produce much stronger chemical reactions. Our concern is that the Geromi can control the reactions remotely although there's been no sign of that. It's likely they can control Hifis and uninfected humans through chemical means, sprays, injections, pills. We believe they can intentionally induce a homicidal rage in Hirsit by conditioned response.

"Animals recovered from a raid on their secret facility in Michigan reveal they were attempting to do the same to Earth animals with limited success. Because of my strong background in veterinary science, I've been assigned to the Hifis research project.

"It's a fascinating study. I'll be one of your personal doctors and all my findings will be available to you with some small exceptions. Whenever I can, I'll be withholding the identity of my patients for their privacy. But some reports need to be made fully, despite the embarrassment it might cause and that's for your fellows' safety.

"Human families behave in a similar way as animals do albeit in a much reduced manner. Hifis humans seem caught somewhere in the middle and those who have a hard time controlling their impulses will protect their Hifis family ferociously. Again, none of that is new information, excepting that we now know what chemicals cause it. Given enough time, we might be able to treat it, and we'll be doing some experiments on our volunteer subjects.

"You three are clearly a family unit, and I'm sure it's a bit discomfiting to have such strong reactions for each other. We don't have many such family units to study, and we don't want to mess with your chemistry until we're absolutely certain we know what we're doing. I don't foresee that happening anytime soon and it won't be done without your permission.

"The Hifis humans who were kept together in captivity display family bonding, including the chemical releases I was speaking of. Prisoners often form these sorts of familial bonds, but Hifis seem to take that to a new level. Sharing dangerous experiences bonds humans. Men who've seen action together will help a war buddy out even thirty years later and feel real affection for a man they haven't seen in all that time.

"But that man will rarely change his life to stay with that buddy in civilian life. They can separate. We aren't certain if the human-hifis need to see their fellows frequently is fear induced worry based on current events and the reasonable assumption that a missing friend could be in grave danger, or a lasting chemical induced effect similar to what a parent feels for their own newborns.

"It's possible you'll feel strong reactions to Hifis you come into regular contact with and we'd like you to report it. We'd also like reports of any unusual behavior from or to anyone in your family group."

Luke said, "What do you expect to happen?"

"You might feel the urge to... den, I suppose is the term I'm looking for. Animals spend a good portion of their time finding safe places to sleep and will protect their dens from others of their own kind. Herds of animals almost always sleep grouped tightly together. Bigger groups of apes will sleep in family clumps within a nesting area that their larger pack inhabits. Humans tend to be more open in who can enter our sleeping spaces but most of us prefer a really secure private space too.

"We've put you into a mixed group purposefully in the hopes it would help your body chemistry remain human normal, but it might not be anything you can control. Being so closely confined with people who aren't family needs to be studied and we need you as active participants. Stress or lack of stress might affect you. By that I mean I want you all to keep track of your urges.

"We discussed keeping our theories from you because we don't want to worry you or inhibit the natural affection humans display. Humans need hugs after a hard day. That's perfectly normal. You're also romantically involved with one of your family pack and it's normal to feel jealous, but if you find yourself feeling in ways you hadn't, come in and talk.

Luke said, "Are you watching us in our rooms?"

"No, but I'm reading all of the reports, and your squad leader has been ordered to report even minor incidents, so I'm aware there was an issue this morning. I didn't think it anything to worry about, and I don't want you worrying either. It's perfectly normal to be angry if someone sneaks into your boyfriend's bath. I'm not quite sure what to make of the disagreement between you and Cadet Lane but it seemed like a perfectly normal sort of exchanged and not really that heated.

I said, "Stephanie is obsessed with him and pesters him all the time."

Luke said, "She's obsessed with one-upping every other woman around her. It isn't me in particular."

I said, "I used to think that too but maybe she really does like you, Luke."

Luke grimaced and said, "Doc, I don't plan on making this public knowledge, but I'm gay. I was trying to keep it from Stephanie because she has a history of gay bashing and I just didn't want to deal with it, but I've been thinking of telling her because I think it will make her really angry if she finds out later and I don't want to deal with that either."

Jasmine said, "There are other gay officers, both male and female, and it's against our policy to ask or comment on anyone's sexual preferences. If she's breaking the rules, then report it and let the proper authorities deal with it.

Luke said, "I hope this morning's argument was enough to straighten it out."

Jasmine said, "I'll be checking in frequently to see how you're doing, and you need to report honestly. Call your Hifis liaison officer or me if you're having any issues. We don't want you to snap and attack a roommate who enters your room."

I said, "Can that happen?"

"We don't know. It appears as if your human intellect can hold back your animal impulses when you're in human form. If you're angry or frightened as a human and shift to an ape, you'll be very angry or frightened and might attack before you can get control of yourself. Anger isn't just a feeling, it's a chemical release that prepares you to fight. We'll be testing all of you and hopefully teaching your animal self to control your animal impulses. Those classes might be embarrassing and maybe even feel a bit demeaning. You aren't animals but we'll be training you a bit as if you are in the hopes that the conditioning holds when you're afraid and angry."

Luke huffed a hard laugh. "Clicker training?"

"That and verbal commands. If we can get you to act instinctively like we can for real animals, then maybe we can save your lives—and ours."

She glanced at her watch, making a face. "Here I am chattering on when we have all these tests to get through. So far your eyes look perfectly normal. This next test will measure how good your distance vision is and I expect to see different results than I would with a non-hifis human. I'll be checking each eye independently in different lights but it's basically the same sort of thing you've been doing all your life. I'll say the line number and you read me the line. Or I'll have you read a card as the letters get smaller. For stage two, you'll have this clicker and you're going to click the instant you can read the displayed word."

I said, "If the word remains in the same spot, I don't think I'll have any trouble reading it. It's when I look away to a new spot that it takes me a second to focus."

"We'll be testing it, but this base line is first. Luke, if you'd stand on the line in the back of the room, please? Mia, just remain quiet in the chair there."

I was able to read everything shown to Luke with no problems and was just beginning to relax when he hesitated. My heart began to pound when he couldn't read the next few lines.

"Very good, Luke," Jasmine said. "Your vision is 120/15. A perfect adaption to x-coms."

"Mia, we'll do you next and then check peripherals."

My heart had resumed a normal rhythm as she spoke to Luke. He was fine.

I was likely farsighted and I could live with that.

Jasmine said, "Just have a seat and remain quiet, Luke."

I read the lines all the way to the bottom of the chart and they remained crisp and clear. I could have read smaller ones and told her so.

She said, "Hold on a minute. I need another chart," and she hurried from the room.

Luke said, "It's your x-coms. I've been talking to Zeus just now."

I'd already figured that and nodded.

He said, "This morning, what were you looking at?"

"The guy in the helicopter. His name tag."

"I could see him, but I don't think I could have read the tag."

"Should I be worried?"

"Maybe. The coms might strain your eyes. If you get headaches or anything let us know."

"Won't shifting fix the damage?"

"I think so but maybe seeing too far would blind you and that could kill you if we were in a firefight when it happened and you couldn't shift right away to fix it.

"That can't happen anytime soon."

"I agree. I also think I could get Zeus to dial it down a bit but let's see how far you can see before we worry about it.

Jasmine was gone for thirty minutes and returned with another woman who introduced herself as Doctor Agnes Hall. We were brought outside where I read charts that soldiers held beneath hastily erected tents.

"Two hundred and thirty yards," Luke said as they conferred. "Is it giving you a headache?"

"No."

"You're squinting."

I shrugged. "I'm trying to see. If I don't squint, I can't read it."

"That's good. It means the x-coms are activating it just like they do for our smart coms."

I said, "I want you to get these coms."

"I can't without an alien form."

I turned away from the doctors to face him. "They decoded the gibberish?"

"We think so. Basically you gave yourself a higher rank. Only Geromi have forms with completely different DNA. We aren't yet certain if Hirsit can't or aren't allowed."

"My vote is can't. It felt like I was falling apart, and it might have been my imagination but I swear I saw flakes drifting away like I was falling to dust in slow motion."

"Never use that form again!"

"It would be a seriously last resort," I agreed.

He hugged me, and I relaxed against him.

We didn't part until Jasmine approached.

"We're going to make a more precise testing station, but I don't think it's anything to worry about. You can see about twice as far as normal Hifis. They want to test the com strength and I'll arrange those tests. Now, let's get this finished up. I'd like to get the hearing and gynecological exams finished today."

I grimaced, and she laughed. "It will be quick and painless, no different than any other one."

"I've never had one."

"I'm out for this one," Luke said.

I made a face at him and could feel my flush.

Jasmine said, "You'll be getting a full body examine too, including a sperm count. It's intrusive but we need a baseline to be sure we notice problems."

"*Ha!*" I said, laughing when he flushed.

Jasmine said, "We can call in another Hifis to accompany you if you prefer.

I said, "I can go alone if he's outside the door."

Luke heaved a put upon sigh. "Let's get it over with."

19

We were released in time to attend evening formation but warned they'd be calling us back. Adan greeted us with smiles but little lines by his eyes revealed his tension.

We headed to the mess hall with the rest of our platoon and then back to our dorm for our mandatory study hour. I opened my Introduction to Hirsit homework assignment, from a class I'd missed.

The first question made me consider that I wasn't observing as closely as I should be. I had no idea how many toes a female Houft had and if they were opposable or prehensile. I clicked on the links and spent the rest of the study period reading about Houft skeletal structure.

The rest of the night was ours to do what we wished with but that included doing our homework assignments. In theory assignments should take half an hour at most. We'd been warned we'd be given projects to do both alone and in groups that would eat into our free time. I knew it was meant to teach us time management and how to work as a team but worried it would take up too much of my homework time. I hoped I could keep up without Whiroon helping me.

I took my laptop with me when I knocked on Adan's door.

Luke exited when he let me in.

"I won't be back until lights out," he said, and I wondered if Adan had asked him to leave or if he felt the tension between us too.

Adan said, "Homework or discussion first?"

"I—homework?"

I sat at Luke's desk put stared at my screen unable to concentrate. I finally said, "How angry are you?"

He flipped his laptop closed, turning to face me.

"I'm not angry. I'm worried."

"We didn't really talk about much after I shut you off."

"Not about that," he said hastily.

My flush felt like fire on my cheeks.

He said, "I expected you to turn it off during that exam." He frowned at me thoughtfully a moment. "I think we need to set some ground rules for using our coms. Let's not use them to watch each other unless we're concerned about something dangerous and let's always say we are. I'll have Luke rig a small light or something that tells us. That way you don't need to be worried we're spying while you're in the shower or anything."

I instantly wondered what had happened in the shower, which must have shown on my face because he exhaled heavily, crossing his arms.

"I couldn't have been any plainer that I didn't want her popping into my shower."

"I know and I'm not mad about it."

"You are. You're mad about this morning too."

"You don't get to tell me what I'm angry about!"

"And you don't get to lie to me, even to spare my feelings!"

"Stephanie's an ass," I snapped.

"On that we agree."

"She's a beautiful one though..."

"She's a slut. And I mean that in the truest sense of the word, not because she has lots of sexual partners but because she doesn't give a shit about any of them. She uses them and discards them and she *tries* to make them miserable about it. She wants her conquests to feel bad that they can't have her.

"I wouldn't even pretend to be her friend, not that I think for a minute that she really thinks she and I are friends, but I'll keep the pretense up because we have to work together. I'll be friendly and polite as long she acts professionally."

I said, "I don't know what to do about her. I never did."

He shrugged. "I don't think you need to do anything. She's ignoring you. You can ignore her."

"She's not ignoring me. She's smirking at me while flirting with you, and you're right, it pisses me off!"

"I won't let her, not even a little bit. I shouldn't have let her to begin with, but I was trying to help Luke."

"And enjoying it."

I hadn't meant to say the last and I said hurriedly, "I'm sorry. I didn't mean that."

He nodded slowly. "Maybe a little but not because of her, just you being jealous. I want you to be jealous of my attention because I'm so damned jealous of yours!" He stared down at his hands on his desk as he said, "You see her flirting with me and turn away smiling like you don't care and that really hurts. I see the worry on your face when she approaches Luke and nothing when she hangs on me, so yeah, when you get angry about her, it makes me happy, and maybe I led her on more than necessary to see you get angry, but I wasn't leading her on today or pretending to be outraged. I don't like her touching me or you or Luke and it has nothing to do with us being a pack but because I know her touch is meant to hurt us. She'd be thrilled to know we're fighting over her."

"We aren't fighting over her but the lack of trust."

"You're right and I don't know how to fix it. I've been thinking about it all day. I even considered asking you to marry me so I could give you the engagement ring and then everyone would know you're spoken for, but I need to trust you to turn away all offers, not limit your offers."

"No one's offering," I said dryly. My heart had begun to flutter when he'd spoken of getting married. I wasn't sure if I were relieved or disappointed that he'd changed his mind.

He said, "Mia, you're a beautiful woman. I think in your mind you're still a gawky girl and that girl is really grateful to Luke for his friendship and support, but you aren't that girl anymore. Luke knows it. Hell, everyone who sees you knows it, including Stephanie. Luke is still hovering and protective because he knows that you don't see it. You think he's there to cover when your insecurities attack when really he's there to keep others from using your insecurities against you."

I snorted, and he rolled his eyes at me.

"How do you think Luke and I became friends? He saw my interest and made it a point to get to know me. He warned me that if I was playing with you, he'd make me very sorry. I'm afraid you're going to suddenly realize you can have anyone you want, and you won't want me..."

"That's ridiculous."

"I love you so much!"

"I love you just as much."

He stood, offering his hand and when I took it, he let out a breath like a sob.

"Are we okay?" I asked when he embraced me.

"As long as you can keep forgiving mistakes we are."

"I don't like to admit when I'm angry because I don't know how to express it without yelling and it wasn't a yelling sort of offense."

"I'd rather have you yell than close me out."

"I'm sorry."

"Me too."

His kiss left me breathless and he moaned as I deepened it, sliding my hands over his back.

His hand closed around mine when I reached for the zipper of his uniform. "God knows I want you, but I don't want you to feel pressured into it. We can just cuddle. I don't expect makeup sex."

I dropped my hand, confused on what he wanted or if he thought I was trying to manipulate him with sex.

We were both tense now and I wasn't sure what to do.

"Maybe I shouldn't have said anything," he finally said. "I'm ruining us by trying too hard. I know it but I can't seem to stop myself..."

I laughed and tightened my grip for a moment then released him. "I'm going to go change and grab a snack for us. We aren't ruined. We're fine. We can take our time until we're both ready."

"I'm ready," he said in laughing breathless voice, but he stepped away and headed to his closet. "I'll change too."

Luke, Lana, and Sinclair were in the main room siting at the table with their open laptops. They nodded greetings or said hi as I passed.

Sutak wasn't in our room. I was relieved that I didn't need to explain or make an excuse. I changed quickly and grabbed two ice cream bars and two chocolate milks from our shelf in the refrigerator.

I'd left Adan's door partially ajar and hesitated before closing it all the way, but I didn't want to talk to or see anyone else, even Luke, so I closed it and handed Adan an ice cream and milk and took my laptop to Adan's bed.

I patted the bed beside me. "You can join me."

"We aren't going to get much homework done if I do."

"Want mine?" he offered, holding out his milk and ice cream.

"Not hungry?"

"I had two after dinner."

I shook my head and he headed into the main room.

I ate my ice cream and drank my milk but I couldn't concentrate on the homework. He returned and sat but I didn't think he was doing his either.

It was worrying me that our small fight had gotten him so upset that he couldn't eat. I set my laptop down and stood to throw out my trash.

He didn't object when I closed the laptop and straddled his lap.

We kissed for a long time before his hands began to wander.

"You're so beautiful, *mi amor*," he whispered as he removed my shirt.

"Whiroon, coms off until further notice," I said, which meant no one could contact us or monitor us.

I wasn't wearing a bra and he leaned back to watch his hands on my breasts. My skin felt feverish. His thumbs lightly trailing over my breasts made me moan and he leaned down to kiss them. We were both naked within minutes, our clothing discarded on the floor by his bed. Warmth pooled in my stomach, following the trail of his fingers and lips.

I'd never imagined sex would affect my entire body like this.

I began to cry, and he stilled, staring down at me and breathing hard.

"Don't stop," I said breathlessly, and he laughed a low husky laugh when I rolled us over to be on top.

"Oh God," he moaned and thrust harder.

My body jerked against his and I forgot we needed to be quiet, moaning loudly as my body tightened around his. My muscles refused to support me, and I fell forward and couldn't catch my breath. I began to cry again, which made it even harder to breath.

He rolled us onto our side and stroked my head and back as he kissed my teary face and made small comforting sounds. I stopped crying but was still breathing too hard. My face felt hot and the rest of me cold. I was embarrassed and afraid I was sinking into a full-blown panic attack.

"Sorry," I whispered when I could finally take a deep breath.

He pressed my hand to his cheek, which was damp, as he said, "It overwhelmed me too." He laid my hand on his heart that was beating as fast as mine, then he brought it to his lips and kissed it. We lay there unspeaking for a few minutes and it should've been perfect—but I was miserable.

Tingles raced over me. I was afraid I'd start crying and have another panic attack. Every time he moved my heart rate accelerated. My fear of an attack was going to make one a reality. The tingles were growing worse. My neck began to feel hot and my face flushed and I knew it was making him uneasy because he was growing tense, which was making me feel worse.

I knew I should dress but couldn't make myself release him. I was terrified and glad we'd turned the coms off because just thinking about explaining it to Jay made a wave of heat pass from my crown across my chest and I began to cry again.

"I'm sorry," I sobbed.

He said, "It's just a panic attack and I'm happy to help you. Please tell me you don't need Luke. *I* want to help you."

I squeezed him so tightly he grunted.

"Damn it, it's almost lights out..."

Nausea suddenly overtook me, making me feel weak and clammy.

"I can't go."

"I don't want you to go."

"I mean it! I can't go! I feel sick." He leaned up on an elbow to feel my forehead.

"You're burning up."

"I'm not going anywhere!" I said shrilly, batting at his hands, and he cuddle me again.

"I think you should shift. Maybe you caught a bug or something... wait—let me talk to Luke a minute."

I closed my eyes against the whirling of the room and nodded.

"Luke, we have a problem," he said a moment later. "Mia is sick. I'm turning the coms on, but she's also having a panic attack and I'm not sure what caused it. We were, ah, intimate for the first time and it was really emotional for both of us, but Jasmine's got me worried. I was thinking Mia should shift, but on second thought, I thought that might be bad. There's no way she can leave our room right now."

My panicky gasps for air began to ease, and he kissed my sweaty forehead.

"She needs to stay here with just me for a bit," he said forcefully, and I relaxed against his side suddenly exhausted.

I must have fallen asleep although I don't remember drifting off. But I woke in a panic. My heart was pounding so hard that it hurt.

Adan growled and Luke stepped back from the open door. Adan growled again and crouched. Luke slammed the door right as Adan leaped.

"Adan!"

He whirled and pounced landing over me and knocking me down.

He licked my face then rubbed his head over me before he became cat-sized and sat on my chest.

I petted him, laughing shakily as I said, "You think it's lowering my blood pressure?"

He sneezed, jumping away to sniff the floor around the door.

"You good now?"

He nodded and leapt back to the bed. *Shift to your cat,'* he texted.

I looked at the time and winced. "How much trouble are we in?"

He snarled and his tail lashed and continued to lash as he paced in circles at the foot of the bed. *'Shift!'* a row of exclamation points appeared before me and I laughed again as I shook my head. "I will. Give me second."

I said, "Luke, how much trouble are we in?"

"None. They cleared the room and brought everyone separately to the medics."

What's going on?"

"You were poisoned."

"What!"

Adan growled, grew bigger, and sniffed me all over again.

Luke said, "Shift to the cat."

I shifted, and Adan snarled and became his panther size to run around the room, slashing at the furniture, ripping the bedding and in general behaving like a spaz.

I taped the icon for Adan and the prerecorded message, *Are you okay?*

Luke said from outside the door, "I can see you guys. The techs want to come in, but he doesn't look up to it..."

Ya think, Wile E.?

Luke laughed, saying, "You would record that."

Adan had stilled but was breathing heavily.

I tapped the message that said, *I need six minutes.*

Adan shifted back and burst into tears when he picked me up.

"Coms off!" he said.

I didn't turn mine off even though I thought Luke and Jay would both be using them. I knew Adan was embarrassed but if we were going to collapse from poison, I wanted them to know it.

20

"Jesus, Mia, I thought you were dead! Are you okay now?"

I nodded yes while taping the, *I'm fine*, message.

He set me on the floor and pulled on his sweatpants while I crawled beneath his covers to shift back. His sheets were gritty. He must have shifted a few times to make them this dirty.

He handed me my sweatshirt and kissed me with trembling lips. "I've never been so scared in my life. You were turning to dust and I thought you were dead.

"I died?" I began to shiver and the nausea returned.

Luke said from my coms, "No. You seem fine."

Adan snapped, "I said turn the coms off, Luke!"

"It's just me," Luke said.

"We shouldn't turn them off if we're going to go poof." My attempt at levity was feeble because my voice cracked and shook.

Luke said, "You're fine but you scared the crap out of us."

"What happened?"

Luke said, "Jasmine would like to talk to you and she really needs some bloodwork. I can come in and take it or leave the supplies outside the door."

Adan said, "I'm sorry, I don't know what came over me. I'd never hurt you, Luke. You can come in. Jasmine can come in. I'm in control of myself. Do they know what was used yet?"

"One second. Let me get them. We have tranquilizers and a net with us in case you lose it. Try not to."

I put my pants on and got up while Adan let them in.

Jasmine wore a hazmat suit. She gave Adan a leery glance as she sidled past him. Two men wearing hazmat suits stood at the door with Luke who was still in BDU.

"How are you feeling now, Mia?" Jasmine asked.

"Normal."

"Great. I'm going to take a quick temperature and then a few vials of blood. I'd like to examine your abdomen."

She shot another nervous glance at Adan who was crowding up against me with a death grip on my hand.

"Okay."

"What happened?" I asked again.

"You were poisoned. Hifis saved you. I think you could've saved yourself if you'd shifted sooner."

Adan said, "I almost fucking killed her! I was listening to you today and thought her sickness might have been some weird reaction to us having sex for the first time and I didn't want her to shift. I thought it might make her less human in her emotions."

Jasmine shook her head but didn't glance up from the vials of blood she was withdrawing from my arm. "It wouldn't work like that. I'm sorry if I wasn't clear earlier. The chemicals we're talking about affect your flight or flight instincts. They don't make you like or dislike people. It might make her more prone to violence when you're injured but it wouldn't alter her affections. She wouldn't cease to be Mia, but it could conceivably make her consider others as her family too, even if she didn't particularly like them. But she has an intellect that can see beyond family. I'm aware of the problems she had with her sister, that she felt family obligation, but that obligation wasn't impossible to act against. It's the same sort of thing.

"You're right in that mating for animals can bond them for life or make them fight other males, but it doesn't bestow or take away affection. Her affection isn't a chemical construct, excepting what hormones do to all of us during the acts of love... although, I suppose, Hifis could be making those chemicals stronger too..."

"Maybe," Adan said doubtfully. "I thought you'd just fallen asleep at first. I didn't want you to go back to your room either. I thought that was worrying you and that when I said you could stay, you'd just relaxed."

"I did. I really didn't want to go. I wouldn't have gone."

Jasmine said, "A strong instinct to seek the help of pack or to stay in your den when injured. Perfectly normal."

"For an animal, maybe," I said unhappily.

"For humans too. We all want our mothers when we're ill. I'd like to take some spinal fluid, and if you'd permit, I'd like brain scans from all three of you. I'd show you the machines and explain the procedures, an MRI and CT"—she laughed lightly— "basically an alphabet soup of scans, but you'd be awake an aware and can be accompanied by a friend."

Adan said, "You've drawn blood already. Did it show anything?"

"Ricin. We found it in the ice cream and in the milk she drank."

"Just mine?" I asked.

"No. All of the ice cream still in your freezer was dosed and we're recalling it all and testing. "Your roommates who ingested the ice cream are being treated and so far are responding well. We think they'll make full recoveries because we caught it so quickly. They hadn't shown any symptoms yet and we're still waiting on test results to confirm poisoning. It's possible not all of the bars were dosed."

"Who bought the food?" I asked.

Luke said, "None of us and we all thought one of us had."

Jasmine said, "Can you lift your shirt so I can examine your stomach, please? I'd like to take a few skin scrapings too if you permit."

"Do what you need to do," I said.

Adan began breathing heavily and his hand tightened painfully on mine.

I said, "Are the needles freaking you out?"

"The knife in her hand is." He put his hand on my stomach and despite the situation and onlookers it sent a thrill down to my toes. I really wanted to kiss him again.

I picked up his hand and kissed it. "Just close your eyes. It will be over in just a minute."

"That's what I'm afraid off... "

I said, "Why am I here and not in a hospital?"

"We were afraid to move you," Jasmine said absently as she listened to my stomach with a stethoscope.

"Jesus, Adan," I said, worried now that he'd lost control so badly that it had endangered us.

He said, "I didn't know what was going on. You were so still though that I got nervous, and when I couldn't wake you, I called Luke and for medics. I was going to put your clothes on you but then I saw..." He shivered, pressing his lips to my temple.

Jasmine said, "The Hifis destroyed the contaminants. It was actually quite a sophisticated response. Your stomach and part of your esophagus was destroyed."

Adan said, "You were turning to dust before my eyes."

Jasmine said, "It took a few hours. I'd have liked to preform tests before you shifted but... I hypothesize that it didn't replace the destroyed organs but just closed the skin and remade essential connections. We weren't certain at first what the cause was but the damage was localized in your abdomen. We decided it was best to leave you because it was clear the damage was contained. There was no blood or apparent discomfort and we hoped you'd wake and be able to shift and thought movement might speed the process, causing an escalating catastrophic effect."

Luke said, "If this happens again, we do the same thing."

"It better not fucking happen again!" Adan snapped.

Jasmine said, "I've seen similar effects in Hifis animals that had been poisoned, but the deterioration was much more rapid."

"Did it die?"

"Within five minutes it had been reduced completely to dust."

Adan moaned, and I patted his shoulder.

I said, "What about Hirsit? What happens to them when they're poisoned?"

"They shift at the first sign of illness or die if the poison is fast acting enough, but it's very difficult to injure them enough instantly with poison, I mean in such a way that they wouldn't realize they were being poisoned."

I said, "I should have shifted when I felt sick."

Jasmine nodded. "I'm going to be speaking with my teams. We need to make a kit of some kind to take a blood sample quickly because all of our evidence would be lost in a shift."

Adan said, "Just shift and worry about evidence after."

I said, "How much time would I have?"

"That's impossible to say. The type of poison, the amount, the administration method, your condition, would all play a role in how fast it would work. How long were you feeling ill before you mentioned it?"

Adan kissed my temple again and I realized I'd been quiet a while as I considered, but I truly couldn't pinpoint the moment my unhappiness over the thought of returning to my own room had changed to real physical discomfort and I really didn't want to talk about our relationship.

Jasmine packed her bag and sat back on her heels. "Maybe you could let Mia and me speak privately for a minute, Mr. Lewis."

"No. He can stay. I was just thinking about it. I really don't know. I was fine but a bit... I'm not sure of the right word. Emotional, I guess. We'd had a fight earlier or more of a misunderstanding, but everything was fine between us, more than fine, and I didn't want to go back to my room. Sometimes when I get angry, I cry and it makes me angrier. I hate crying like that. It really embarrasses me, which can give me a panic attack. I haven't had an attack like that in years although I did have one from fear recently or maybe the HGTRF injection caused it... I lose my breath and feel sick and weak and dizzy.

"I wasn't angry, but I *was* crying, and it embarrassed me, and I thought I was having a panic attack until I felt nauseous. Adan said I had a fever and it scared me, but he was there, and I knew he'd take care of me, so I let him..."

"Were you aware?" Adan asked in horror.

"No. I meant I just relaxed. You didn't seem repulsed by my attack or angry, and to be honest, I was glad you were going to arrange things so that we could stay together longer even though I knew I should go back to my room."

"You're staying with me," Adan said firmly.

"I'm fine."

Adan stiffened, and I added hurriedly, "I'd like to stay but I don't need to."

Luke said, "We're all being moved to new rooms while they investigate ours."

Adan said slowly, "I want to cooperate and follow orders but the thought of leaving her right now is literally making me break out in a cold sweat. I know this is a court martial offense but I'm not leaving her— even if she wants me to."

Luke laughed a short unhappy bark of laughter. "We didn't even last a full day."

Jasmine said, "It isn't an offense. It's a Hifis need *and* a human one. You were almost murdered. I'm sure that rates a day or two of leave. This isn't violence in the heat of battle on a battlefield but an attack in your home. As your doctor, I can order time to rest, and I'm doing so. I'll arrange for you to have a room together because of your Hifis needs, but I expect you won't take advantage of this and will return to duty as soon as you're able to."

"And what good is a soldier who falls to pieces like this?" Adan asked bitterly.

"We're exploring this phenomenon because it does impact your effectiveness. We believe your instincts would demand you fight if there was a threat to fight. Animal instinct is a tricky thing and humans have it too. We'll leave you alone for two days and see if you're feeling more yourself. If you feel better sooner, all well and good, but you have two days leave.

"We have another young couple who has an injured partner. The male's anxiety can cause the female to shift. Leaving them alone for a day, well actually, my theory is that sleeping together, and I don't mean sex but sleeping, relieves the anxiety that the other is hurt. That relief is enough that she's able to shift back and he can function normally until she displays signs of injury again."

I thought it very likely Jasmine was speaking of Alex and Molly.

Jasmine said, "I'm hoping if you both can relax that there won't be as much emotional trauma to trigger either of you to shift at a later date over this incident. So, I prescribe rest and naps in front of the television. I'd also like urine samples whenever you urinate. I'll leave the specimen cups in the bathroom that you can leave right outside the door, which will be guarded."

Luke said, "Is this house arrest?"

"Not at all. You can come and go as you please. You could go to your classes if you're up to it. You seem okay to me, but I'm not a psychiatrist." She winked at him and said, "I'd probably be better able to judge your mental health in your animal form."

Luke said, "I'm shaken and angry but I'm in control of myself. I'll stay close if they need me but I'm okay away from them for a day or two. I can go to class, but is that safe?"

"That, I couldn't say. They might keep you out much longer than two days. I'm just medical, not security. I was speaking as a doctor when I said you could go to class, not that you *should* go to class." She wrinkled her nose at him. "I warned you my bedside manner is in need of work. I'm not really used to working with patients that can speak... I've spent most of the last six years in my lab with patient interactions limited to observations as they undergo my experiments. Part of that process was brain scans but they weren't allowed to know what I was seeing..."

I said, "I'd feel better if you weren't out wandering around, Luke. Now I'm going to be worried about you..."

"I can study from my room or maybe I can use this opportunity to visit Zeus? I have some ideas I wanted to run past Jay, and this might be a good time because we need access to Zeus to try them."

"X-coms?" I asked.

"Yes."

Jasmine said, "You have my medical permission, but check with security."

21

They moved Aden and I back to Fort Bliss into a tiny apartment with three rooms, a bedroom with a full-size bed, a bathroom, and a kitchen-living room combo that had a small couch with a coffee table, one chair, a television and two barstools under the kitchen counter.

"Let's take a shower," he said as he yanked off his sweatshirt. He dropped it by the door and kicked off his sweatpants and sock booties he wore instead of shoes.

We'd had to leave everything behind for security to check and had been given the new sweats and booties to wear here.

When he was naked he hugged me, sliding his hands beneath the waistband of my pants to slide them down. He began breathing harder and lifted me, pressing me against the closed door to make love. The door rattled and I whispered laughingly, "There's a guard right outside."

He growled and took two steps into the room then laid me on the floor. His passion made me feel shivery and weak.

I forgot we should be quiet again and didn't even realize I was making noise until he collapsed across my chest breathing hard.

"Sorry," he said and began to rise.

I pulled him back down and kissed him hard, putting my legs around him to keep him there and we kissed a long time while his hands wandered until his breathing became ragged and we made love again. "Shower now?" he asked, and I shook my head.

"I need a minute." My legs were trembling and my heart pounding, but in a good way. I just wanted to hold him close.

I fell asleep and woke when he picked me up.

"You can sleep. I'll wash us both," he said gruffly. "My pack weighs more than you."

His voce made warmth flush my skin and my muscles tense in anticipation. "Kiss me," I said breathlessly, and he moaned when our lips touched, laughing as he staggered to the bathroom.

"This is perfect," he said as we made love again. "You're perfect."

"I love you," I said, and he laughed a happy laugh that changed to a hoarse shout when I called his name.

It was a good thing he was holding me up or I'd have fallen. He didn't bother with a towel just carried me to bed and rolled us in the blanket.

I was asleep in seconds and slept deeply.

When I woke, the room was mid-day light and he was kissing my breast.

"Morning," I said.

"*Mi amor,*" his voice caught and he sat, running his palm over me, making me shiver. I was a bit embarrassed he was staring so intently. But it also excited me. His skin was silky smooth and he shivered and leaned into my caresses.

I said, "I don't think two days is going to be long enough," and he laughed and moaned and made me cry out his name again.

22

I winked at Adan over my shoulder, grinning at his return grin, and headed to my pristinely clean room.

The security who'd swept our room for poisons had cleaned every surface. Our fridge had a new lock on it as did all of our cabinets and the door to my room.

I pressed my thumb to the pad and the door unlocked.

"Daffy!" Sutak exclaimed, jumping up from her desk to give me a hug.

"I'm going to kill him," I said as I returned the hug.

"I was so worried," Sutak said as she held me at arm's length to examine me. "How the hell didn't it kill you?"

I glanced at the door I'd left open and leaned closer to whisper, "Can this be just between us?"

She nodded and drew me further from the door.

"We were fighting over Stephanie's bathroom visit, and I got so mad that I threw my milk at him." She looked a bit confused and I said, "Wait—did you know it was in the milk?"

"Yeah, they told us poison was in the milk, the orange juice, the fruit on the counter, and the ice cream."

I felt bad about the lie I was going to tell her, but I'd been ordered to lie to keep my hifis status a secret.

I said, "I'd only had a few sips before I chucked it at him, and he got me so upset that I vomited. I was so fucking embarrassed when I kept vomiting... but then I was feverish, and he called a medic."

"Thank goodness," she said then frowned at me. "And why is this secret?"

I glanced back at the door. "Because I didn't want them all to know I was angry about Stephanie. She doesn't need to know Adan and I were arguing about her."

"Well, they won't it hear it from me."

My heart began to pound.

The use of nickname she'd never called me was one thing, but the Sutak I knew wouldn't have just let a Stephanie comment drop without making her support clear. The lack of—that bitch—in that sentence was too much off from normal to ignore.

She turned back to her desk as she said, "Do they know why we were targeted in particular?"

Tingles swept from my feet to my head. I tapped the icon to send an alert to my entire security division.

"I'm guessing the ship," I said while I picked up my laptop while triggering the prerecorded response on my coms that said alien infiltration followed by the one that said wait.

Adan came to the door and knocked once as he stepped inside.

"Hey, Sutak, it's damned good to see everyone alive and well. They didn't tell us what was going on for hours."

Sutak shook his hand while I typed feverishly. *She'll be alive. Don't tip it off. It must be bugged and in communication. Let's give the real Sutak a chance to slip us some information. Get Sopon in here to conduct a security check. We can pretend to believe the answers and maybe Sutak can tell us what she knows about where she is.*

Sutak said, "I'd just gotten back and hadn't eaten a thing."

I knew it was a risk to send the message. The aliens could probably hear our communications. Zeus had assured us it was secure, but I doubted he'd meant from themselves, but I hoped it was. The fact that they wanted a spy gave me hope that they really didn't know where Whiroon was, and maybe if we gave Sutak an obvious chance to send us false information, she'd be smart enough to take it.

Luke said, *"If we warn them and the others are also compromised, it will tip our hand."*

Adan said, "Steph is the only one who tested positive, but she seemed okay."

Sutak turned to me to say, "Maybe she did it to get rid of you."

I'd considered that too but thought it unlikely she'd go to such extremes but maybe I was wrong about Sutak and it had been Stephanie. Adan shrugged at me and said, "I can't imagine her doing anything like that but maybe they infiltrated and it isn't even her."

I said, "I think we need a security check."

Sutak said, "They already cleared us."

I said, "I'll know if it isn't her. We have history and I can read between her lies."

Adan said, "We all have history."

He left our room to go bang on Stephanie's door.

Sutak's expression hadn't changed. She still looked worried and a bit confused.

Luke said, *"Security is on the way. They want a few minutes."*

"We can handle one Houft," Adan said. He banged on Sinclair's door as Lana opened theirs. Adan said, "We're having a meeting. Everyone in the main room! Luke, that means you too!"

Sutak said, "Do they all know about the ship?"

"I have no idea what they know, but I doubt it. We can talk later."

She followed me from the room.

Sutak said, "Everyone take a seat. We're all nervous about how the ricin got into the room. Maybe one of you is an alien and you managed to get the passwords or bribed a guard or something. So we'll take turns asking some questions to verify we are who we say we are."

Luke said, "Stephanie, when did we kiss for the first time."

I rose an eyebrow at him, and she said, "Freshman year, on like the third day of school right before gym class."

"Wrong."

I jumped to my feet along with everyone else and backed away from her.

She said, "We did too! Lana, what was the perfume you spilled?

Lana said, "You spilled it and it was my perfume, Fleur Rose."

"And that shit stank," Felipe mutter as Stephanie said, "See, how would I know about that?"

Luke said, "I'll give you a hint. Darcy."

Stephanie laughed and said, "Oh my god. I completely forgot about that. Darcy Markowitz's birthday party and spin the bottle. I thought you meant a real kiss."

Luke nodded and everyone laughed nervously.

Felipe said, "Sinclair, what color were your socks when we met."

Sinclair said, "Purple with pink hearts."

"Really?" Stephanie said, and she and Lana laughed.

Adan said, "No one help him with this because some of you know the answer. Felipe, what did Major Grant say we should do if we knew there was a spy but that spy didn't know you knew."

Felipe hesitated and said, "Report it at once by secure channels."

Sinclair's eyes narrowed. He glared at Adan and then Felipe who was biting his lip and had paled.

Luke said, "Mia, what did my mother give me for my last birthday?"

"A bank account intended for your college expenses."

Sinclair stood and said, "Move away from the door a little, Adan."

Adan held up his hands and stepped away from the door to the room.

Sinclair said, "What was your score on the first obstacle course we ran together?"

"I came in twelve seconds after you."

Luke said, "I was three seconds behind Adan."

Felipe said, "I fell and was last."

Sinclair said, "No more fucking questions about our security protocols! It's just dumb to give a spy a heads up!"

Lana said, "None of us are spies. Mia, what could I smell in the air when we met?"

"Romance," I said, and Sutak laughed.

It made me shiver. It sounded like her—but it wasn't her. There was an emptiness in it that I hoped our security who was watching this through my coms noticed.

Stephanie said, "Someone ask Sutak something. I don't know her well enough to have anything good."

Luke said, "Where did I kiss you for the first time?"

Stephanie jumped to her feet, "Seriously? You've got to be kidding me! Her?"

Adan said, "She's a beautiful woman. Why not her? Get a grip."

Stephanie glared.

Adan smirked until she finally thumped back into her seat.

271

Sutak said, "Under the bleachers. But we're not dating or anything. It was just the one kiss."

Stephanie crossed her arms, turning her glare on me.

I turned to Sutak. "When are we going skateboarding this Saturday?"

Adan said, "Everyone knows that. It's on the board here."

Lana's eyes widened and she leaned forward. Felipe said hurriedly, "Don't tell her."

I rolled my eyes at Adan and said, "Okay, *where* are we going skateboarding."

"Everyone knows that too," Adan said. He grabbed Sinclair's shoulder and said, "Don't tell her the answer."

Stephanie said, "I don't, and how come I wasn't invited if everyone else was?"

Lana said, "Cause you weren't in the room, but come if you want."

Sutak said, "The saloon. We can use the obstacle course whenever we want."

I hit the icon that said, *Got it.*

Lana stood and practically ran to her door as she said, "Well, I'm satisfied, and I have a ton of homework to do. You coming, Steph?"

Stephanie said, "Seriously, it's just shitty that you guys gang up on me so much! You want me to treat you like friends, but you ignore me and laugh behind my back. Did you all know Sutak and Luke were whatever the hell they are?"

Luke said, "You're acting like a spaz. I kissed her once and she wasn't interested. Get over it. Believe me, I'd like to know why more than you do!"

Sutak said, "I like you a lot, Luke, this just isn't the time or place. Maybe someday."

Stephanie stomped from the room.

Sinclair said, "Now what?" His gaze flicked over us. I was worried he'd give away that he knew Sutak had screwed up.

Adan shrugged. "Nothing, I guess. We let security handle keeping us safe."

Felipe said, "I'm not sure they're up to the job, but Lana is right. I have a ton of homework to catch up on too."

Sinclair crossed his arms, glaring at Adan. "I don't like this one little bit."

I said, "I think I know why we were targeted, but I can't say anything about it until I get permission, which I think I'll get because some of you already know a bit and telling you more can't make much difference. Besides, it's dumb to not reveal everything we know when we all have top secret clearance."

"Dumb or not, rules are rules." Felipe headed into his room. Sinclair glared at us all before following.

I said to Adan, "We have a few hours before lights out. Let's say we study in your room?"

He laughed, giving me a heated glance that made me flush even though I knew he was faking it.

Sutak headed to our room, calling over her shoulder, "I have homework to catch up on too."

Adan closed the door and I typed, *'When we first got here, Sutak said this was a one horse town and that the bar they were closing down across from the campus was so old it should have had the word saloon over it. She might be there. Or maybe she meant in the town beneath a field somewhere there would be bleachers? Or maybe she meant the obstacle course, but would she have said that straight out?'*

'Under the saloon, would be my guess,' Adan typed back.

"Mine too," I said as I ran to his window.

Jay said, *"Security is on it."*

I typed, *'Security has been fucking up! How the hell did they take her with no one the wiser!'*

Adan said, *"Let them do their jobs."*

"I'm going. If we're close enough, Zeus can use our coms to scan. Jay, send us some Hifis backup.

Luke entered the bedroom as I slid the window open.

"Squirrels," Adan said. *"Chimps when we get there."*

Jay said, *"Hang back and let the professionals handle it."*

I said, *"We should have had Zeus moved closer."*

Luke said, *"Go back in your room and tell her Zeus blew up or something."*

"If I do that, they might kill Sutak."

Adan laid his hand on my cheek and whispered. "They'll likely kill her anyway the minute they know they're compromised. Tell her the ship is gone and maybe she'll report that and we can trick them into thinking we found her out some other way."

Jay said, *"She might attack you if you give her the information she came for... I don't like this."*

Luke said, *"Not if she believes her cover isn't blown."*

I hesitated at the window. Adan was right but it felt like a betrayal. I was giving up on Sutak if I spoke to the alien, trading her life for the slim chance of fooling the aliens and protecting myself.

I said loudly, "If we're sneaking out to meet O'Connor for a late night party, I better tell Sutak that I'm staying over."

"Will she cover for you?" Adan asked

"She said she would. She'll be pissed if she catches us sneaking out though..."

"She won't catch us," Luke said. "And even if she did, she's cool and wouldn't rat us out."

"Wait for me," I said and ran for the door. I forced a calm expression and hurried to my room.

"I know you said you'd cover for me, and I'm going to take you up on it just this once and stay with Adan tonight if you're still okay with it?"

She nodded, and I grabbed my sweats. "Thanks. All these secrets are so dumb. I can't believe they never told you what happened to the stupid ship!"

"What did happen?"

"Nothing much until the night those grots tried to infiltrate our camp. It said- emergency protocols activated- and flew off. It was off radar in seconds and they're worried it went to wherever it came from. We have another one but so far it hasn't turned on at all. Both Adan and I tried, and it didn't do a thing."

"Do they know why the ship spoke to you to begin with?"

"Yes, but that's another classified secret I'm not supposed to tell. I probably shouldn't have mentioned the ship, but you were there and saw it take off too. Don't say I told you until I get the official clearance."

I paused at the door and turned back to say, "And don't write Luke off so quickly. Sure, the timing sucks but it's not going to get any better. He really does like you a lot. I know the whole Stephanie thing is a nightmare, but it isn't his fault."

"I'll think about it."

"See ya in the morning."

I hoped Sutak got my message that we were coming—that it wasn't too late.

"Night."

I wanted to kill this alien thing that dared wear her face. Instead I forced a smile.

I closed the door and ran back to Adan's room.

23

The boys were already squirrels and sitting on the nightstand.

I turned away to remove my clothes and shifted quickly. We scampered down the wall and across the grass. Whiroon was displaying a map of the town and had highlighted all of the bars. I tapped the one closest to the cemetery.

Jay said, "I'm sending units there but it's going to take them a few minutes.

I tapped the prerecorded message, *hang back*. Then I stopped to type, *'Let us scope it out before they show themselves. We're just fury rodents that they shouldn't even notice.'*

Jay said, "*I still don't like it. Be careful, Mia. They could have ways to detect Hifis.*"

Luke was typing as I was and little yellow specs began to populate the map around us. I tapped one and an image of a field mouse appeared. It was laying on a bed of twigs and leaves, nibbling a piece of bark. Writing appeared beside it, listing the heart rate and size. It was just a foot away from us.

I typed, '*Without Zeus here we're going to have to be really close.*'

Luke replied, '*We can triangulate and get heat signatures and heartbeats much farther apart. I'm having it weed out all earth animals and focusing on houft and human shapes and sounds. I know they might be able to take Earth animal forms even though Zeus hadn't known of any, but I'm hoping we can narrow it down quickly.*

'*Split up and go to the spots I mark. Stand on the dots. Zeus will use our coms to scan. So wait until I mark a new spot before moving because if we see something, I'll need to check it and it will work best if the signal is sent from the same exact location.*'

Adan texted, '*Wait until we're off the campus to get bigger.*'

Luke replied, '*It would be better to stay smaller, but it will take too long to get there.*'

Jay said, *"I'm getting you a vehicle. Go to gate three. They'll be expecting you. The jeep will slow when it passes the building right before the bar and you can jump out."*

Luke began running and I followed. We stayed on the grass bordering the sidewalk and weren't trying to be stealthy. No one was around until we reached the parking lot. AFAR soldiers, our fellows who hadn't made the cut for officer, were guarding the entranceways and greeted our appearance with nervous mutterings and whispers. A jeep was waiting.

Captain Hendricks and another Ranger-X were sitting in the backseat. We climbed onto the passenger side seat.

The driver gave us a skeptical nervous glance as we exited. He drove slowly down the road. The two rangers in the backseat wore the short-sleeved version of our BDU and carried bags and weapons. I hoped we had more backup than them but didn't say anything because I didn't want to be ordered away.

The buildings we passed were all in the process of being torn down. The entire street had been requisitioned for the war effort. Construction had started on a large cement building, but no one was working. It was dark and quiet. All of the roads around the school were closed to through traffic. The nearest buildings had been all been commandeered to house

AFAR soldiers who mostly wore Army uniforms. I figured the locals were probably pissed at this intrusion into their town or maybe they thought a military presence would make them safer.

Jay said from my coms, "Her last flight was a training run, and they have her landing about half a mile north of your position. There's a house and outbuilding about a quarter mile north of that.

"She was off radar for eight minutes. Long enough for a switch, but not long enough for anyone to get concerned. She goes off frequently when she's showing her students how to land. Her student is under surveillance. We're leaving him alone. Maybe he'll try to contact others."

I typed, 'We'll check the house next.'

Hendricks said, "We have teams heading there."

I crawled to the top of the seat to look at him.

He said, "Your coms are better equipped, but my men are more prepared. Don't rush in halfcocked. We're surveillance. If we see her, we wait and make a plan! Am I clear?'

I nodded and saluted, and he laughed.

Jay said from my coms, "None of you might be able to wait. This is the first real contact, and your animal instincts might take over."

"I'm aware, sir," Hendricks said.

Jay said, "You might even fight each other, so give each other plenty of space."

I showed my teeth, made a muscle, and winked, making both men laugh.

Jay said, "All clowning aside, Mia, it's a real possibility, and if you begin to feel anxious, or see them begin to be aggressive, run away."

Jay sounded pissed.

I gave him a thumbs up.

Adan pulled my tail, and I climbed back down. He chittered at me, grabbing my paw.

The driver gave us a nervous glance.

Luke hissed and pulled our paws apart then crouched, putting his butt in the air and focusing pointedly on the road. I crouched beside him, jumping when he did.

We were going slow, and I rolled with it, hopped to my feet, and scampered to the first marker on my map. Whiroon guided me with a glowing strand of light that only I could see.

The night remained dark and still. The jeep's taillights faded into the distance.

'*Move on*,' Luke ordered.

I crept forward slowly, sniffing the air and pricking my ears. The bar was still standing with recently broken windows. I flicked the icon to see my pack. Adan was already inside the building. Luke was climbing a lattice on a wall on the next building. My mark was the back door.

I sniffed hard. People had passed but I couldn't tell when or how many or even how recently. Stale alcohol and urine were the predominant smells.

I stayed where I was until the next light lit and reluctantly left the bar behind.

At my next destination, which was the next building over, I typed, *'How accurate is it? Would it have seen her if she were in a cellar?'*

Jay said, *"Yes if the cellar was no more than twenty feet down and the material between us was less than three feet thick. We mapped a cellar, and it was empty of anything moving."*

I was on my way to the next marker when I smelled fresh blood. I slowed to type, *'I smell blood.'*

"Follow but go slow and carefully," Jay said.

I crept forward and the scent grew stronger.

Adan joined me and we sniffed the ground together.

'A rat would be better.' He shifted before I could answer.

He sniffed and ran forward, darting across the empty street. I ran after him. He ran beneath a bush right against a building.

He texted, *'The house ahead of us. Those were footprints. Someone walked past recently. I'd say it wasn't an animal from the length of the stride. I can smell lots of blood and shit and I hear something... I'm not sure what it is.'*

I heard it too. A soft mechanical whir. I could also hear insects and birds and soft rustlings of other rodents. Luke joined me as Adan crept forward.

"Contact," Jay said. *"Surround the building and let's see if we can map it."*

I ran for the dot that appeared on my map.

"Houft," Jay said a moment later.

A man said, *"We're headed to your position."*

Hendricks said, *"Mia, wait for Sergeant Garcia to get in position."*

"Three Houft, six humanoid, and one Hiff," Jay said a minute later.

Luke typed, *'Radio signals and electricity.'*

Hendricks said, *"Check the surrounding buildings."*

Jay said, *"You have twenty-four allies heading to your position. I'm marking them on your map. I can see them and you. I'll warn you when they get within radio range but ask before engaging. They're com silent until we engage."*

I tapped the button that said, *Roger that.*

Firt x-coms would auto connect to other Firt. I had no idea if that was true for x-coms that Whiroon hadn't made or not, but it seemed likely.

Adan texted, *'Six minutes.'*

Jay said, *"Stay the rat and circle the house while Luke and Mia get readings on the next building."*

I hesitated but then ran to my next mark.

Whiroon said, *"Metal concentration, explosive material, point eight yards."*

I stopped to type, *'I've got a mine here. Be careful, Luke.'*

I ran up a spindly tree, jumped to the top of a rickety iron fence, and ran along the top of it until I could jump to a stack of boards leaning against the wall. The wood of the building was old and dry with plenty of cracks to wedge my claws into. I climbed to the roof and then down to reach my assigned spot.

Whiroon said, *"Contact. Probable humanoid. Thirteen-point-three-feet northwest, heading in your direction."*

I typed it in and then told Whiroon to make all reports to the entire security team on the base until further notice.

Whiroon said, *"Contact grot. Probable Hifis. Northeast one hundred feet and closing."*

I turned to scan and saw it. It likely saw me too, so I picked up a stick and began chewing, angling my body away from it so it wouldn't see the shine of my x-coms through my fur. It slunk low to the ground, passing within feet of me, heading to the house Adan was at.

The first contact hadn't moved. I waited until I could no longer see the grot and climbed the house again, crawling into the gutter and trying to act like I imagined a squirrel might act, digging through the leaves and sticks caught in the gutter, chewing them as I eased forward.

"*Houft,*" Whiroon said but I could see that it was. It was crouched against the chimney of the next house over, using a spyglass to scan the field behind the house.

'*It has eyes on the field and most of the road,*' I typed.

Luke replied, '*I'm going to the next house. Keep an eye on it.*'

Adan said, '*The grot entered and is sitting by a closed door that I assume leads to the cellar.*'

Whiroon said, "*Five humanoids in the cellar. Consistent life sign for human*"

'*Five? What happened to six?*' Luke asked before I could.

"*Life signs terminated.*"

"*Fuck!*" Jay said. "*Don't rush in! It's too late to help whoever that was!*"

My heart pounded hard. I wanted to rush in but knew Jay was right.

'*Houft is moving,*' I warned. '*It's circling the chimney. That device it's using can likely see heat.*'

I scampered down the drainpipe, darted across the road, and up the drainpipe on the house the Houft was on.

"Mia," Jay said warningly.

'Get down from there, fool!' Adan texted.

I ignored them and ran across the roof and to the chimney where I crouched with my back to it and typed, *'Whiroon, can you block radio transmissions from Hirsit radio dots?'*

"Removal required."

'Jay, how close is my backup?'

"Four are holding on the cellar steps in the last house on the left. The rest are running south. I estimate six minutes before they're in range to help."

I hit the prerecorded button that said- *'Adan hold position.'* Then typed, *'Whiroon, using closest English approximation, identify the device Houft is holding.'*

Whiroon said, *"Computer enhanced, line of sight, long range, thermal imaging device with automatic lock on triggered by movement within set parameters. Parameters unknown. Capable of multiple target acquisition, computing probable destination by rate of travel with laser guided assistance for—weapons dispersal."*

The slight hesitation meant it didn't have a more exact word, which gave me pause.

24

I typed, '*Luke, just check the rest of the roofs then come to me. I need a squirrel distraction. I'll get behind it and pull the radio off and you attack from the front.*'

Jay said, "*It likely has a weapon.*"

I typed, '*We need to take it out to get our men close. I'll wait for our teams to get as close as they can. If it gets a signal out, we're in no worse position, but if it doesn't, we'll have a strategic advantage.*'

A minute later Jay said, "*Security here agrees, but check the rest of the roofs and buildings.*"

'*Five more to check,*' Luke said. '*There's a wire in the road here and I don't know if it's them or us.*'

Jay said, "*Us, but maybe they can tap it, so don't step on it.*"

I continued to scan around me, spotting an animal waddling into the bushes.

I typed, '*Whiroon, identify what I'm looking at.*'

Whiroon said, "*Taxidea Taxus, Badger. Estimated eighteen pounds. Normal habitat. Normal behavior. Probable non-Hifis.*"

I typed, '*I can't see it now. I think it went underground.*'

I crept around the chimney as the Houft did, keeping the bricks between us. It was a *firt*, and if its coms were like ours, which I was pretty sure they were, it wouldn't be able to scan me. It could send and receive but not scan with less than three dots. It hadn't given the slightest indication that it had noticed me.

'*Whiroon, interrupt communications of Houft radio dots as soon as possible. Priority action. If at all possible, I don't want the other Hirsit to realize the communication signal has been compromised.*'

"*Acknowledged.*"

Whiroon had sounded tense or excited.

I hoped I was projecting as I was both tense and excited too. I wanted to rip the dot from the houft's shoulder badly and knew it was my squirrel's lack of intelligence that was keeping me so focused on it but knowing it couldn't make me switch focus.

Me and the Houft circled the chimney three more times before Luke finally joined me. The grot had remained motionless in front of the cellar door. I wondered what it had been up to before it came back. I worried about there being more of them that I couldn't see. I worried that they'd kill another of the humans they'd taken before our team were in position. I worried it was already too late for Sutak.

Jay said, *"We're in position. I'm marking on your map where you should go next but use your common sense!"*

'Got that, Daffy?' Luke asked.

I taped the prerecorded message, *Har har, Wile E.,* grinning to myself over the expression I imagined was on his face.

'I'm coming up,' he said a few seconds later.

I shifted into my chimp form and hit my six-minute timer.

"We go in six minutes," Jay said.

I was tempted to ask who was there with him but decided it didn't really matter. They were letting us handle it, and I suddenly wondered if this entire thing was a training exercise. But it was a real Houft on the roof and a real grot in the building with Adan, and I couldn't imagine a way they could have real ones working with us.

Luke and I circled the chimney, keeping pace with the Houft. I pointed to the gutter, and he saluted and ran to begin digging through the leaves caught in it. The Houft halted to examine him, and I crept behind her.

"Life sign terminated," Whiroon said. *"Four human life signs remaining."*

I was sure that time he'd sounded tense—angry even.

My heart pounded with adrenaline. I jumped forward as Luke screeched, chittering angrily, throwing debris from the gutter to the ground.

The Houft lowered the device, making a hissing noise that I assumed was to scare what it presumed to be a squirrel away. I threw an arm around its neck, grabbing for the x-com on its chest, ripping away a hunk of fur and flesh as Luke shifted to his chimp and leaped forward.

The com felt red-hot. I yowled as the Houft grabbed my arm and threw me. I rolled across the roof, and Luke jumped over me, grabbing the Houft.

A wild cacophony of sound filled my head. It was so loud and unexpected it paralyzed me. I lay gasping on the roof unable to move or make a noise of my own. Flailing limbs knocked me over the edge of the roof.

I landed hard. It knocked the wind from me but the pain in my paw and the noise in my head was dimming.

I realized I was hearing Hirsit or maybe even Geromi transmissions, but I couldn't understand a word of it because there was so much sound it was impossible to make out individual words. Jay must have noticed I wasn't moving and reported it, but I hadn't heard him. I wasn't sure if that was because the noise had been too loud and confusing or that I was now on a different frequency— and I was afraid to ask.

I lay there for a minute while the sound slowly faded, which I thought —or at least hoped—was my coms lowering the volume. I could still hear it but it was a whisper now,, a continuous hum of noise as if a million radios were playing at once.

I ran around the house to climb up the drainpipe and reached the top as Luke bit a chunk from the Houft's neck.

The Houft snarled. The scent of blood was thick in the air. I ran forward, grabbed at the arm around Luke's neck, and bit down as hard as I could. The houft made a muffled screech and the arm broke with a sharp crack.

I released the arm to bite a leg. A kick knocked me back and rolled me over, but I was up and biting again in seconds. It was stronger than us, but we were faster. I was able to get my hands around its neck and I squeezed it until the feet stopped kicking at Luke.

Luke released the Houft to hiss at me. I shook my head, tapping my chest where my coms were.

I thought the Houft was dead or at least out of commission for a while, but I was afraid to use my coms to ask Whiroon.

Movement caught my eye. I slapped Luke's shoulder and pointed. We both watched Hendricks team take out the grot by the doorway.

Luke gave me a thumbs up then made a soft questioning sound, laying a knuckle against my lips.

I shrugged and mimed listening and then pointed up.

He tilted my head, leaning close to sniff me then ran his fingers through the fur of my head and then over my chest, parting the fur and searching.

I slapped his hands away and he hissed and signed *No. Looking*. And I let him groom me again as I signed *Mia okay*.

He held up a finger, tapped his ear, and turned away. I scampered to the other edge of the roof to examine the street. Eight monkeys ran along the edge of the building. They carried machine guns and wore AFAR uniforms, including bulletproof vests and headgear. Luke joined me, pointing to the house Adan was at, then giving me a thumbs up. We climbed down and joined the other monkeys crouching against the side of the building.

Luke's coms whispered aloud, "Mia, Zeus says you can deactivate local coms the same way you turn ours off. Just tell it to turn off all coms within fifty miles, except for crew. You have another black dot orbiting the larger one and he says they can hear you if you turn it on and it will auto translate. You can hear theirs too and you can order it to auto translate but if they look, they'll know we did it. I think I can have Zeus listen in and translate second hand but it's a risk that I don't think we need to take right now. Just turn the com off and turn crew coms on. Zeus will ask you to authenticate. Just say I authenticate."

I gave him a thumbs up and began typing. A second later the x-com on the monkeys' chests flashed and Whiroon said, "*Authenticate control access Pfsirt Purfit Charsinissf shut down fifty-mile radius.*"

I typed, '*Authenticate.*'

"*Authorized.*"

Whiroon had sounded amused or maybe smug. It made the fur on my back lift. I no longer thought I was projecting because I was scared of the dots.

'*Good job, Cadet Sutton,*' Captain Hendricks said. '*Lewis, can you get close enough to the grot inside that building to clamp it's muzzle shut?*'

'*Affirmative.*'

"*Sutton, Melton, stay behind my men.*" He handed me a forty-five, gesturing for the monkey beside him to hand one to Luke.

'*We'll handle the enemies. You handle the tech.*'

Two monkeys darted across the street to my left. I tapped the icon to turn on my map and examined the positions.

Jay said, *"You have air support waiting. Zeus doesn't know if they can use the spy glass devices without coms but says it's probable, so keep a sharp eye out. They only work in line of sight so you'll see them if they can see you but they likely have other devices."*

'Roger that.'

I followed Hendricks, staying low and darting from cover-to-cover, keeping a 3D map of Adan's position in front of me. He was creeping along the baseboard behind the grot. It made me pant to see him in such a dangerous position. The grot could kill him in one bite in that form and grot where fast.

Hendricks said, "Okay, Crane, you're up."

Crane was a sert like Hendricks. He had two radio dots. He shifted into an orange cat.

'On three, Lewis. Crane will distract.'

Hendricks put his hand on the door and counted down softly.

He opened the door, and I ran past him, becoming as big as I could get to leap on the grot Adan held.

Hendricks and his men ran down the stairs as I savaged the grot, ripping at it with my teeth and claws.

We savaged it to pieces. I'd have kept clawing the corpse, but a gunshot sounded below me followed by a long, prolonged blast of gunfire that grabbed my attention.

"Three human life signs," Whiroon said.

I screamed a chimp scream of defiance and ran down the stairs. The room was lit with a blue glow that I wasn't sure was my Hifis eyesight, my x-coms, or a combination. A brighter white light emanated from a tank of water that bubbled slowly. Tentacles like Whiroon's but much thinner and smaller writhed at the back of the tank.

Monkeys rolled on the floor with two Houft. Three obviously dead human corpses were stacked against the wall with a pile of dead animals. They'd all been tossed aside like garbage, which made me flush with anger.

The Hiff had been shot and lay in a growing pool of blood. A female Hirsit stood between two metal gurney-like tables. She hadn't yet shifted and held a metal box in one hand and a bloody knife in the other that she'd just obviously used on the man tied to the table. Sutak was strapped to the other table and hadn't moved or made a sound. I jumped forward and the hirsit's eyes widened. She dropped the box. A human who'd been kneeling with his hands behind his head screamed "Shoot her!" followed by a spat of Geromi words.

The Hirsit began to squeal a high-pitched sound between a scream and a whine that rose the hair on my arms.

One of the monkeys knocked the man to the ground and bit his neck and another leapt over the table to help savage the man.

Whiroon said, "Order them to stop!"

I shifted to human to yell, "Drop the knife!"

To my surprise she did.

I kicked the nearest Houft and said, "Don't move, that's an order!"

The Houft snarled at the chimp holding his arm but he stopped fighting. The other Houft stared at me with wide eyes and lay panting on the floor. Chimps began gathering the weapons while two tugged on the straps holding the bleeding man to the table and a third tried to wrap the gash in his neck.

He was trying to talk but the wound in his neck made it impossible. He pushed the monkey away to wrap his hands around his own neck and gasped out, "Puppet master."

I didn't think he meant me because he was glaring at the man the monkeys were mauling. He reached a bloody hand to me, closing his eyes when I grasped it.

Luke had shifted to human and was pushing away the monkey tugging on the straps that held Sutak.

I said, "No one touches her. What is that, Luke?"

"I have no idea."

"Is she..."

"Alive. Her chest is moving. These aren't just straps though."

The hand I held was lax and cold. I thought the man on the table had died. He was just a bit older than me with a shaved head. I vaguely recognized him from basic. I released his hand and pulled the other loose from his neck to press a bandage to it that a monkey handed me. I closed his eyes and said, "Do we have anything to cover him with?"

Hendricks shifted to human and said, "Get the captives tied for transport and be careful of the equipment."

I said, "Leave coms on a few. I need to test."

"Yes, ma am." He saluted me jauntily, but his smile faded as his gaze rested on the dead man on the gurney. They narrowed as he turned to examine the corpse of the man the two monkeys had killed. Both monkeys were crouched over the body with their lips raised and teeth showing. One snarled when Hendricks made eye contact.

"Shift back," he ordered and they both did as one of the other monkeys laid a sheet over the body and placed another bandage on the neck.

"Sorry, boss," Crane said.

Hendricks sighed hard and said, "Shit happens. We'll work on it."

All three men bent over the corpse on the floor.

I said, "Whiroon, is this human crew dead?"

"Unknown. Life signs negative but possible Hifis reactivation."

Jay said, "It can't tell from here if he's Hifis."

I said, "I don't think he is." I absently accepted a sheet one of the monkey's handed me and wrapped it around myself as I leaned closer to examine the bonds holding the corpse to the table. "Whiroon, using closest human equivalent, what am I looking at?"

"Restraints, medical readout... nervous system manipulator... answer machine."

The long pause told me there was no Earth equivalent, but I got the idea.

"Torture device."

"Affirmative."

"How do I remove it?"

"Key on the floor, one foot to your left." A grid map appeared over my vision with the metal box that the Houft had dropped highlighted in soft yellow. I picked up the box and a ghostly image of my hand sliding the box along the outer edge of the restraint appeared.

I said, "That's sort of spooky."

"What?" Adan asked as he hugged me.

I returned his embrace and would have hugged him longer, but Hendricks loudly cleared his throat.

"It's showing me how to use it."

Hendricks said, "Ask it if using it will notify anyone. Ask it if using it will harm you or us. Ask it if it will harm her." He gestured to Sutak who was now covered with a sheet.

Luke said, "Go ahead and use it. I already asked."

A clunk and low whirring sound was accompanied by the light in the tank brightening. I jumped, letting out a startled eep of surprise that changed to a horrified scream as a misshapen flattened version of Lana appeared in the tank.

Hendricks beat me to the tank, holding out a hand to stop me, but I'd already realized it wasn't really Lana but an empty shell. It had grown as quickly as a Hifis shift. Nausea rose in my gut and I wiped my suddenly sweating brow.

Small tentacles were wriggling into the body. We all stared in horror but the body remained inanimate.

Adan said, "Whiroon, tell me what I'm looking at."

"Fabricated humanoid shell."

"What is the purpose of the shell?"

"To repair or reskin for a more—pleasing appearance. Incompatible with Hirsit hifis."

I said, "He called the dead guy a puppet master. This must be how they replace us."

Hendricks said, "Can you read the writing here?"

He gestured to a toothbrush laying on the small table beside the tank. I examined the articles laid on the table with mounting horror.

I said, "That silver brush is Stephanie's."

Adan said, "The toothbrush is mine, I think."

"Jesus..."

Hendrick's motioned us back. "Don't touch any of it. Maybe we can pull some prints and find out who stole them."

"We should turn this machine off." I rubbed the goosebumps on my arms.

Hendrick's said, "Getty, cover this tank carefully. Mia, as disgusting as it is, we can't turn it off. Maybe we can learn how they do it and then we can use it to help our injured."

He gestured me back to the table with the dead private. "Let's get him unhooked."

Adan was whispering to Whiroon, asking questions about the tank and sending replies to different labs. I knew he must be speaking with Jay or maybe even the doctors directly because he was asking some pretty technical sounding questions that I doubted were his idea.

It was hard to turn my back on the floating body. Even though I knew it wasn't really Lana, it somehow felt as if I was leaving her in the aliens' hands. I was thankful the machine hadn't made Adan. Just contemplating it made bile rise in my throat. I ran to the door to vomit, but the nausea passed quickly and I returned before I embarrassed myself.

I said firmly, "Whiroon, show me again how to use this box to remove the restraints."

I slid the box along the path the ghost hand showed me, and the restraints fell to the side.

"Careful, Mia there's little wires here." Luke pointed to barely visible filaments entering the man's neck.

"Is she still out?"

"Yes. Do him first in case we make a mistake."

"Whiroon, how do I remove these wires that I'm looking at without damaging anyone or alerting anyone, except my crew."

Again my ghostly hand appeared and I had to squint to make the hand movements clear.

I said, "There's a panel there that looks like part of the table but it wants me to push it up with two fingers. It's showing a small spot of green amid pulsing orange, which makes me think if I screw it up, I really screw it up."

Luke said, "Wait a second. I have some questions."

Hendricks said, "Mia, ask if we can move the equipment without losing power to it."

He leaned over my shoulder and I suddenly felt naked. A hot flush covered my face as I considered I'd stood here naked for a few minutes in front of all of them. I hadn't been thinking of them as men but as monkeys. My flush grew hotter as I considered what they probably thought of me. I pulled the sheet tighter, crossing my arms over my breasts and leaning away.

"Get away from her," Adan said, pulling Hendricks back.

All of the monkeys stopped and stared.

Adan flushed, saying gruffly, "Give her some space to work."

He was naked as was Luke, and the monkeys suddenly seemed threatening. I hadn't been paying attention to them but to the alien devices and their nakedness had been hard to see among the clutter of equipment and odd lighting, but now it seemed glaring.

"You need a gun," I said.

He lifted any eyebrow, glancing around.

"You need a gun!" I repeated louder.

Hendricks backed away, offering his machine gun to Adan.

"You okay?" Luke asked.

"I'm... You're defenseless. Get a gun."

"I'm not defenseless, but fine.

"We're all on the same team here," Hendricks said.

I nodded and tried to smile but I really really wanted Luke and Adan armed.

"Just do it," I said tightly to Luke.

Hendricks said, "Finian, Getty, give Lewis and Melton your uniforms and guns and then help load up the houfts. I'll have more gear sent out."

"I'm on it already," Jay said. "Mia, your heart rate is really elevated. Take a few deep breaths. Let's just get our people out and then you can take a few minutes outside to catch your breath."

I'm fine," I said tightly. "I would like some clothes though."

"Crane, give her your—"

"I can wait," I interrupted Hendricks "I don't want to wear his clothes. Let's get this shit out of this poor guy's head."

Luke said, "Whiroon told me that the table has a trigger there that can dust Hifis. Hiff can see in a different spectrum, and don't even think about it, Mia. We can get lights and glasses to see in it too. But be careful touching anything because this stuff is made for Hiff and will have control pads that we can't see.

"Those filaments are feeding him Hifis chemicals to allow them to dust him at will. They're making him a sort of pseudo Hifis so they can operate and he'll recover, but he has no control over it, they do. He might have enough to bring him back. I don't think we should remove it yet."

Jay said, "Our specialists are headed to you. Let's see if we can bring him to Olympus."

"I can't just leave her like this!"

Jay said, "It's the best thing to do for her now."

"Whiroon, designate the human I'm looking at as Nika Sutak."

"Acknowledged."

"Can you tell me the condition of Nika Sutak, specifically what the devices attached to her are doing?"

"Negative."

"Is there a device here that can tell me what the devices attached to her are doing?"

"Affirmative."

I grit my teeth and said, "The health of Nika Sutak is a priority. Do nothing that might deactivate Nika Sutak. Show me the device that will tell me what the devices that are affecting or monitoring or interacting in any way with Nika Sutak are doing."

Luke said, "Nice and slow. We got this, Daffy."

25

Five hours later I stepped from the basement to stretch and breathe deeply of the cool night air.

I said, "Jay, if we don't get back soon, it's going to know its cover is blown if it doesn't already by the com silence."

"We need another few hours. Your roommates are safe and know to remain locked in their rooms. We have three agents in Adan's room. The apartments on either side of yours have armed agents waiting to go in. We're going to try to get you back in time, but this is the priority."

I taped the icon to see through Luke's x-com. He stood in a well-lit room with a group of men who were pouring over large printouts that I couldn't make heads or tails off although I knew it was computer code. I didn't interrupt them.

Adan joined me a few minutes later and pulled me into his lap. He leaned on the wall and I leaned on him. My tense muscles relaxed as he rubbed my back. He woke me by kissing my temple. I groaned and snuggled closer and he laughed ruefully as he said, "Sorry. I'd like to let you sleep but duty calls. The food's here though."

The street was lined with Jeeps. Two trucks with oversized metal boxes had parked right in the yard and one was being loaded with the table the dead private lay on. I was surprised I'd slept through the arrival. I wasn't that tired or even that hungry but I was thirsty. I willingly followed Adan back inside.

The room was now lit with a reddish glow. I accepted the eyeglasses I was offered and put them on before taking a water bottle from a box of them beside the door. I drank the entire thing and finished two more before my thirst was sated.

Adan said, "You should've said you were thirsty. They carry supplies with them."

"I'm fine. Where do you want me?" I asked the room at large.

Men and women wearing white hazmat suits were examining the room.

Jasmine smiled at me over her shoulder, waving me forward. "Here, if you have a minute. Ask what these marks signify and what made them and how long ago, please."

She was crouched over the remains of a pair of jack rabbits. A tech beside her was carefully vacuuming up dust from the floor.

I said, "It looks as if they were trying to Hifis the rabbits."

Jasmine pointed at a dark swath in the rabbit's fur.

I squinted at it, taking a minute to find and tap the button that said record and forward to Lab Three.

"Whiroon, what am I looking at?"

Whiroon said, "*Lepus californicus,* American desert hare, Black Tailed Jack Rabbit, four point two one pounds, male, deceased. Indicated mark probable result of restraints. Unable to determine cause of death."

"When did it die?"

"Unknown. Sample required for more in-depth analysis."

Jasmine pointed to the base of the ear, and I squinted at it. Black marks that I hadn't thought a thing of became tunnels that I knew were tiny pinpricks.

I said, "You have very good eyes. Whiroon, what am I looking at?"

"Puncture marks. Distinct patterning, probable cause diog. Further testing required to confirm diagnosis."

I knew the diog was the machine that injected Hifis-like chemicals. I'd spent the last few hours learning about every machine in the room.

I said, "Why would they want to control it?" I'd been asking Jasmine, but Whiroon answered.

"Common procedure to ensure Hifis adaption."

I said, "Can you estimate how many Hirsit have failed to adapt by the amount of dust on the floor?"

"Rough estimate.... No known positive adaptation."

Jasmine said, "They can't adapt but keep trying?"

I said, "Show me the dust you collected."

Jasmine said, "There's lots of dirt mixed in."

"I can see the dirt if we spread it out on something."

The tech said, "It isn't a priority. I can get it sifted and weighed and send you the information."

I said, "Whiroon, what causes the adaptation to fail?"

"Unknown. Suspected error in original formulation applied to Hirsit."

Sweat sprang up on my palms.

Jasmine said, "It sounds amused."

I'd thought so too and grabbed her arm hard.

Her eyes widened and she whispered, "Is it... doing something?"

I said, "Whiroon, are you sentient?

"Gertigi class ships are not allowed to be sentient."

I shivered at the anger in the reply.

Jay said, "Drop it, Mia," but he needn't have. I knew I was treading dangerously.

I said, "Whiroon, ignore any question that would comprise your function or clash with your programing."

"Acknowledged."

The calm machine-like quality had returned.

I said, "Thank you for your help."

"Acknowledged."

The reply was definitely said in softer tone.

I said, "I like you, Whiroon."

Jay said hurriedly, "Make no offers of assistance. Don't humanize it. Our actions will need to speak for us."

"Understood." I said, "Jasmine, what can I do to help you?"

Jasmine bit her lip and took a deep trembling breath. "You're a good friend, Mia. We'll figure out how to free human Hifis and keep our DNA from being artificially manipulated and save all of our friends."

Jay said, "That's enough chatter, get back to work."

I could practically feel Whiroon's tension and knew we were skirting dangerously close to programing that would make it react in ways it didn't wish too. I was certain that it was sentient despite the prohibition against it.

I said, "Jasmine, did you examine the Hiff?"

"Just in passing. Hiff are Doctor Jenner's specialty."

"Can you find out if the eyes are the same for Houft and Hiff? The two Hiff I've seen have been at least fiss. Granted I've only seen two of them but the one at Olympus had five radio dots. This one had two. If one form is Hirsit and the other is Hiff, I think it isn't Hirsit at all but Geromi or something else. The Hirsit form would be his second one, with the original form a Hiff. Not the other way around. Can you find out what spectrum it can see in when it's that flat shape?"

"Yes. But what makes you think it's the real shape?"

"It can change its appendage length in both forms. Only Geromi change the Hirsit form appendage length. Grot can shift appendage size but not in Hirsit forms. It's possible we misunderstand the significance of the number of radio dots and it has another form but maybe it doesn't. Maybe Hiff are a type of Geromi. I don't think Houft can see in the spectrum that the controls are in because these ones here had glasses to use, so why are the controls in that spectrum?"

"Maybe grot see in that spectrum like cats."

"The table would be awkward for a grot to use, so I don't think controls are meant for it. Zeus has the same sort of surfaces and we know it can manipulate those tentacles. It just seems logical that the creatures with the tentacles can see and use the hidden controls. Houft practically have to be an engineered form. Most of them have just the one dot. The original Hirsit form and the engineered Houft form. Why not engineer in the eyesight necessary to use the devices unless you don't want them to use it?"

"True, but maybe the forms are given as training progresses?"

"I agree that it's likely, but my point is that the natural ability to see in that spectrum is lacking in most of the Hirsit we have."

"Cats are Earth animals that can see in different spectrums."

"True," I said and slumped. I'd been sure I was onto something.

Adan said, "I think we need to have another chat with Bill."

I'd forgotten Bill had a Nuhoah form, and I frowned thoughtfully as I considered.

I said, "Bill and Bob both have Nuhoah forms. I saw Bob make his Hirsit arm longer. Maybe he isn't really Hirsit either but Geromi.

Jasmine said, "I'll mention your theory, and we'll retest vision on all of them."

I said, "I haven't asked Zeus about Hiff or Geromi since I got the new coms, and I don't think I should. At least not until we know more. His response in the past has been to say unauthorized but it was clipped and hurried. Maybe he can't speak about the higher ranks without triggering safety protocols like we would trigger if we asked for clearance to read documents above our grade."

Adan said, "I'm forwarding this conversation to Jay. Don't ask it about anything with more dots than we have."

I said, "I wonder if this new dot would be gold color if I took the form?"

"Don't," Adan said hurriedly.

His flush was both guilty and worried. I narrowed my eyes at him.

He said, "You don't want to know."

"I do now..."

He wrinkled his nose at me. "I asked and there's a ninety-nine percent chance of catastrophic mis-adjustment resulting in deactivation. When Zeus said the Houft here couldn't take a rabbit form, he meant it. One chance out of hundred is terrible odds."

"I did it. Maybe humans have better odds."

"That was the human rate and that was an optimistic estimate. There's no known successful adaptation, except for you."

Sweat sprang up on my brow.

"Don't do it again," he said gruffly.

I nodded.

Jasmine said, "We've upped the survival rate for Hifis considerably. We only had one death in the last batch of fifty."

"That's great news!" I said enthusiastically.

"It is but it's also bad news. People who've had minimal to no exposure to artificial sweeteners, certain medicines, and caffeine have a much higher chance of surviving because of the type and strength of phosphodiesterase enzymes on covalent bonds. This is a genetic trait, a change to your DNA that happens in utero that as far as we know can't be altered. We can test for it and if it's present, we believe your chances of survival would be much greater, but we can't help those without it.

"Persons possessing the correct bonds can lower their chances of successful adaptation by taking certain medicines, unbalanced blood sugars, and a myriad of other ways. But without those bonds to begin with, you're basically doomed. I'd die if exposed to Hifis." She waved at the empty space where the tables had been. "But they have other forms of it and maybe we can make a vaccine."

I said, "I want my sister tested."

Jasmine said, "I'll see what I can do. The testing is expensive and won't be revealed until we know more. This is all new information, and we need to be certain our findings are correct before the general populace hears about it and acts on the information."

Adan said, "Your worried about food manufactures? You should be worried about lives!"

"Those manufactures employ millions of people. We have billions of dollars invested. We need to be certain. I can assure you, it isn't at all comforting to know I won't survive their return. Imagine the panic of the people who find out they'll die if exposed to Hifis. If we take away their hope, what have they got?"

Adan said, "Imagine the people who will die needlessly because they didn't know to avoid foods that might hurt their chances."

"The president is aware of the problem and will be addressing it but in an orderly manner. Who does it hurt if the switch in food production and medicine usage is handled gradually enough that the people can keep their jobs, eat the foods that are already produced and begin weaning off of harmful medicines? Or would you rather see them riot and starve?"

"No one if we have enough time to switch, but it could kill them if we don't."

I said, "Civil unrest is more likely to kill them. I'll ask for the president to put out a general service announcement that they believe good health will positively affect your chances to survive Hifis infection.

We can tell them to eat healthier without hurting anything."

Jasmine said, "I'm certain they're already working on it."

She turned the dead rabbit and held up a paw. "Ask Zeus what made these marks, please."

26

An hour later Luke interrupted my discussion with Whiroon on how long it had taken to set up the equipment in the room.

Luke said, "I think we've reworked the message system enough that you should test it out. Zeus needs your permission to change the smart-x features already in place for your x-coms. I have some volunteers here who've been cleared to attempt to get updated coms, but before they attempt to shift to one of the alien forms, I want to be sure Zeus can update. I get an access denied message when I ask."

I said, "I told Zeus to ignore any questions that could comprise its function or clash with its programing."

"Then it shouldn't hurt to ask," Luke said.

"Is it urgent? Or can I finish here?"

"Finish there. I think you can activate my new smart-x program by just telling it to use the ones I'm using. I was able to do everyone's, except yours. It should make it easier for you to report. When you have the coms in battle mode everything you see will be sent to our mainframes and then on to the appropriate division. It will be recording around you and sending that too.

"I hate this idea... I'll be standing around naked. And what if I forget to turn it off?"

"I'll see if I can make it blur us or use an avatar."

"Give me a way to push urgent discoveries to the correct division head. I mean a way that ignores the protocols in place for that. If I see something that I think Jasmine or whoever should know about, I don't want her to wait for it to be sent if I think it's urgent."

"That's already a feature. I'll walk you through it when we get a minute and anything you don't like I'll change. I'll work on having it turn off automatically, but I don't have time to do that right now. It will probably be a few days. For now, I'll just have Zeus remind you every hour that you have battle coms on."

"Fine," I said grumpily. My modesty wasn't worth someone's life, but I hated the idea that strangers would be watching me run around naked. "Whiroon, activate Luke Melton's battle coms program."

"Activating...Activated."

It took me a moment to notice the change and I stood to examine the room, playing with the new features as I did so.

It reminded me of a video game HUD.

He'd left instructions that disappeared when I flicked them and in minutes I was able to make the information displayed brighter or dimmer by staring at it and pretending to turn a dial. He'd added in a range display and a collapsible information panel that told me who was receiving the information both actively and passively, which reminded me that I had an entirely new radio channel to worry about.

I said, "What are we doing about that other channel?"

"Nothing yet since only you can access it. Jay is looking for someone to monitor that channel. Until then, don't do anything."

"Monitor it... couldn't Whiroon do that and report?"

"That's just it, he needs to report to someone of the right rank. That info you hear is info for an admiral's ears only—or so he informed us."

"Yeah... but I can order him to tell anyone I want, can't I?"

"What if you're hearing his ship?"

"Oh..."

Goosebumps rose on my arms as I considered that. If that was Whiroon's mothership that I was hearing it would be dangerous in ways I couldn't even imagine for him to hear it too.

"Just be careful, Mia."

I said, "Whiroon, crew segment Jay Baurr will be assigning a new segment to monitor the new com channel. This segment's purpose is to translate and record that information. I don't want to listen to it myself right now. Please render all assistance."

"Understood, Purfit," Whiroon said.

I shrugged at Luke who grimaced at me.

I said, "They'll know something's up when they realize they can't hear their segments here."

"I don't think they'll know for sure why this is a dead zone. We have teams out looking for the other grots that Zeus thinks brought in the equipment. I think we should make a sweep around the entire perimeter and I'm laying that out now. We really need more personnel who have these same coms."

"I agree but the success rate... can't we use the equipment we took from here?"

"Yes, and Zeus can give us equipment but he doesn't have unlimited stores. We need to be able to manufacture it ourselves. Our priority needs to be keeping Zeus safe and by extension, you."

"Have they figured out who the human informant is?"

"Not yet."

"How many people knew she was going on that flight?"

"Anyone who wanted to look. The rooster was right on the wall."

"But who knew she'd be practicing landings there?"

"I don't think they had to know that. Is all they had to do was watch her helicopter when it lifted off and make it to her landing site before she took off again. Or hell, maybe they have a way to force it to land."

I said, "I'm supposed to go up with her Saturday. I bet she'd be willing to take me if we don't tip her off."

"Are you crazy?"

"She'd probably take me to their base."

"Exactly! That's nuts!"

Jay said, "I have to agree."

"Who asked you?"

"Your battle com did. Mission planning is me."

I said, "Well, that needs tweaking, Luke. That was a private conversation."

Luke said, "He's right. Mission plans need to be vetted by professionals, which we're not!"

I said, "Fine. Loop them in. But think about it. It takes me up in our helicopter. We can put whatever we want on the copter. She doesn't know I have the x-coms."

"You think she doesn't. It isn't the same thing at all."

I ignored the interruption. "She flies me wherever and our teams follow. I was able to order the Hirsit here to stand down. I might be able to order other ones too. But let's say I can't. They'll want to know what I know. They aren't going to kill me right away."

Adan snapped, "You think they won't, and it isn't the same thing at all!"

"They don't know I'm Hifis—"

"Another assumption," Adan said angrily.

"My point is, I'm not helpless or easy to kill."

"My point is, you're an idiot! They could have a working ship and fly away with you! No! You aren't doing it."

"I could do it," Luke said thoughtfully.

"No way!" I snapped, flushing as Adan snickered.

"See how crazy it sounds?"

I said, "It might not try to take him."

"That's hardly a downside," Adan said dryly, and my flush grew hotter.

Jay said, "I've ordered you transport back to your rooms. I don't know if they'll approve this mission or not, but you need rest anyway."

"Like I'll be able to sleep with it right next door," Adan said.

Jay said, "It had no weapons, and the rooms were thoroughly searched. It can't break down your door."

"You think it can't," Adan muttered.

I rolled my eyes. "It can't and even if it could we have backup right next door and can fight it." I stepped closer to rest my head on his shoulder. "I'd really like to get out of here."

"Two hours isn't much time to rest," Adan said grumpily but he took my hand and headed for the door.

Outside was remarkably quiet. The jeeps and trucks had left, except for three. A driver brought us back and dropped us in front of our dorm.

We let ourselves in and the men who'd been in our room climbed out the window.

"Battle coms off," I whispered and pulled off my borrowed clothes to hug Adan.

I meant it to be a quick hug but his kiss made me forget everything except the feel of his lips on mine.

He walked us away from the window, and broke from the kiss to say, "Luke could be back at any minute."

"Ah huh," I murmured as I began to remove his pants.

He was naked and pulling me down to the bed when we heard the door beep.

"Eep!" I exclaimed as I yanked Adan's blanket around us, and he laughed as he rolled us over.

"Sorry," Luke whispered.

Adan said, "Don't worry about it just throw her a clean sweatsuit from my drawer."

"I could rat up and sleep in the closet?" Luke offered.

I said, "Don't be silly. We were just changing. I have no idea whose clothes I was wearing. I really want a shower, but I guess it needs to wait."

"Get some sleep, *mi amor.*" Adan helped me pull his sweatshirt on and tucked my head beneath his chin.

He hadn't dressed and I had no pants, but he kept his hands above the covers. I was both relieved and disappointed.

Luke picked up our scattered clothes and stuffed them into a laundry bag then went into the closet to change. He emerged dressed in BDU, put another sweatsuit on the night table with a stack of hooah bars, and laid down in his bed.

I figured he planned to stay up and relaxed against Adan perfectly content.

A knock on the door woke me.

Adan kissed my cheek quickly then pulled on a pair of sweats to answer it.

Sinclair said, "I'm making, eggs. Want some?"

"We'll eat later, thanks."

Adan closed the door and leaned against it, whispering, "He's pale as a ghost. I'm going to grab a quick shower."

He grinned invitingly, and I threw the pillow at him.

"Tease," I muttered as I yanked the blanket over my head.

Adan had left the door ajar and I could hear Felipe and Sinclair.

Adan's laughter made me grin, and I closed my eyes to stretch out. The bed was warm and comfortable. I wasn't at all worried about the alien in my bedroom. She'd either attack or play along. Either way worked for me.

Luke yanked the blanket from my head.

"What time is it?" I grumbled.

"Time to get up."

"Don't want to," I said and pulled him down to hug him. He laughed as I forced him down to lay my head on his chest.

"You make a good pillow too."

He kissed my forehead, resting his head against mine as he dropped my sweatpants on my chest, making me giggle. His eyes softened and he gave me a real grin.

"I love you so much," I said as I brought our clasped hands to my lips.

"Does Adan know that?" Stephanie asked bitterly.

Luke started and half rose.

I pulled him back down.

"What Adan knows about me isn't any of your business." I kissed Luke on the lips and sat to slide my pants on beneath the blankets.

She continued to glare. I brushed past her, turning back to blow him a kiss.

He laughed and stretched out, crossing his legs and putting his arms behind his head.

I went to use the bathroom. Adan was exiting the shower when I finished. Stephanie was still standing in their doorway.

I wondered if they'd been arguing. I hadn't heard them at all over Sinclair and Felipe talking with Lana who'd just gotten up.

"Excuse me," Adan said to Stephanie and then in a laughing voice to Luke, "Last one out makes the bed."

Lana said, "Steph, we really need to talk. You can't keep ignoring me! This is important!"

I headed to the shower and used Adan's soap. When I was done, I put his sweats back on.

326

"Battle com's on." I was hoping Sutak would exit our bedroom. She was probably hoping I'd enter so she could press me for details on Whiroon—or attack me with the door locked.

27

Jay whispered in my head, *"They've tentatively okayed the mission. Go to reveille like normal then report to hanger five. Ignore your orders on the laptop."*

I sent back acknowledgment and headed to my room. Adan trailed me. The rest of them stared at us nervously, except for Stephanie who was glaring. Her face was bright red, and I thought it was anger at me and Luke and not fear of the alien, which worried me anew how obsessed she was with him.

Sutak exited the room right as we reached it. I grinned at her as I brushed past.

"I'll be right out. Give me three minutes to dress and we can go!" I called back as I ran to our closet. Adan leaned on my bedroom door and said, "Cool boards. Whose is whose?"

Sinclair said, "Mines the one with the devil on it."

"Mine's the flowered one," Lana said, "I ordered you one just like it but with pink and red flowers, Steph."

My battle coms were showing the room and transmitting their voices, but the focus was on Sutak who was examining the skateboards hanging on the wall. All of our boards now hung beside the television. I wondered who'd hung them and how they'd gotten them so fast.

Sinclair said, "Which is yours?"

Adan said, "Tweety. It's a long story."

"No it's not," Luke muttered, and Adan huffed in exasperation. "Fine, then it's a private story!"

Luke laughed.

Sutak said, "I don't have one."

The hair on my arms rose. She sounded different, nervous and worried and childlike somehow.

Lana said, "We can take turns. I've never done it and am sure to suck."

Luke took his down and said, "This is the only important move." He did an ollie, and Lana groaned.

Luke laughed. "I'm kidding. The only important move is landing on your feet."

I exited the bedroom, and Luke kicked his board up to catch it and laid it on the table.

"Good to go?" Luke asked.

Felipe exhaled loudly, jerking the door open. He hadn't said a word and his smile was ghastly as he held the door for Lana. She gave him a hard glare, and he licked his lips, his eyes darting to Sutak and then Adan.

Felipe said to Sutak, "Are you leading us there again today?"

I was watching Sutak and knew the second she realized we were onto her. Her expression was bewildered. She cocked her head as if listening. I was guessing she didn't know the proper reply and was waiting for her handler to tell her. Her fists clenched and teeth showed in a silent snarl, and I figured she'd Houft up any second.

On my coms, Adan said, *"We're blown."*

I grabbed Luke's skateboard and swung—and Stephanie hit me, making the blow hit Sutak's shoulder and not her head.

"She doesn't know!" Lana screamed as I lowered the board to block Stephanie's kick. I stared at her in shock for the second it took her to knock the board from my hand, and she kicked me again as she grabbed my arm, pivoting and throwing me to the tabletop.

Uh oh, I thought in a corner of my mind. Her moves were quick and I knew she'd had training. We'd just begun to learn close quarters combat in basic. I'd seen real professionals in hand-to-hand combat fight, and I knew Stephanie had way more training then me by the ease and quickness with which she'd flipped me.

Adan and Sinclair were fighting with Sutak. Adan had grabbed one of her arms and Sinclair the other. Sutak snarled and snapped at them, but she didn't Houft up. Felipe grabbed Lana's arm, pulling her back from Stephanie and inadvertently blocking the door, keeping the armed men trying to enter it out.

Lana continued to yell, "She doesn't know!" as Stephanie and I rolled over the table and crashed into the floor hard enough to knock the wind from me.

Luke grabbed Stephanie's arm, and she elbowed him hard in the face.

"It's Sutak, not Mia!" he yelled, and I saw the recognition and new resolve in her eyes. She'd heard him and understood but was going to kill me anyway. Her grip on my neck tightened. She banged my head against the ground, grinding the arm she knelt on into the floor. If I wasn't Hifis it might have killed me, but I pried one of her hands loose as Luke grabbed her and threw her, saving her eyesight because I missed my swipe by a second. I sprang up to grab at her, and Luke yanked me back.

"Down on the ground!" one of the men in the doorway barked.

I knelt and laced my hands behind my back, glaring at Stephanie who looked smug and angry.

"You're the traitor," she snapped.

I knew she didn't believe it.

She shook her hair from her eyes as she knelt like I was and turned her glare on Luke. "You're fucking an alien!"

Luke said, "You're a fucking idiot! I'm gay."

Her mouth dropped open and despite my anger or maybe because of it, I laughed. "You should see your face, skank!"

Adan said, "Are you okay? You're neck..."

He turned to glare at Stephanie, and Luke grabbed him in a hard embrace.

"You're fucking him? Jesus, I should've known. You were always hanging out with Milo and his crew."

One of the soldiers yanked her up and zip-tied her hands.

Luke said, "She isn't helping Sutak."

A hot flush crawled up my chest. I'd forgotten the damned alien.

She'd remained in her Sutak shape but was hissing and snapping at the men who were carrying her out.

"Sutak is an alien?" Stephanie said, sounding shocked.

"I thought you said they'd all been warned, Jay!" I said angrily.

Stephanie glared at me over her shoulder then turned to examine all of the men present, likely wondering which one I was talking to.

Jay, said, *"They were. We texted all of them and they all acknowledged receipt."*

I said, "You knew, you fucking psychopath!"

Lana said from the hall, "She wouldn't listen to me last night. She was pretending to sleep with her headphones in, and when I handed her my phone, she batted it across the room. It wasn't like I could yell the information with it right next door, and then she got the text telling us what we were supposed to do, but I'm not sure if she read it or not..."

"I didn't," Stephanie said quickly.

The soldier pulling her up, said, "You acknowledged an official communication without reading it... I seriously doubt that. We know they have humans working with them. Come clean now and you won't be executed. You might even be rewarded if the information you give us is good."

Her face drained of color. I think mine did too. I'd forgotten the new severity of our laws. If she were convicted of treason, she'd be shot.

Luke said, "It's just like her to do something like that, isn't it, Mia?"

I smirked at her, and she bit her lip. I let her sweat, enjoying the reversal. I could have her killed and she knew it.

Her eyes narrowed and lips pursed. "Mia, you seriously aren't going to let them arrest me, are you?"

"Like you seriously weren't trying to kill me?"

Her face paled even more, and she licked her lips again, her gaze darting to Luke and Adan and then the soldiers. "I thought you were attacking Sutak! That she'd been the target all along." She turned back to me, glaring hotly. "Why in the hell would anyone target you. You're nobody!"

Adan said, "I fucking hate you!"

Stephanie gave him a sexy pout, lowering her eyes and shaking her head to get her hair to fall over her shoulder.

I wondered if she'd practiced the look.

She said, "You know I didn't know. I wouldn't have hit her if I had. I didn't know you and Luke—that the three of you were a couple. I have no problems with that, I'd share him too if that's what it took."

I said, "Jesus fucking Christ! This is serious and you're still flirting! You're unbelievable!"

Stephanie said, "But I'm not involved with this alien shit."

The soldier holding her arm pursed his lips at me.

"She probably didn't know," I said grudgingly.

Hendricks said, "Let her go," and I flushed again as I looked at the door. I hadn't noticed his arrival because I was having a juvenile spat.

I said, "Steph, just so we're clear here, if you attack me again, I'm not going to let it go."

"Any time, bitch."

Luke pinched the bridge of his nose. "Just let this go, please."

I had no idea if he was talking to me or her but supposed it didn't matter.

Hendricks said, "Do you need medical attention? Our medic can see you in your room."

"I'm fine."

He stepped into the room to tilt my head and examine my neck. "Get some ice on that right away and it should fade quickly."

I stomped to our freezer, dumped the ice tray into a handful of paper towels, and headed to my room.

Adan said, "Use ours. They'll want to search yours again."

Hendricks said, "And leave the laptop. You'll be issued a new one."

Stephanie said, "What did it want with us?"

"We'll find out. Sweeny, uncuff her and take her statement. Report her infractions. Her platoon leader can handle this."

"Yes, sir," the man cutting Stephanie loose said.

She cast me a last furious glance as he led her from the room.

I peeked into the hall. Our roommates were being led away. Armed men were herding our classmates to the stairs at the opposite end of the hall.

Hendricks closed the door to the room. "I saw the recordings and I'm not convinced of her innocence. She seemed serious about strangling you even after she was told you weren't involved. She might have just been scared and focused on the fight and not the people around her, but I don't like it."

Luke said, "Stephanie has absolutely no sense when it comes to getting what she wants. She hates Mia because she thought Mia and I were involved. I think she just took this opportunity to hurt her. I don't like her, but I don't want her to pay with her life because I never told her the truth about me."

I turned away to shift to my cat.

Adan helped me free of my clothing and picked me up to cuddle me. His worried gaze stayed on Luke. We both knew Luke felt guilty about Stephanie and his guilt would be worse if we pressed the issue. If I said she'd have killed me regardless, he'd feel even worse, and now I wasn't sure of what I'd seen. I might have been projecting or misunderstood. An expression I'd seen for seconds seemed like a flimsy reason to pursue it. And truthfully, I didn't want her death on my conscience either.

I tapped the button to make my texts audible and typed, "She'll stop now, Luke. I'm okay and you don't need to feel bad about any of it. Our lives are none of her business. She needs to learn that she can't have everything she wants."

Hendricks said laughingly, "I'll make sure your platoon leader teaches her that. Should I get her transferred from this room?"

"We can live with her," Adan said.

"How long do you need?" Hendricks asked me.

"Just a few more minutes," Adan said before I could answer.

I nodded agreement, and Hendrick's said, "Be in the main room dressed and ready to go in ten."

He laughed when I saluted with my paw and let himself from Adan's room.

Adan kissed the top of my head then set me down to grab a broom from his closet and began to sweep the floor.

"Maybe we should ask for a different roommate," Luke said worriedly.

Adan said, "I don't give a damn about her. It makes no difference to me where she sleeps. I bet they move her anyway just to be on the safe side, but asking for her to be moved will make them think we can't control ourselves or that we'll expect special treatment and I don't want to limit our chance to be assigned to Zeus if they decide to use him as an actual ship and not just for information."

Luke rubbed his face hard and nodded. When he dropped his hands he said, "We think he can fit a crew of eight aboard but the space behind the forward bulkhead might be equipment."

Adan said, "We should just ask it."

I shook my head.

Luke said, "She's right. We have no idea what Zeus will do if we breach the interior. It's better to use him this way."

It amused me that Luke was calling Zeus him now and not it.

The boys left the room so that I could shift back and dress.

Hendricks examined me quickly when I appeared, nodding slightly as if he was happy with what he saw and gesturing me to the door. "Let's go see what Sutak has to say for itself."

"Can we call it something else? It gives me the creeps to call it that, and how is Sutak? The real Sutak?"

"We'll be heading there after we talk to Operative S. The doctors want your help running a few more tests, and then we'll try to release her from that damned table."

Adan said, "And Private Undine?"

"Has been declared officially dead and will be cremated when the autopsy is complete."

Tears filled my eyes. "Damn it! I'd hoped Zeus could help him."

"He was DOA. Zeus confirmed it."

Luke said, "I'd like to go ahead if you guys can handle interviewing Operative S without me."

"Sure." Adan gave Luke a quick hug. "Are you okay?"

"Pissed but I'm always pissed after dealing with Stephanie. I need to talk to Zeus in person."

Jay said, "I have all the supplies you requested ready and waiting."

I glanced at the icon that would tell me who was listening or watching us and had to hide my grimace at the amount. Three hundred people had just witnessed this embarrassing adolescent encounter and they all probably thought we were a threesome. I kept forgetting the battle coms were on despite the tiny flicker of light that appeared to float as far from me as the room allowed.

Squinting at the flicker the barest amount would make the HUD pop up and I scrolled through it quickly to see the latest reports.

I said, "Luke, make us a dead spot to change in and make the showers and bathrooms auto turn off coms."

"Already working on it," Luke said absently.

The world turned red for a moment warning me the next thing I heard was private, and Adan said, *'Let's leave him be for a bit. Send him notes instead. He's trying to hide it from us because he feels bad and knows we'll feel bad that he does. She really messed with his head more than I realized. I'm really worried, but hovering over him isn't going to help.*

'I'm not sure if he just wants space from us or if he really needs to work with Zeus, but he was tense as hell when I hugged him. He wasn't ready to be so outed. I think we should just let him work.'

I was really worried now too but I forced a smile, nodded, and resumed reading the reports as we walked to the car, which was harder to do than it sounded, and I made Adan snort with annoyance and then worry as I bumped into walls and doorways.

"Sorry, reading and I need to practice it."

Hendricks snorted with laughter, and I rolled my eyes. "I meant walking while doing it."

"Uh huh."

Adan chuckled and even Luke smiled for a second.

He got into a different car than us, and I tried not to let it worry me.

28

Dawe greeted us as we entered, holding out a hand for us to shake, saying, "It hasn't said a word. X-rays have revealed what we believe to be a radio dot in the right shoulder blade. The dot doesn't trigger metal detectors like yours do, so it's probably made of something different. I'm hoping you can get it to speak to you.

Jay said, "You're cleared to reveal your x-coms to it."

Armed men and women stood in clumps in the hallway, keeping a close eye on the white-coated men and women who hurried from one partitioned alcove to another with a sense of urgency that made me nervous.

The walls were thin enough that I caught snatches of talk, but I didn't understand it other to know they were speaking of biology.

Dawe led us to a partition, and I halted to examine the room. Operative S sat on a metal chair, shackled by her hands and feet to a metal table inside a chain link cage. Four men carrying assault rifles and incendiary grenades were spaced around the cage, but I wasn't paying them any attention.

I glared at Carr as he rose from one of the three seats facing the alien.

"What the hell is he doing here?"

Dawe said nervously, "He's the expert on—"

"I don't care if he's the smartest man you ever met! I won't work with him! He should be in jail somewhere!"

Carr said, "I appreciate your sentiments, but I wasn't aware of the gross misconduct of the guards. I assure you, I was investigated quit thoroughly."

"My fucking sentiments! Are you kidding me? And what's with the injured tone? You did it to yourself! I had nothing to do with it." I turned away from him to glare at Adan who'd remained silent. "There's no way he didn't know. Either they're lying about investigating or they're so incompetent that we can't possibly trust them with our security."

Jay said, "They investigated and I'm sending you the reports. He was perfectly aware that torture was being used but unaware that the guards had begun torturing for their own reasons."

"I can't fucking work with him!"

My vision flashed red, warning me were speaking privately. Jay said, *"He's an expert and like it or not he gets results. We have to work with men and women we dislike, and his help might make a difference. So suck it up and get on with it."*

I whirled back to the cage, but Adan dragged me backward. "No fucking way is she going in there with him."

Jay said, "I'm watching and at the first indication that anything hinky is up, I'll wake the gods."

Carr said, "I'm not the danger here."

I ignored him and pushed the chairs apart to pull one directly in front of Operative S.

"Do you have a name?" I asked.

She glared at me and it made me both angry and sad. I hoped I'd get to see the real Sutak glare again. That this creature had stolen her away and dared wear her face made my hands clench in anger.

I stood and unzipped my BDU. Lines appeared by her eyes. I knew she was puzzled. I pulled off my t-shirt and her eyes widened, and she jerked backward.

I was wearing a sports bra that clearly revealed my x-coms. She leaned forward to stare at them.

"They're real," I said dryly. *"Whiroon* is under my command."

She made an abortive attempt to cross her arms. "You're lying. Humans lie."

"Humans lie but you know I'm not lying."

"It must be a lie!"

"Because you don't want it to be true or because you're afraid to hope that it is? This building is just a temporary holding cell. You'll never escape from the cell where we're bringing you and you know that's true because the Geromi we've got in captivity are still in captivity.

"If the Geromi possessed a way to escape us, they would have. Those Geromi have been written off by their fellows. The Geromi directing you doesn't care about them. It cares about *Whiroon.*"

I let her stew on that a moment and said, "Battle coms off. Carr, make sure we can't be heard by any means because I don't want word reaching Zeus."

"One minute," he said and stepped into the hallway.

Adan sat beside me and opened his BDU to take off his t-shirt.

Her lips narrowed and compressed, and she tried again to cross her arms but the chains wouldn't let her.

We stared at each other until Carr returned.

I said, "All clear?"

"Yes."

"Whiroon is helping us, but you already know that. You must be aware that there are factions in your ranks. What the Geromi have planned for us is wrong. What they've done to the Hirsit is a tragedy and we'd help them if we could."

She said, "That is a lie. What humans do to each other is an abomination. You should be destroyed completely. Whiroon is not helping you. Whiroon is helping itself. He knows that to mix your *Dersct* with ours is an abomination. You will sully us and make us as evil as you are, unable to bond, forgotten scraps of flesh."

I said, "That might be true and all the more reason you should cooperate with us. We don't want to mix our DNA with yours. Help us rid our world of Geromi, and you and all of your kind, including Whiroon, can leave here peacefully. We'll help you leave. Believe me, we want you gone."

Her gaze darted over us and she licked her lips but her voice was firm as she said, "If left to fester on this planet, you will destroy us. You must be assimilated if we are to survive."

Adan said, "So there's three factions. Ones who want to leave us alone, ones who want to use us, and ones who want to wipe us out. But you have to see how impossible it would be to assimilate us. We won't be contained in a small grouping. The segment who has us will be the segment that subjugates you all. Our knowledge will make it so despite whatever intentions the segment has when it assimilates us. Humans will never submit to slavery. We find the very idea of living as Hirsit do to be revolting. But if left alone we have neither the means nor motive to seek you out."

She frowned at him.

I said, "Battle coms on."

Her gaze jerked back to me and her mouth opened then closed as she stared at my x-coms.

I said, "Wiping us out would be evil and you know it. You came here. We didn't come to you. And while it's true that we're a violent race, it's also true that we love each other and we're learning to get along. If given time we might be able to master ourselves and live together peacefully. Large groups of us do it now with only small segments that chose differently, and we value that choice. We only revile it when it leads to violence against others of our kind."

Carr said, "Many of us keep the lesser smaller creatures in our homes and treat them kindly and make them as safe as we can. We fight among ourselves because we have segments who bond with nothing and no one, and those segments need to be stopped before they harm our planet or the beings that dwell on it. Sometimes fights between humans grow confused and large and do great damage, but most humans would live peacefully if left in peace."

"More of your segments than not are corrupted beyond saving."

She'd said it all in a rush as if it were a memorized response.

"Who are you to judge?" Adan asked angrily. "Your actions are corrupt, and by your own words you know it, and yet you do it. You lie and murder. You use our friendships against us. This body you're wearing was chosen to hurt us with our own affections."

She stared down at herself with a puzzled expression, saying, "It's just a shell."

"You have no right to it!"

I laid my hand on Adan's arm, and he snapped his mouth closed.

I said, "Is your true form just a shell? If I were to tivp that form and leave you this one would it be a small loss?"

She inhaled sharply and said, "You would unmake me?"

The tone reminded me that she was a young animal with no real comprehension.

I said, "Can you fly a helicopter?"

She pursed her lips but nodded.

"How did you learn to?"

Her face flushed and her eyes narrowed and darted about the room.

I said, "We won't teach you anything new. I have the tools to teach but not the disposition. You've seen us, so you know that I like some of my crewmates more than others, but I wouldn't do that to any of them, even Stephanie."

Adan snorted, and Carr's brow wrinkled.

I said, "Humans choose to learn or not. The effort is their own. How they live, who they live with, how they spend their time, is their own choice."

She said, "Learning is necessary for the good of the Geromi."

"But not your good."

"Ge—I—am the Geromi."

"I think you mean you will be someday if you serve them well. But if I destroy your body, there will be no part of you left for the Geromi."

She began to whimper, and I felt like a bully.

Adan said, "We won't do that. We can put you with your crewmates and you can live together untroubled by Geromi until they come to retrieve you."

I said, "You wish to obey, and they'll see that you've done as you were ordered to do. They'll have no reason to destroy your dersct. It will live on with them, and you will live on with your fellows. It's your duty to obey me. If the Hiff that sent you in didn't know about me, then that's on him, not you. You must obey me if I rank higher. You have no choice."

"But you can't be a Purfit. I can't obey a lie..."

She was so clearly confused that again I felt pity. She was smart enough to recognize the conundrum she found herself in but not smart enough to abandon a life of training.

"Don't!" Adan yelled as I shifted to my grot form.

She screamed, cowering away from me.

Adan snapped, "Goddamn it! Mia!"

I used my speech to text app to say, "Your name is now Sue. Tell me where Sue was trained to fly a helicopter."

The shivery feeling of falling apart remained until I shifted to my cat six minutes later.

Sue told use everything she was asked and the crowd watching and listening grew to over two thousand.

Stealing that radio dot and being able to hear that com signal had inadvertently given myself the highest rank Geromi had—I'd made myself a Purfit able to order all segments if I could catch them—or at least Sue believed it to be true.

I knew from the thoughtful weighing glances Carr was giving me that he was debating the wisdom of letting me try—or maybe worried I would.

Luke said, "This is the breakthrough we needed, Mia."

I typed, *'We still have to capture them all. They'll be prepared for me. This won't work again once they know I'm here.'*

"But now we know what we face."

'Twenty-six years until they return, if the fight between themselves doesn't hold them back. And if we don't stop the ones here, it won't matter if they return or not...'

Sue had been taught here on Earth. She'd been grown here and trained her entire life to be a spy in the military. Her form was a product of surgery, not Hifis. She wasn't Hifis at all but fully Hirsit wearing a human shell. According to her, there were four large enclaves of Hirsit, and numerous smaller settlements scattered around the globe. And for eighty years there were humans who knew it and were helping them.

I shifted back to human and dressed, hoping Luke had gotten the program running to blur me out.

Sue knew few names, but she knew how the Houft were being trained. It sickened me to hear it. She was a creature bred for war but with a gentle soul that had been twisted to hate. She hated with a fanatical passion but a sort of confusion that was heartbreaking. She hated because hating was the only thing that allowed her moments of peace with her family. Her rare moments of rest in the family burrow were clearly her driving force.

She loved them as I loved my pack. The similarities of our situation weren't lost on me.

Luke said, "We have more tools now and can copy them. Zeus is working with us on the coms and we have a rough prototype that might save the men from trying to get a grot form."

"*Don't,*" Adan whispered, and I gave him a wan smile.

He said, "You've done enough, risked enough. There's no need."

I brought our clasped hands to my lips.

We both knew that taking a Geromi, Nuhoah, or Hiff form might be the form that let the war end before it even began.

He said, "It won't matter in the long run. We'll still develop the weapons and tech, and they'll still come here. It won't take them long to change their protocols. You'd die for nothing."

He released my hand. "If I think you're going to do it, I'll do it first."

"I won't," I said instantly, and he smiled sadly as he leaned down to kiss me.

"I won't." I repeated against his lips and his relieved sigh misted my face.

"I love you so much," I whispered.

"Mia Sutton, will you marry me?"

I smiled against his neck and felt his body relax.

"I will," I said.

EPILOGUE

I nervously twisted my engagement ring and made myself stop.

Carr said, "This is a risk but if we do nothing, she'll remain in this condition—and likely die of it."

I didn't spare him a glance. I hated that he was even in the room. Every report that remotely involved Sutak was a priority for me. I likely knew more than he did about her condition. I examined all of the human machinery in the room and the doctors who waited to use it.

Carr had no machines just a notebook.

"Why the hell are you here?" I snapped.

"It will be invaluable to my research to speak with her immediately before she has time to consciously adjust. Initial reactions might tell us if she's been compromised."

"Fine! Just back the hell up! She doesn't need you looming over her!"

"Is everyone ready?"

Jasmine said, "We are. Mia, I can use the table if you prefer?"

I shook my head. "I have the best chance of being able to help if something goes wrong."

Jasmine pursed her lips but nodded. I wasn't certain that was true either. Whiroon would talk to anyone with the new coms wearing an AFAR medal that the ship had seen me pin to their collar.

The new coms were rough, a bulky black box worn at the waist, and not anywhere near as efficient as mine, but I thought in time they would be. They were made entirely by materials we developed, and we'd done that in days with Sue's help. Sue herself knew next to nothing about how her equipment worked but Zeus would answer if we knew the questions to ask it, and it happily answered in detail when asked about the words she told us. We'd found the loophole in its programing. Zeus couldn't volunteer restricted information, but it could answer when asked to clarify a definition.

I was sure there were tons of things Sue didn't know anything about, but she knew enough to keep us busy for a good long while. We were already planning attacks on the bigger compounds. We didn't know where they were exactly other than the details of foliage and climate that Sue knew, but we'd find them, and when we did, we'd have access to even more of their devices and tools that Zeus would happily teach us about.

My pack wouldn't be allowed on those missions, which was fine with me. School was our priority. I planned to keep shift free for nine months, not because I wanted to have a child but to prove to myself that I could. Adan professed that he didn't care, but I did. I wanted us to be a family someday, and if I could do it now, I could do it then and I'd be able to marry him with one less nagging worry.

I leaned down to kiss Sutak's brow and then slid my fingers along the table to release the diog. I could have used the diog to speak with her, but the thought gave me the willies. Making her aware enough to know these might be her final moments seemed the height of cruelty—and I was afraid she'd choose death over becoming Hifis.

The table made the faintest humming noise and red lights flickered along the outer edged. I hesitated, taking a few deep breaths.

I'd practiced the sequences that Zeus had told me would revive her. I knew what sections of the table to press, and my battle coms were also showing them to me, but I knew that the next button I pressed might kill her. She might be unrevivable and then my only choice would be a full Hifis injection. Trying to revive her without a full Hifis injection might kill her before I could inject her with Hifis.

She was one of the few who had a chance to survive but she'd also been given God knows what to keep her contained and cooperative. I knew what the compounds were all called and what they did but not how they would affect Hifis adaptation. The choice of treatment had been left to me.

I pressed the buttons.

THE END

About the Author

S.M. Savoy is an artist who lives and works on the family farm in New England alongside her husband, two grown children, and a very spoiled dog. Most days, when she isn't working on her art, she spends her time writing. An avid reader since childhood, she appreciates work in all genres and likes to mix it up a bit in her own work, writing romantic thrillers and paranormal romances under the *nom deplume* C. M. Conney.

Books by S. M. Savoy

***Valo**r, a Fantasy Series by S. M. Savoy*

When lightning irradiates Team Valor, led by Charlie Hayes, five professional video game players find themselves able to use the magic of their game characters. But there's no time to plan, practice, or recover from the lightning that transformed them. ISIS has kidnapped a squad of Marines and is beheading one soldier every eight hours. And Charlie's brother, Rick, is one of those Marines.

Valor
A Warrior's Fury
A Sun Priest's Magic
Beyond Valor
A Rogue's Passion
Hidden Nature
A Vow Unbroken

*Books in Related Series: **Return of the Fae***

Medieval England is a nightmare for a modern woman. Luckily for Jen Frey, when she arrives there through a magic portal, she possesses magic of her own. But now she's trapped with no way back to her own time. She's determined to make a safe place she and her fellow time travelers can live, one where women are equal and using magic won't get you burned at the stake.

Return of the Fae
Enter the Frey
Danu's Children
Upcoming Book Forged by Lightning

The Makers: *A Science Fiction Series*
By S. M Savoy

A previously unknown gas rises from the ocean floor and sweeps the Earth, reducing every manufactured item that it touches to its base elements, leaving a devastated world in its wake. But there are some survivors. And among them are those who can capture and use this gas to reform the elements to their will— They call them the makers...

Essence of the Storm
Storm Wrought
Eye of the Storm

A NEW SERIES: **DUSTED**

Dusted by an alien pathogen, Mia Sutton can now transform into a rat. The government is searching for people like her and making them disappear—she has no intention of becoming their lab rat.

Dusted
Hifis
Purfit

Books by C. M. Conney

Military Romance
The Real Deal
Take the Shot
The Deep End

Rubenstein-Wong
Ms. Denali
Danxia: Losing Faith

Company L: *The Enemy at Home*

Books set in the **Realms of Man**
Suggested Reading Order:
Moon Caught
Heaven Scent
Pact Mates
Qarahpyr
Seethe
Lord Blackwood
Anima Whispers
Cassandriel

———————————————————